all done in w~~hite leather~~ ~~~~ MW01123905 ~~~~
faint scent of vanilla. Under the shimmer of the small
chandelier overhead, my dress looked scarlet red. I
swallowed and smoothed out the fabric around my
waist. This was the worst place to tell him about his
ex's plans. I plumped myself on the sofa, and a few
pillows dropped to the floor.

"Oh, sorry." I bent to pick them up.

"Leave it." Cole caught my hand. He unbuttoned
his tuxedo jacket and sat. Out of habit, or cowardice, I
inched over to my left to make room. He gave me a
bright smile that said *nice try*. "Make up your mind,
Valentina. I can't take this any longer."

I melted a little every time he said my name, a hot
puddle of unrealized desire. I squeezed my legs
together and scooted some more. This sofa wasn't big
enough for the two of us. "I don't know what you
mean."

"Do you want to kiss me or not?" He slid across
the cushion, closing the space between us. "Ask me."

I adjusted my weight on the seat. He tightened his
hold on my fingers. God, even if I had wanted to flee, I
didn't think my legs would respond. Cocking his head,
he rubbed his thumb across the inside of my wrist
where my pulse was visible.

"I want you." The words left my lips of their own
accord.

Love Over Lattes

by

Diana A. Hicks

Desert Monsoon Series, Book One

Love Over Lattes

Cover Art by *RJ Morris*

The Wild Rose Press, Inc.
PO Box 708
Adams Basin, NY 14410-0708
Visit us at www.thewildrosepress.com

Publishing History
First Champagne Rose Edition, 2018
Print ISBN 978-1-5092-1944-5
Digital ISBN 978-1-5092-1945-2

Desert Monsoon Series, Book One
Published in the United States of America

Dedication

With love to David, Logan, and Victoria.
Best family I could ever ask for.

April,

Cole says
hi!

Happy Reading!

Acknowledgements

My deepest gratitude to the entire The Wild Rose Press family. I'm proud to be a Rose.

A shout-out to the Georgia Romance Writers chapter, a group of incredibly strong women who generously give their time to help new writers reach their goals. My first romance writers' conference ever was the Moonlight and Magnolias Conference. That Saturday night, while dancing in a roomful of women (and like four guys), I realized I'd found my tribe. Thank you for welcoming me into the fold and for your friendship. Thank you to Pam for reading an early version of *Love Over Lattes* and encouraging me to do better.

To Brenda Drake and the #PitchWars family, thank you for helping me become the writer I am today, for the support, writing advice, and everything else. To my critique partner, Piper Grayson. Thank you for talking me off the ledge so many times and the late-night chats. Thanks to the authors @Authors18 for all the support. We're in this together.

This one is for my parents and their blind and unrealistic faith that I can do anything I set out to do. To my sisters, Dalila and Yadira, for your strength. To my daughter, Victoria, who was the inspiration for Max. Thank you for the mac and cheese. To my son, Logan, who taught me that matching socks are overrated. And finally, thank you to my husband and partner in crime, David, for believing in me and acting impressed even when my first manuscripts were complete crap.

Chapter One
Café Triste

Valentina

Mr. Quad Americano rounded the corner across the street at a trot. When he reached the curb, he tapped his watch and wiped sweat off his face with the hem of his T-shirt.

"Thank you." I let out a quiet sigh and sipped my nonfat latte.

Every morning before E-Commerce class, I sat by the bay window at Cafe Triste and waited for him. The man never disappointed. Always on time. Always incredibly gorgeous—mesmerizing in the way he sauntered toward the coffee shop as if he had nowhere else to be but here with me. The familiar adrenaline rush and hot blood pulsing in my ears kicked in a second before he glanced in my direction. I didn't flinch or anything. I simply darted my gaze to my laptop screen and typed gibberish on the keyboard.

Smooth.

I'd been doing this for a while. Ever since he first barged into Cafe Triste six months ago. That day the man had been out running in the pouring rain. He changed direction midstride and stood at the intersection across the way, jaw clenched, hands fisted at his sides, and looking as intimidating as all hell. But when his blue eyes met mine, he relaxed his stance. In the end, a flash of lightning ripping across the sky followed by a particularly loud thunderclap made him rush into the coffee shop.

Rainwater dripped down his face and arms as he shuffled to the counter, ordered a quad americano coffee and an iced water, and plopped himself at the table next to mine. Holy shit, the man radiated pure testosterone, and all I could do was sit there and stare. Like an avalanche, out of nowhere, a hum in my chest spread and filled me with a kind of desire I'd never felt in my life. The kind I'd never thought could be for me.

The next day he'd come back, and then the next, and the next. Same time. Same order. Same table.

True to form, he was back this morning. Across the street, Quad Americano placed both hands on his slim hips, where his black sweats hung low and sexy. His gray T-shirt bunched up under his long fingers, exposing a bit of skin. I'd bet it was smooth and warm. No one ever looked this good in workout clothes, certainly not me. My guess was he'd spent hours at the uber-fancy gym a couple blocks away at the edge of campus. Or maybe this was his usual look, ripped and sweaty.

The traffic light turned green, and he sprinted straight toward the entrance, where the barista stood at attention as soon as he crossed the threshold. A little too eager in my opinion. Wait. Was that what I looked like ogling the guy? Shit. I darted my gaze away from him and back to my screen.

"How're you doing this morning?" he drawled in a deep voice that carried through the small restaurant.

I had no idea where he was from, but an accent like

that stood out in a college town like Tucson. Deep South was my guess. All smiles and blushing cheeks, the barista asked for his order.

"Quad americano coffee, please…"

And an iced water, I mouthed along with him. The breakfast of champions.

Blowing out air, he sat at his usual table, his over-six-foot frame turned toward me, elbows braced on his knees. I slunk in my seat to hide behind the laptop screen. Not that it mattered. He never saw me. Too busy looking at the world outside the window. But I didn't care. This was my favorite part of the morning—when we got to share a bit of peace.

I peeked over my computer again, clicking at random stuff on my friend's blog, mesmerized by the biceps stretching the sleeves on his T-shirt from the small effort of removing the lid from his cup of water. He downed half of it in one go. A slow smile formed on his lips before he caught a chip of ice between his teeth and bit on it hard.

Jeez, Valentina. Do the decent thing and look away.

Easier said than done, especially when the slanting sunrays skimming his profile invited me to stare. Sometimes he came in clean shaven, but today he had stubble that glinted a mix of light and dark brown on his cheeks. Same color as the hair dusting his chest. That T-shirt of his left nothing to the imagination. Not that I needed help in that department. This guy had my mind dreaming up things I was pretty sure were physically impossible.

His phone rang, and he stared it for several rings before sending the call away. He rubbed a hand over his face and into his hair. The strand trapped between his fingers caught the sunlight and gleamed like gold. An all-American boy, if I ever saw one. Two seconds later, his phone rang again. This time he sent the call away with a quick tap, brows furrowed, lips pursed. Whoever had called was definitely on his shit list. He slumped in his seat, and I had a strong urge to scoot two chairs over and asked him if he was all right. *Okay, no.* I had to get out of here. I shook my head to clear my thoughts. Mommy time was over.

Focus. Get your shit together and get your ass to class. Like right now.

With a sigh, I checked the time on my laptop. Yep, time to go. I downed the rest of my latte, drumming the bottom of the cup to get the foam to slide into my mouth, slurping a little when the froth slithered slowly and touched my lips. The first and last sips were always the best.

I grabbed my bag and stuffed my laptop in the front panel. My gaze darted toward the hot stranger sitting next to me. On round three, my phone buzzed for a second before it blared out the song "Titanium." It might as well had been an electric shock the way my body jerked in response. Why did I get so jumpy when he was around? I wasn't doing anything wrong. He was way over there, and I was way over here in my own world, doing the right thing, even though I'd spent the last ten minutes thinking about all the wrong things.

Heart beating fast, I fumbled through my bag, trying to kill the ringer, while making a mental note to switch it to a normal ringtone—and change the passcode so Mom wouldn't mess with my phone. Again.

"Hi, Mom," I answered.

"Oh, thank God, Valentina. I caught you before class."

"Barely. If I don't leave now, I'll be late." When Mom cleared her throat, my mommy instincts kicked in immediately. "What's wrong? Is Max okay?"

Mom never called during the week. Not if she could help it. She wanted my attention on school. That was the deal I'd made with my parents, or rather the deal they talked me into making with them—my son, Max, would stay with them until I finished college. If she was calling, something happened. I leaned forward, pushing my bag to make room on the table. My empty cup fell to the floor, but I didn't bother to pick it up. I gripped my phone, mouth dry. If anything happened to Max, it'd be my fault. He needed to be with me all the time, not just on weekends.

Quad Americano picked up the cup and offered it to me. "You finished?"

I waved him away, nodding.

"Valentina. Relax. He's okay." Another pause. A long string of static hummed in my ear before mom spoke again. "I'm sorry, honey. But your rental application was denied. The owner of the house called. Sounded like your credit is questionable? He went with the next applicant on the list."

"What? Why didn't he call me?" I ran my cold fingertips across my forehead. I'd spent months looking for a rental house I could afford. Tucson wasn't an expensive town, but finding a decent and affordable rental had been a real challenge, even after taking into account the job I had waiting for me after graduation. This place had been a true miracle to find. It was in the right school zone, close to my new job, cutest yard, and more importantly within budget.

"He did. But you didn't pick up."

Right. I'd been too busy being selfish, ogling a hot stranger. "Don't tell Max. Okay? I'll call the owner back and find out what the problem is."

"Oh, honey, do that… I'm sorry, sweetie. Take care."

I ended the call, scrounged through my bag, and pulled out my to-do list from a year ago. The one I made when Max had asked me why all the other kids in his preschool class lived with their moms. Why he had to live with grandma while I was away all week. My answer that day had been a promise to bring him home. I promised him it'd be just the two of us after graduation.

With a tightness in my chest, I glared at the list. *Find a house* was already crossed out. I took a deep, calming breath, tapped on the Recents icon, and immediately spotted the house owner's number. Dammit. He had called me first. I hit his name on the screen and waited for him to answer.

"Hello."

"Hi, Mr. Mendez. This is Valentina."

"You got my message," he said, his voice a monotone. He didn't want to deal with me.

Hell if I cared. "I did. I thought the rental agreement had been settled. What changed?"

"Your credit."

Tears stung my eyes. I blinked and wiped my cheeks while a lump churned in my stomach. I couldn't lose this house. Maybe if he knew why I had such a huge debt, he'd understand. People in the coffee shop shot furtive glances my way, at the girl in the corner having a moment. Two chairs down, Quad Americano gazed out the window—the only one in the restaurant who didn't notice me. I turned in my chair to face away from him and switched to Spanish. I had Mr. Mendez's attention for thirty seconds, tops. I had to make it count.

I squeezed my hand into a fist, crumpled my to-do list, and buried it in the folds of my skirt. I had to ask a complete stranger for a break, a favor. I squared my shoulders and swallowed my damn pride. "Listen, my five-year-old son had a fall last year. He's fine now, but his leg surgery wasn't cheap. I promise you the medical bills are the only debt I have, and I've never been late on payments."

"I didn't know. I already moved on," he said curtly.

"Please," I begged.

"Lady, don't make this difficult. Not my fault." He hung up.

Dammit.

A sound between a whimper and a hiccup escaped my lips. I pressed my face against the soft flannel lining of my messenger bag the moment the first tear trickled down my cheek. Crying in public was embarrassing, but at this point I didn't care. I had failed Max. My stomach rolled at the thought. How could I tell him he had to stay with grandma until I could either fix my credit or get a raise? An image of his big brown eyes fluttered in my mind, trusting and caring.

No. I made him a promise. I couldn't let him down.

God, an apartment didn't sound half-bad now. But if Mr. Mendez, a regular homeowner, had a problem with my credit, I was sure an apartment complex would be the same. If not worse. Eyes itchy and probably already puffy from crying, I ripped the old list into tiny pieces, took out my notebook, and wrote at the top of the page in all caps, going over the letters three times to make them stand out.

To-Do List

1. Get through finals week.

2. Make a list of new rental prospects. Two-bedroom unit, with a yard. Stay north of Speedway, if possible. Ask for a raise?

I scratched that last part. Who asks for a raise before starting a new job?

3. Find more rental money in the budget.

Maybe if I offered to pay two or three months in advance, my credit wouldn't be an issue.

4. Find out how much I'm spending on lattes. How much to brew at home?

5. Research schools in other areas.

6. Schedule tours for ~~late~~ early next week.

I called Mom back to give her an update.

Max answered. "Hi, Mom." A few weeks ago, I was Mommy. Max was growing fast, and I was missing it.

"Hey, buddy. What are you doing?"

"Packing," he said, his mouth full of food. "I have seventeen days before I can come live with you. No, wait. Sixteen days. Today doesn't count."

My lip quivered. Placing a hand over my mouth, I swallowed my tears. "You're going to love our new house." I closed my eyes and pictured the house I'd lost just ten minutes ago. Holding on to that image made the lie feel a little true. I still had time to turn this around and start making up for lost time and all the mistakes

I'd made. Max would be proud of me this time.

"It's going to be epic. 'Kay, here's Grandma. Love you, Mom."

"I love you too," I said, but he was gone.

"You got it taken care of?" Mom asked with real glee in her voice.

I shook my head, chest tight. "No. Please don't tell Max."

"Oh, honey, you know I won't. But I have to say it breaks my heart to see him packing for a move that may not happen." She paused for a moment while I sniffled. "Don't be so hard on yourself. You know you can always come stay with us. Just until you find another place."

"Thanks. But I can handle it, Mom. Really."

"Would you at least let us help you pack up your dorm?"

"I'm fine." I forced a laugh. "Don't worry. I still have two weeks before I need to move out. Plenty of time to find a new rental." That last bit came out way too bubbly, a big fat lie. But Mom didn't push it anymore. She knew that if I failed, I'd wind up in her house. Again.

"Okay, honey. I'll see you Friday."

I ended the call, tears blurring my vision. Mom would never say it, but she'd been silently hoping Max and I would come live with her and Dad in a more permanent capacity after graduation. Her dream was my nightmare. I was twenty-four years old. Moving in with my parents would be a major step back. I'd be stuck in Casa Grande, a town where I'd always be the girl who got knocked up her first week in college. My muscles tightened as I pictured their looks full of pity and disappointment, as I remembered all those months I spent hiding in my room.

Moving in with my parents wasn't an option. I had to keep moving forward. Even if that meant lowering my standards a bit. Okay, maybe a whole lot. I regarded my list and added a comment to item two.

2. Make a list of new rental prospects. Include apartment complexes.

Then I added a final item in huge letters.

7. Pick a home for Max.

Chapter Two
We Were Strangers

Cole

I rubbed my hand against the front of my T-shirt, fighting the urge to walk over to the woman sitting in the corner of the coffee shop. That long dark hair of hers spread on the table, a thick curl touching her bare knee. What'd happened to make her cry like this? No, I couldn't care about that. *Today's not the day my resolve to stay away from her crumbles.*

"Would you like another water?" the barista asked, standing next to me.

"Sure. Thanks." I handed her my cup and followed her back to the register. I needed to get out of here before I did anything stupid like talk to Valentina—the name embroidered on her laptop bag. The name suited her. Crossing my arms, I leaned on the counter, stealing another glance at her.

She'd found her composure and played with a long tress as she wrote in her notebook, her pretty brown eyes still wet, high cheekbones red and blotchy. To my disappointment, the dimple that'd appeared when she was on the phone was gone. When she let go of the strand of hair, it bounced and wrapped itself around the swell of her breast. My nerve endings stirred, and my pulse beat hard. I stepped toward her.

"Here you go." The barista touched my arm, something between a pat and a caress. I turned to face her as she offered me the water.

"Thanks." I took the cup from her and headed for the door. I had to get out of here. The last thing I needed right now was more female problems. Was she making a list?

Don't get involved.

Wasn't curiosity the thing that killed the cat? Great. Now I was comparing myself to a damn cat. Pirate would appreciate that. Useless cat. Valentina could deal with her own goddamn problems. I had my own. Plenty of them. I blew out air and dashed out of the coffee shop. I was an asshole for not offering her a bit of kindness, but letting her be was the right thing to do.

Lately, everything I touch turns to shit.

When I reached my car at the end of the block, I stuffed my hand in my pants. "Fuck my life," I said through gritted teeth. My key was gone. I punched the entry code in the car keypad and climbed in. I looked everywhere for the damn thing, in between and underneath the seats, and even in the trunk. Nothing. I made a mental list of where I'd been since I parked. There were only two places.

The fancy by-invitation-only gym I'd joined last year stood at the end of the parking lot. With a bit of luck, not that I'd had much of it lately, I'd dropped the key there and not back at Cafe Triste. I let my head fall back and took a deep breath just as my phone rang for the tenth time this morning. I answered it without looking at the screen. "What?"

" 'Bout damn time you answered, man," Dom, my lawyer and best friend, said.

"I was busy."

"Or maybe you thought I had bad news. No, man, just wanted to check in on you. I'm leaving New York in the morning. We'll talk when I get there. Okay? Sorry it took so long. Had a lot of crap to take care of before the move."

After more than six months, I'd finally talked Dom into coming to work for me. If anyone could get me out of this goddamn nightmare, it was him. "Thanks for doing this."

"Don't mention it. Which reminds me. Did you get Bridget's latest bullshit proposal?"

"Hmm." I pinched my nose, squeezing my eyes shut. I'd seen yet another legal envelope sitting on the mounting pile of mail in the kitchen, but I didn't bother to open it. They were all the same. One thing was clear to me—this divorce would cost me everything I'd worked so hard to build. Breathing through my mouth to make the tightness in my chest go away, I curled my hands into fists. "No, what do you think?"

"I think she's a conniving, coldhearted bitch." He paused on the other end. "But you're talking about the proposal. Well, I think it's bullshit. The question you need to answer is how badly you want this woman out of your life."

"I want her out of my life in the worst way possible."

"Okay. I spoke with her lawyer and made it very clear that you were done conceding to her…because you are. Can we agree on that? No more Mr. Nice Guy. For now, she's agreed to let you keep your house."

"I don't give a shit about the house. She can have it all for all I care, but not my company."

"None of this was your fault, man. Can you get that through your thick head? Stop saying she can have it all. This is exactly why you're in this fucking mess. Just like you, all she wants is CCI. You made it easy for her when you walked out."

"I needed distance from her. You know that." When would this be over? "And I didn't walk out. She convinced the board of directors I wasn't fit to run the company in *my state.* They voted in her favor when they saw pictures of the cottage."

Goddammit. My muscles tensed, and I slammed the heel of my palm on the steering wheel. What would it take for Bridget to let go of the company? A lot of people depended on me and the success of CCI. How long before she ran it into the ground just to spite me?

After a long pause, Dom cleared his throat and said, "Sorry, man. Didn't mean to put this on you. She does have a damn good case. Don't get discouraged. Now that we know exactly what she wants, we'll be able to figure this out. For now, don't talk to her, and for Christ's sake, don't let her in your house. Or you'll lose that too. I'll call you when I land." He hung up.

Drawing a slow, steady breath, I rubbed my forehead and hit the ignition button. Nothing happened. I climbed out of the car and headed for the gym to look for the key.

The receptionist greeted me. "Mr. Cole, welcome back."

"Hi again, Sam." I tapped my fingers on the counter. She ducked her gaze, blushing. I smiled to ease her nerves. "Any chance someone turned in a BMW key in the last couple of hours? I seemed to have misplaced mine."

"Let me check for you, Mr. Cole." She took off.

I paced the front lobby, and then it hit me. I knew exactly where I'd dropped the damn key. It fell out of my pocket when I picked up Valentina's trash. Damn it.

Sam came back. "I'm sorry, sir—"

"Yeah, I know." I spun and reached for the door. "Thanks, anyway," I said over my shoulder.

I stood at the corner, waiting for the light to turn green. It was past eight, but Valentina was still here. On the other side of the coffee shop window, she sat at her table, writing furiously. How did she do that? Fifteen minutes ago, it looked as if her whole world was crumbling around her. But now she was focused, scribbling away as if her life depended on it. I crossed the street and shouldered the door open.

The key lay a few inches from her sandaled, pedicured foot. Even her feet were pretty. I raked my hand through my hair, cursing under my breath, my gaze moving up to the short ruffle skirt tucked between her legs, revealing a muscled thigh. I swallowed. This was getting way too close to the fire. Maybe I should get the barista to help me look for the key. A polite girl like her would never refuse. Then it would be easy to point her in the right direction and…. *What the fuck am I doing?* Talking to Valentina couldn't hurt anything. All I had to do was keep it brief, explain I dropped my key, and move on. Better to get it over with quickly. I was already late for a day of doing nothing.

I marched to her and kneeled at the edge of the table to pick up the key. Anyone spying on us would think I was trying to look up her skirt. She certainly thought so. When I peered at her, she had those big brown eyes trained on me. Her full lips, red and swollen from crying, formed a perfect *o*.

Oh, sweetheart. My heartbeat picked up the pace, and blood rushed to my toes and fingers. Just like that, with one look, she washed away all the bad. How did she do that?

As I balanced on my knee, her eyebrows came together in a frown.

"I dropped my key." God, I sounded like an idiot.

She nodded and scooted her chair back. I had an odd urge to grab her leg to stop her. Women normally didn't run away from me. What the hell? I rose to my feet. Her eyes followed mine until her long neck and smooth collarbone were exposed. Sexy. It was my turn to take a step back. I placed my hands on my hips to keep myself in check.

Our gazes locked, and I swallowed, feet glued to the wooden planks. "Hi, I'm Cole." I offered her my hand. "Derek Cole."

Valentina arched a perfectly shaped eyebrow. She wore no makeup, but her skin was soft and radiant.

My fingers itched to touch her, give in, and… "I mean, my name is Derek, but my friends call me Cole." That usually came out a lot smoother.

"Nice to meet you." She placed her hand in mine. Gardenias. She smelled like gardenias. "I'm Valentina de Cordoba."

Her hand was small, but she had a firm shake. Here was a woman who knew what she wanted, who wasn't afraid. Why was she crying? The Spanish name explained her smooth, brown skin. But nothing more. Like the first day I saw her, a smile pulled at the corner of my mouth, and a blast of adrenaline rushed through me. A feeling I only got when I wrote code. I released her hand as if it suddenly turned into a hot coal.

"Well, I gotta go." I showed her my key. The universal sign for *this is the only reason I came back*. I had to go before I made a complete ass of myself and broke the only rule keeping my head above water right now—no attachments, especially of the female kind.

"Good luck with your list." I turned to leave.

"I'll need a little more than luck to get my house back," she muttered, eyes brimming with tears.

Fuck. Damn it.

Through the window, a cloud rushed across the sky, covering the sun for a moment. Shit. This was a bad idea. I chucked any fantasy I've ever had about Valentina from my mind before I walked to the condiment bar and grabbed a couple of napkins. When I returned to her, I forced a slow gait, taking my time as I pulled the chair out, waiting for her to send me away. She gawked at me but didn't ask me to leave, so I sat, with her bare knee inches from mine.

"What happened?" I offered her the bunch of napkins. I couldn't get involve and drag her down with me into this never-ending divorce, but that didn't mean I had to be an asshole. *Five minutes and then I'm gone.*

Unshed tears made her eyes look like a perfectly brewed espresso. Her hand reached for mine, her gaze focused on my fingers. As if she were afraid I'd yank the napkins away.

"It doesn't matter." She took the napkins and pointed to her list, forcing a small smile. "I'll find another one."

The fake bravado tugged at something in my chest. I understood the desolation I found in her expression well. But as much as I wanted to help her, I wouldn't know how. Dammit. She'd be better off calling her mom back. Yeah, I'd eavesdropped before when she was on the phone. She had a nice accent.

Tears rolled down her face again. She tipped her head down to hide them. A few drops fell on her flower skirt, while a couple scurried down her thigh. *Please don't cry,* I wanted to say, but instead I glanced toward the door. She wiped her face on her cardigan sweater, tore the page off her notebook, and folded it in four. The creases on the paper were even and neat. You could tell a lot about a person by how they handled their personal effects. Everything about her was tidy and organized. She was driven.

When she stood, she shouldered her computer bag and stuffed her list in one of the outer pockets. "It was nice meeting you, Derek."

I jerked to my feet. "Please call me Cole." I shouldn't have said that. We weren't friends. We couldn't be. A year ago, maybe. But now I would just hurt her. And she obviously didn't deserve that. I rubbed my jaw, tapping my fingers on my lips. Valentina spun and headed for the door.

My pulse raced, and something heavy settled in my stomach. She was leaving. If she lost her home, who knew when she'd be back to Cafe Triste? And I needed her here. I needed her to break up the days, to give me a reason to get up in the morning and leave the house. But she didn't know that. To her, I was a stranger. We were strangers. She didn't owe me shit. I pinched the bridge of my nose. I'd hit a new level of rock bottom and turned into a selfish asshole. *Let her go.*

Biting my lip, I rubbed the back of my neck. "I have a rental you might be interested in," I blurted out.

She spun around, frowning, mouth slightly open. *Fuck.*

Chapter Three
The Cottage

Valentina

God, he had a sexy voice.

Dumbfounded, I stared at him. Did I hear him right? He was offering me a place to live? Things never just fell on my lap. This kind of sheer luck didn't exist. *So what was the catch, Derek Cole?* I continued to stare.

He opened his mouth slightly and closed it, looking over my head toward the door, both hands on his hips. His T-shirt went up a bit. Oh, there it was, that patch of skin. It definitely looked smooth from where I stood. His full lips formed a smile before he took a step back. He'd changed his mind. Of course he did.

"This is where you ask about the rental." He peeked from under his eyelashes. Like a kid waiting for me to say yes to that candy he'd asked for. "Unless you already have other prospects." He didn't move, as if waiting for me to jump up and down and thank him for his generosity. This was by far the most uncomfortable conversation I'd ever had with a stranger.

"I'm sorry. I can't."

"Why not?" He swallowed hard, his expression blank.

People in the coffee shop slanted glances our way. I

didn't really have a good reason for saying no other than my gut told me this guy was trouble. The last thing I needed was to fall for the wrong guy again. It was one thing to admire him from afar, but having him as my landlord would mean he could visit me. Hot landlords did that, right?

A warm tingling sensation blasted across my belly and in between my legs. Derek Cole in my bedroom, tall and handsome, shirtless—now that was a sight. Why did I always end up *there* with him? Jeez. Wiping my sweaty hands on my skirt, I cleared my throat and lowered my voice. "I don't even know you." Wasn't that the truth? I turned away from him, my chest aching.

He leaned in to catch my words. His smell was intoxicating, a mix of body wash, lemon and verbena maybe, and manly sweat. He was in my personal space, and I didn't care. The room had gone from frigid to hot, and I wanted nothing more than to take off my sweater, touch him.

But I didn't dare move. Instead, I balled my hands and hid them in the folds of my skirt. Breathing through my mouth, I said, "And you don't know me. For all you know, I have ten people living with me."

"Good point." He nodded, his face inches from mine.

Okay, break it up. On three. One, two, three.

"Thanks anyway." I made for the exit.

He grabbed my arm before I reached the doorknob. His warm long fingers on my skin sent another adrenaline-induced surge through me. I stood still, fighting the urge to turn my body to face him. An inch to the left and his forearm would brush against my breast. Bad idea. Terrible.

"Wait." He gave me a brilliant smile, straight white teeth, eyes a little puffy, as if he hadn't slept much the night before.

Why? Nope. I didn't care if he slept or not. *Run*, my gut screamed.

"If you think about it," he said, "you don't know the other property owners either."

"Good point." I looked down at his hand.

After stealing another glance toward the door, he released me. I had to squeeze my fists tighter to stop myself from reaching out. He wanted to flee. I recognized the look on his face because I felt the same way. But for the life of me, I couldn't understand why I was still here, basking in the heat emanating from this gorgeous stranger.

He gazed into my eyes. "The property was built recently. It just needs a few touch-ups." He waited for me to comment, but I didn't say anything. "It's about eleven hundred square feet, two bedrooms, one bathroom. With a bathtub." He added that last bit as if that would seal the deal with me. Not all girls like baths. Running two long fingers across the stubble just below his jaw, he caught his bottom lip between his teeth for a moment. "What else? The kitchen is small, but the living room has good space and lighting. The cottage was meant to be an art studio. But I'm sure it will suit your needs."

I stifled a sigh. This cottage sounded like a dream come true. "Sounds decent."

We stood in the middle of the small coffee shop, near the door. Customers bustled in and out as the daily morning rush came into full swing. Derek sidestepped a woman to clear the aisle and let more people in.

This close, I had to look up to keep eye contact. "Are you an artist?"

"No." He thumbed the palm of his hand. "It was built for someone else. But that person no longer has need of it. So I figured you could use it."

"You mean it's not listed?"

"No. Of course, it is." He crossed his arms, his gaze on me. "I just meant that it might be something you could use. Even if you don't paint."

"I don't paint." I shook my head. "At all."

He hunched down a bit, eyes trained on mine. "What do you do? I mean, I can tell you're a student. What's your major?"

"Oh." I'd never had anyone look at me like this, as if my answer was important, as if it meant everything to him. "Information systems." I tried to move back, but the line to order had spilled into the sitting section. This was why I always left fifteen minutes before eight. The place was a madhouse, loud and crowded.

He laughed, shaking his head. "Computer stuff, huh?"

"Yep. I already have a real job waiting for me. I mean, I have real job now. Just, you know, not a career." Why did I tell him that? I didn't need his approval.

He nodded, as if he knew exactly what I meant. "Impressive. Not everyone gets a *real* job right after graduation."

"I started interviewing last semester."

"Let me guess. That was on your list. Find job. Check." He drew a check in the air, doing a combination of a small chuckle and mischievous grin.

Holy shit. This gorgeous man was flirting with me. I smiled at the floor as flutters sprung from my center. I glanced at him, doing a bad job of hiding my laugh. "Hey, don't mock the list. That's how I get things done."

"I wouldn't dream of it." He hid his hands behind his back. His gaze moved from my eyes down to my cheeks before it settled on my lips, and my stomach did a quick somersault.

"Excuse me," a short guy said, squeezing in between a table and me.

"Watch it." Derek pointed behind me.

I shuffled forward and held my breath when my side pressed against Derek's torso. He used his free arm to create a barrier between the guy trying to get by and me. Technically speaking, I was in Derek's embrace, my hand resting on his muscular chest, hard and warm. I inhaled and took in his smell. I wanted to run my hand up his biceps and bury my face in the nook of his neck and shoulder. I wanted it so badly my skin felt hot and alive. Oh my God, he was dangerous. I needed to get out of here.

"It also has a private yard," he whispered in my ear.

"Okay." I did my absolute best not to shut my eyes and melt into him.

"Okay, what?"

"I'll add you to my list. Your property, that is." I stepped back, ignoring the pull, the strange need to be in his arms. It'd been too long since someone held me this close.

He nodded and exhaled. Had he been holding his breath?

How could someone I barely knew make me feel this way? Admittedly, he wasn't a complete stranger. I'd seen enough of him over the past months to know he was courteous, but not too friendly. He stuck to his morning routine religiously and drank watered-down espresso shots. The man intrigued me. What made him stay and talk to a girl crying her eyes out in a coffeehouse? Any other guy would've run out. I knew this from experience.

I wanted to know more about him, but I couldn't pluck up the courage to ask. His clean-cut look said he was successful in whatever it was he did, educated. And he carried a six-hundred-dollar wallet in his sweatpants. The one he always placed on the table next to him, with a BMW key on top of it. Did men really buy expensive wallets for themselves? Derek didn't strike me as the type. Or maybe someone gave it to him as a gift. I glanced at his left hand. No ring. No wife. Not that I cared.

"So where is this amazing rental located? What's the monthly rent?" I raised an eyebrow, a move I learned from Mom. The woman could command a room with just her eyebrows.

His chest expanded slightly, and I could swear his body temperature had gone up a few degrees. He relaxed his stance and dug into his front pocket. His sweatpants slid down to where his V-line dipped below the waistband. I wiped my sweaty hands on my skirt, a raw current stirring up a storm inside me. Could I really accept his help without getting close to him?

If his offer was viable, I owed it to Max to at least consider it. I should ask Dad to run a background check on him. Check for priors. Dad was a retired cop, but he still had a lot of friends in the force. All of them more than willing to run background checks if he asked.

Derek pulled out his wallet, reached for my wrist, and placed his business card on the palm of my hand. His touch, warm and soft, traveled all the way down to my toes. I rubbed the thick card stock between my fingers while I peered at his name printed in off-white letters against a dark gray background. When was the last time I accepted a guy's number?

Max's dad's menacing voice echoed in my head. *You were nothing when I found you. And you're still nothing.* My fingertips went cold as I cradled my cheek and welcomed the ghost pain—a reminder of how mistakes could hurt the people I love. My insides quivered, and suddenly I couldn't catch my breath.

Dammit. What was I doing? Falling for the wrong guy once was enough. Derek seemed nice, but that could change in an instant. No, I couldn't accept his help, and I couldn't call or email him. I didn't need this kind of distraction in my life, the kind that could easily turn into pain.

After all these years, it was time for Max and me to be a real family. The *get job* item on my list had been checked. I just needed to find a house. We were almost there. I couldn't make any more mistakes. Max was my only priority, and that left no room for anyone else. I couldn't falter now just because a beautiful stranger with a chiseled jaw flashed me a dazzling smile. Love wasn't for me, and I was okay with that. I'd come to terms with it a long time ago, before Max was born. I couldn't lose sight of what was important.

"Are you okay?" Derek tipped his head. A crease formed across his forehead as his hand reached for my face, only to stop halfway when I nodded and stepped out of his reach. "Email me at that address. I'll forward you the details, and we can set up a meet." He'd turned on his business voice, deep and determined.

"Thanks." I put the card in my bag, just to be polite, and turned to leave. His fingers brushed my elbow, but I didn't let him stop me this time. Without another glance back, I scurried out the door.

Good-bye, Derek Cole.

Chapter Four
Patch Up This Hole

Cole

Well, my gut was right.

Another day and she hadn't come back to Cafe Triste. Two weeks had gone by since Valentina ran out of the coffee shop. I'd offered her my cottage in a moment of goddamn weakness. And, yeah, at the time I'd kicked myself for doing it and even wished I hadn't done it. I'd spent days thinking of ways to get out of it. Excuses I'd make if she called or emailed. Excuses I never got to use because she never contacted me.

I leaned back in my chair and looked out the bay window. The image of her crossing the street that day was tattooed in my mind. Her long hair, her skirt flowing wildly with every step, exposing toned legs. Like an idiot, I kept my eyes fixed on the street corner, as if my sheer want could make her suddenly appear.

I checked my phone again. By now, I was sure she wouldn't email. And here I thought I'd been extra charming that day. Maybe I'd lost my touch. Or maybe she was stubborn as hell. Stubborn and beautiful. Valentina was gone, and I couldn't stand it. The notion took me by surprise. It shouldn't matter to me if I saw her again or not, although I'd give anything right now to know what'd kept her away the last two weeks.

"Would you like a refill on your coffee?" the barista asked, clearing the empty cups off the table. Her knee brushed the outside of my thigh as she leaned forward to wipe the table.

"No, thanks." I pushed my chair back and stood.

She pressed her lips tight, and a look of disappointment washed over her face. That made two of us.

I shouldered open the coffee shop door and plodded to my car. I wasn't in a hurry to get home to another day of doing nothing. The days kept getting longer and longer. Without Valentina to break them up, time had stood still. To top it all off, I hadn't heard from Dom either. Not after he'd called to let me know he was in town and handling things.

Rush hour was almost over, with heavy traffic only at main intersections, but I managed to drag out the drive. I beat my previous record and added almost an hour to my commute back up north. In my mind's eye, I saw Valentina's big brown teary eyes staring at me. I gripped the wheel tightly. Why did she say no? As I understood it from her call with her mom, she needed a place to live. Bad. Bad enough to make her cry. I'd offered her exactly what she wanted, and she refused it. Why?

The idea of Valentina in the cottage, so close, made me feel whole again. Without meaning to, I'd open the Pandora's box that was the small house in my backyard. If I had to be honest, I wasn't ready to deal with what I'd left there. But I had to face the past sometime. I'd spent a lot of time thinking about the cottage, my divorce, and my next move. Even if Valentina never called, I still had to clear out the place and somehow

29

start moving forward.

It was fucking time.

I pulled into the driveway. Gravel crushed around me as the tires rolled half a mile up the hill. I parked the car near the front door and went in to look for my housekeeper.

"Good morning," Em said, setting the table in the breakfast room.

I had no idea how early she got up every morning. When I left before five, she was already dressed in that gray uniform she insisted on wearing, her white hair up in a proper bun. God, I didn't pay her enough to take care of me. And my fucking mess. My eyes fell on the now-spotless living room. The night before had gotten out of hand. My head pounded when I tried to remember what happened after I left the bar.

After Bridget moved out, I went out with other women to pacify this fucking loneliness that wouldn't let up. And for a while it worked. But no amount of sex could ever fill the void or make up for everything I'd lost. All I wanted now was for people to stop asking about what happened, to stop feeling sorry for me. I wanted to show them I'd moved on, even if it wasn't true. I was still angry, still felt like an asshole for what happened.

"Good morning." I glanced around, scratching my temple. "Who's the second setting for?"

Em narrowed her eyes before she whispered, "Your houseguest. I figured she'd be hungry."

I winced. "Shit. I forgot."

"Clearly." She walked to the kitchen and came back with a boxful of mail. Several legal-size envelopes stood out. "I threw the new mail on top. In case you feel like going through it today."

"Tomorrow. I promise." I bit the inside of my lip.

"It's time you got your life back, don't you think?"

"I need a shower." I pulled my T-shirt over my head. "Could I ask you for two huge favors?"

She gave me a knowing smile. "I'll take care of *Tuesday*…. Oh, I'm sorry. Today is Wednesday. I'll take care of *Wednesday*. What's the other favor?"

I deserved that. I let out a slow breath. "We didn't do anything."

She threw up her hands. "That's your business. I just work here."

I rolled my eyes. Em was more than a housekeeper. She was family. "Could you clear the cottage? I need everything gone before the end of the day."

And there it was. The pity in her eyes filled the room. "Of course. Consider it done. What should I do with the stuff?"

"Donate it, burn it. I don't care." I dashed upstairs to get cleaned up.

I didn't know why I felt as if I needed a cold shower. The thing about Arizona was that cold water was just an illusion. Nothing was ever cold here, not like back East. I set the water temperature to sixty degrees. It'd never get there, but the system would at least try.

Placing both hands on the tiled wall, I let the cool shower hit my neck and back. The water sprayed my sore muscles, and as usual, my mind formed a picture of Valentina. This time the feel of her hands on me, her scent, and the smoothness of her skin were there to complete the image. I'd gotten too close that day. And now my body craved more.

I was glad she had decided not to take me up on my offer. She was a complication I didn't need. *Stop thinking about her.*

I shut off the water and grabbed a towel off the rack on my way back to the bedroom. The french doors were wide open, letting in a bunch of hot air. On the terrace, just outside my bedroom, Em had breakfast set on one of the stone tables. Probably so she could make up some bullshit story for Nikki, or *Wednesday*, as Em called her. She'd use the standard excuse. *Mr. Cole had to rush to the office for an early meeting.*

I winced, rubbing a hand over the stubble on my cheek. This thing with Nikki had to stop. Donning a T-shirt and jeans, I wandered onto the terrace. With the sun on my face, I plopped myself down and ate. I had to. Otherwise, Em would nag me about not eating later.

I chewed on the goat-cheese-and-tomato omelet, not really tasting anything. Across the backyard, at the edge of my property, Em worked on the cottage. She had several garbage bags filled with clothes and God knows what else. I strolled to the low wall and straddled it.

Minutes went by. Or maybe it was hours. Who knew how long I sat there, pity party of one? Numbed, I watched as Em directed a couple of security guards to haul away the trash bags. They rolled their eyes every time she dumped more stuff for them to take. Manual labor was beneath them, but they wouldn't dare say no to her. They'd have to answer to me if they didn't do what she said.

Back in the bedroom, my mobile rang. I didn't move at first. It was too early, and I was too damn sober for socializing. The phone stopped its nagging ring. A few minutes later, it rang again. Who could possibly want to talk to me at this hour? Except for… My stomach clenched as I dashed to the bedroom and reached the phone in time to see the missed call message appear.

The call had come from an unavailable number. I exhaled and waited for it to ring again. It didn't. This was ridiculous. I needed to get Valentina out of my mind. I took the terrace stone steps down to the backyard. The high-noon sun shimmered across the pool, and the air was still and hot. A bit of rain would be great right about now. We needed the relief.

"Come to help?" Em asked when I reached the cottage front door.

I shook my head, leaned my shoulder on the threshold, and peeked inside.

"I could use some help," she said over her shoulder, carrying a stack of papers and canvases to a trash pile out on the lawn.

Everything looked exactly how I'd left it six months ago. The massive hole in the wall, the broken furniture, and the scattered papers. Maybe it was a good thing Valentina didn't call. Crossing my arms, I trudged to the middle of the room. I felt disgusted with myself. To think I almost killed a man here. For Bridget.

Ignoring the hole in the wall in my peripheral vision, I picked up a large paper off the floor. It felt heavy in my hand, expensive. A self-portrait of my soon-to-be ex-wife. Bridget, the painter and business manager extraordinaire. I lifted another sheet. This one was a nude, another self-portrait. That was all she cared to paint or draw, it seemed.

I followed the trail of papers around the house,

stuffing them all in a trash bag I found in the kitchen. I'd made quite a mess that day. I've drunk a lot of booze since then to make the details of that morning go away, although the gut-wrenching anger was still there. I wanted everything gone, including the memory of her and what she'd done. I hurled the trash bag at the wall.

In the bathroom, I eyed the crack on the tile. The broken showerhead and the incessant water drip. Just like that day, his face was inches from mine again. So close his stale-beer breath puffed against my flared nostrils. A loud tear, the front of his shirt ripping under my grip as I slammed him against the wall, echoed in my head. I squeezed my eyes shut and tried to erase the sight of the two of them in bed together.

Sitting on the floor, I blinked until the image was gone. What an idiot I'd been, but it was over now. Done. If Valentina called, this place would have a purpose again. I stood, picked up the trash bag, and kept going until every drawing was off the floors and walls. The work felt like closure. The coffee table and broken chairs were next. I dumped everything outside, ignoring Em's big smile. I wasn't in the mood for her pity. She opened her mouth to say something but closed it when my phone rang again.

"What?" I answered. The words came out like a roar.

A sigh echoed on the other end, followed by a throat clearing. The sound definitely belonged to a woman. "Mr. Cole, good morning."

My body reacted, blood rushing. Tension mingled with… *Jesus*.

"It's Valentina de Cordoba. You probably don't remember me, but we met at Cafe Triste a week or so ago."

Oh, sweetheart, I remember you. And it's been more than a week.

I strolled back into the cottage, away from Em's prying ears. "Hmm. I'm sorry. I don't." I was being a jerk. I knew it. Why did she make me wait this long?

"Well, you said you had a rental I might be interested in. I have your business card."

She sounded desperate but hopeful at the same time. I wanted to hold her. "Oh yes. Yes. You're the computer major looking for a house. Is that correct?"

She cleared her throat again. The sunlight hit the kitchen window and illuminated the room. Picturing her big brown eyes and that little dimple on the side of her mouth warmed my insides.

"Well, if the property is still available, I'd like to take a look at it. Now."

Now? Her tone was so subtle I almost didn't catch it. She was giving me orders.

A heavy weight lifted off my shoulders. I smiled, looking at my bare feet. "I'm terribly busy right now. But let me check my schedule and see when I can squeeze you in."

"Sure. I'm available every afternoon until Friday. I'm going out of town then."

Where was she going? My pulse quickened. "Well, in that case, how does tonight sound? How early can you get here?"

"I work until five. I can leave here as soon as I'm done."

She was at work. I looked down at my mobile and saved her number to my contacts. Just in case I needed to reach her later. I wasn't about to make the same mistake as before. Back in the coffeehouse, I'd assumed she'd call right away and didn't think to get her number before she walked out on me.

"That should work."

A sigh and the scratching of pen against paper hovered in my ear. Or maybe I imagined that part. No doubt she was adding notes to her list.

"Should we meet at the property?" she asked. "What's the address?"

I cringed. She might run away again if she found out the cottage was inside my property. "Sure. I'll text you the address." That was vague enough.

"Perfect. I'll text when I leave work."

"Perfect," I echoed her words. "I'll see you tonight, Valentina de Cordoba." I gulped a lungful of air. It was good to breathe again.

"What is going on?" Em stood in the threshold. The lines around her mouth hardened into a quizzical frown. I'd take that over pity any day of the week.

"I'm heeding my accountant's advice to rent out the place. It's a good tax write-off."

She pressed her lips together. The woman's sixth sense was intolerable. What would she say if she found out I had a recent grad moving into the cottage?

"Who is she?"

I did a double take. Might as well get it over with and tell her now. "Recent grad. University housing kicked her out after graduation. She needs a place." I shrugged.

At least that was what I'd gathered from Valentina's five-minute call with her mom and that guy who made her cry. She had a job, but no place to live because of some medical bills. My Spanish wasn't that great, and she'd talked incredibly fast that day. Probably on purpose so no one could follow her phone conversations.

"So after months of parading women through this house to fill that void in your chest, you figured the way to really fix everything that's wrong with your life right now was to patch up this hole." She pointed at the wall. "With an actual person."

"My life doesn't need fixing. Yes, I've been going out a lot lately, but that's because I have nothing else to do. Remember? I have no job to go to anymore."

"Hmm" was all she said. I really didn't need this kind of grief in my life.

With a sigh, she came toward me. "I know. I'm sorry." She wrapped her arms around my waist, and I hugged her back. Her head barely reached my shoulder. "Promise me you won't hurt this woman. She sounds very young. Too young for you. I get that you need some kind of connection. But you need to take care of what's inside here first." She dug her finger in my chest. "Then you can start thinking about love again. Do you see that?"

"First of all, I'm twenty-eight. I can't be that much older than her. And two, who said anything about love? I'm not looking for any kind of relationship. Not with her or anyone. Just thought it was time to put this place to good use." I put my hands up. "She looked like she needed help. I'm just helping."

Em narrowed her eyes at me. "Okay. You're the boss. And if this rental agreement is getting you to face all this"—she gestured toward the hole—"I'm all for it." By the time she finished her sentence, she was smiling with less pity in her eyes.

"Where do you need me?"

"I'll get started on the bathroom." She laughed. "You finish up in here."

"What?"

"I don't think I've ever seen you clean up one of your messes. But if I may speak freely—"

"No, you may not speak freely."

She waved her hand at me, shaking her head. "If there ever was a mess you needed to clear, this would be it." Her eyes sparkled before she turned and walked down the narrow hall to the bedrooms in the back.

I rubbed my hand over my face and into my hair. "Em."

"Yes?"

"She's not here to patch up any holes."

"Of course not."

Chapter Five
Just Sign

Valentina

Quad Americano, or Derek Cole, didn't text me an address. Instead, he sent me long and complicated directions on how to get to the rental. I was surprised he hadn't included singing trees and dancing pineapples. The directions took me way up north, farther than I wanted to be. But if the price was right, a long morning commute to work would be a small price to pay. Not to mention that after two weeks of looking at apartments, my options were pretty slim. At this point I could live either with my parents or in that Miracle Mile complex with the bug-infested carpet. Both options made my stomach roll. I loved my parents, but Max and I needed our own place. I promised him.

I turned right on Skyline Drive and left on Craycroft. From there, I swore he was trying to confuse me so I wouldn't find my way back. Small roads took me higher up the mountain. The last named road was *Las Nubes*. The clouds. Another left led me to an unnamed road that finally put me on Cole Drive. The name of the street was his last name. This meant either he was the first one to build here or his house took up the entire street. A half a mile later, I pulled up to a hidden private gate that opened when I approached.

Crap. He owned the whole street. I leaned on the steering wheel to take a better look. The jitters I'd had at the pit of my stomach since I left the dorm soared to my chest. Why did this feel like a bad idea? My leg trembled over the gas pedal as I gave Gris, my gray Honda Civic, a nudge to keep going. As soon as I entered the driveway, his house peeked in the distance, up on a hill. Following the gravel road, I circled around a water fountain and stopped in front of the Andalusian-style home, complete with solid hand-carved double doors.

This was his house?

He lived in a house straight out of an *Architectural Digest* magazine. The Catalina Mountains stood majestically under a sky covered in shades of pink and purple with white clouds smeared across the landscape. Despite the incredible view, several alarm bells went off in my head. I sighed as the realization that I didn't know Derek at all washed over me.

I climbed out of the car anyway. Just to take a peek. How could I not? I was already here. Gris looked like a scared house mouse, out of place sitting on Derek's driveway, just like me. I didn't need to do much research to know the schools in the area were the best in the state. No way I could stay. This was asking for trouble. Stealing one last look at the incredible view, I dashed back to my car.

"Running away?" Derek's deep voice called from the threshold of his hacienda, or whatever it was he lived in. Mansion, palace? "I thought you were made of something tougher."

"I don't know what gave you that idea." Really. I was bawling my eyes out when he met me. *Tough* couldn't be what he thought of me. I turned to face him.

He had his arms across his chest, shoulder leaning against the doorframe, those blue eyes trained on me. I didn't think it was possible, but he was better looking than I'd remembered.

He shrugged and pushed away from the door. I hadn't seen him in weeks. Watching him shuffle down the stone steps, barefoot, in worn jeans and a very thin white T-shirt sent an intense rush through me. Gosh, I'd missed him. I'd missed seeing his face. And damn if he didn't look good sauntering toward me. Those long legs took their time with every stride, as if we had all night. We didn't.

"I'm sorry. This isn't what I had in mind when I called you. I thought you said you had a rental and that we were meeting there."

"I do. And we are." He flashed me his all-American-boy smile. "Come on." He waved for me to follow. "I assure you I'm not a psycho. Are you always this suspicious?"

"I have to be."

He was now inches from me and for some reason, grinning. "It's good to see you again." He offered me his hand.

Without thinking, I reached out to shake it. When I pulled away, he tightened his grip. His hand was warm and soft. The gesture felt intimate, and for a moment I wished it were real.

"Come on. Let me give you the tour and then you can decide."

I let him pull me toward his house a couple of steps before I took my hand back. My pulse quickened. How did we get here? A few weeks ago, he was just Quad

Americano. And now I was here, at his home.

He ushered me through the vaulted front entry and into the great room. His feet slapped on the colored polished-concrete floors as he made his way to a coffee table, which sat in front of the massive stone fireplace. The kind of fireplace I'd only seen in movies, very European looking and antique. Expensive.

Instinct had me looking back at my car. Or maybe I just needed to make sure I knew the way out. To the right of the entrance was a set of stairs that led to a loft, a library with wall-to-wall shelves filled with books and leather club chairs along the arch window.

Jeez.

Through the opened door, I saw Gris. If we were in a cartoon, it'd be shaking in its tires right about now. I looked down at my trembling fingers. *Go. No. Run as fast as you can.* Good idea. But before I could take a step forward, Derek planted himself in front of me, blocking the view to my car and the only exit. His manly scent was such a distraction.

And there it was again, that hum I felt the first time I saw him. I wanted to lick that nook between his neck and shoulder, see if he tasted as good as he smelled. *Wait. What?* I shook my head a bit, tried to focus on what he was saying.

He gave me a half smirk, handing me a large envelope. "The lease agreement? We kind of need one. Take a look before I show you the cottage. No sense in falling in love with the place if you can't afford the rent, right?"

I swallowed and took the papers from him. After spending a month looking at rentals, I was getting good at reading contracts. The lease agreement was pretty standard, and the rent was right within my budget.

A door creaked below the library, and out came a blonde bombshell in her underwear. At six in the evening? She looked sleepy but flashed Derek a bright smile as soon as she saw him. That was definitely a bedroom she'd come out of. I couldn't even imagined what they did in there. Actually, I could. And did. Dammit.

"Hey." Derek gave her a half frown before he stepped to his right. "Em?" He called out.

"Well, this is awkward," I said.

It was hilarious. The man looked like a child who'd been caught with his hand in the cookie jar. A tall and incredibly hot cookie jar. I squared my shoulders to stand taller. At five eight, not exactly short, I felt small next to her.

An older lady came out of nowhere, suppressing a smile. "Would it be three for dinner today, sir?"

Derek narrowed his eyes. "No, Em. Thank you. I'm in the middle of a business meeting."

"I forgot." She gave him an innocent look.

Hot Cookie Jar finally realized she wasn't supposed to be here. "Oh, I'm sorry. I'll just go if you're busy."

With an apologetic look, she turned and trod back into the bedroom below the stairs. Not once did she try to cover up. Beauty and confidence. Good for her. So that was Derek's type. Basically the opposite of me. Knowing he couldn't be interested in me made things easier, even if it stung a little after all the flirting he did back at the coffee shop. I smoothed out my gray pencil skirt, wishing I had worn something trendy. But I'd come here right after work. I'd been so nervous about seeing him I didn't think to bring a change of clothes. Not that it would've made a difference compared to the hot, naked blonde in his room.

Feeling deflated, I plopped myself on the sofa. The fancy chenille material felt soft and welcoming, like his whole house. Something about it was very homey, complete with the smell of fresh-baked cookies.

"I can come back some other day if you need to tend to your naked-girl issue." I couldn't even be jealous. He wasn't mine. He'd said it right before. This was a business meeting.

"No. Don't leave. We didn't... She sleeps like that." The tip of his tongue touched his bottom lip before he bit it. "This looks bad. I know. Please don't leave."

How could I say no to that? I sat frozen in place as he turned to the older lady.

"Em, this is Valentina. She's interested in renting the cottage."

"It's really nice to meet you, dear." She gave me a warm smile and shook my hand gently. "I'm sure you're going to love the house. Now if you'd excuse, I need to take care of *Wednesday*."

"Em." His tone was laced with warning as he watched her leave the room.

"She seems nice," I said.

"She can be. Shall we?" Derek pointed to the floor-to-ceiling windows on the opposite side of the great room. "I promised you a tour."

I stood, smoothed out my skirt, and stepped out onto a covered patio. The Catalina Mountains were in full view from here. A great expanse of beautiful desert. Serene. Complete with sounds of running water and birds singing, although I couldn't see the source of the noise anywhere. A set of stone steps led to a zero gravity pool and a green lawn. To my left was a stone grand staircase that wrapped around the house, which probably led to a fancy terrace of some sort.

"There's a side entrance you can use and parking on the other end of the cottage" He kept his distance, but still, his deep voice sent a chill down my arm. "It's just beyond the pool."

The path next to the pool ushered us by the grand staircase and down more steps toward a courtyard. Tucked in the corner was the cottage. I hugged my belly to keep myself from squealing or jumping up and down. It was perfect. And too good to be true.

"Why are you doing this?" I asked.

"I need to rent the place, and you need a place to stay. I'm doing it for the money."

"Because you obviously need more of that."

"Everyone needs more money. That's what money does." He dug his hand in his back pocket. In the stark sunlight, he might as well be shirtless. The thin material of his T-shirt didn't do much to cover his muscled torso, and I got lost counting the ridges on his abs. "Go ahead and take a look."

"I'm sorry. What?" I cleared my throat.

He showed me a key. A knowing smile appeared on his face for a split second. "What are you here to see?"

"Oh." If I didn't know any better, I'd say he was flirting. As if. I shot a glance back to the main house and the hot cookie jar waiting for him in skimpy underwear. I took the key from him and went into the house, ignoring the sweat running down my back.

The front of the house was one big room, with a

small kitchen on the left and a cute fireplace centered on the right wall, next to a huge hole.

"What happened here?" I peeked inside it.

"Normal wear and tear."

He didn't have to explain himself to me. But I couldn't help but wonder what'd happened. He was letting me see something very intimate. Why did I feel an urge to hold him, stroke his cheek?

"Really? 'Cause it looks like you took a sledgehammer to it."

He laughed, an irresistible, deep belly laugh that melted my insides. "My fist. But it'll be fixed before you move in." He waved toward the Sheetrock patch kit and other materials sitting in the corner of the room. "It'll be good as new."

Derek was offering me a dream of a house for Max. The least I could do was help with this small job. I'd patched a few walls in my lifetime. This one reminded me of the time when Max drew a baseball on Mom's living room wall for batting practice. The hole that little boy left behind was commendable.

"Don't worry about it. I can fix it for you."

His face turned serious, with tired lines on either side of his mouth. "You don't have to do that. I can take care of it myself."

"It's your house." I shrugged and strolled down the hallway, where the terra-cotta floors continued. They were beautiful and fairly new. The first door on the left was a full bathroom with a tiled shower and bathtub combination. Someone had ripped the showerhead and let the water leak for months. "More normal wear and tear?" I asked with a smile.

"It'll be fixed before you move in. I promise. The

master bedroom is at the end of the hallway here." He gestured for me to follow.

The room was a good size, with a walk-in closet and a sliding door that led to a private yard in the back. A woman had obviously designed this place. I looked at his hand again. Still no ring.

I pursed my lips to hide my smile. *Wednesday* didn't live here.

"Eleven-hundred square feet, two bedrooms, and a bathroom," he said. "As promised." He opened the door to the second bedroom. "If there's anything else you need, just ask Em or me." He bit the inside of his bottom lip. Again. Was he nervous?

My chest filled with bubbles when I saw what would be Max's room. It had a big window and a small closet. The space was perfect. I didn't know when, why, or how, but I was ready to sign his contract. Something about Derek was trustworthy. He meant well. His hotness would be an issue, but all I had to do was stay away from him. This property was big enough. Keeping him out of our lives shouldn't be too hard.

We strolled back to the main living area, where I smoothed out the contract and set the papers on the kitchen island. "One last thing." I took a deep breath.

"What is it?" He closed the space between us. His voice was gentle, as if he didn't want to scare me away.

"Okay." This was as good a time as any to tell him about Max. "My son, Max. He'll be living with me." I'd been waiting five years to say that. God, it felt good.

He smiled, bracing his arm on the granite. The light coming in through the kitchen window touched his face and made his eyes look like sapphires. Did natural light just follow this guy around?

"So that's it. That's why you were crying?" The way he asked the question, he made it sound as if Max was this big secret I'd been keeping.

I nodded. "He's been waiting a long time to come live with me. I couldn't fail him with this."

He took a deep breath. "Well, I'll have to run an extensive background check on him. But if he clears it, I don't see why he can't live here with you."

"Ah. Well, if you find anything, let me know. Who knows what he and my parents are up to during the week when I'm not there?"

"I'll make sure and do that." He stepped forward to turn the page over. That sexy smile of his on full blast. "There's a personal information sheet on the back. You'll need to fill that out too."

My legs turned to jelly, and I squeezed them together. *Stop staring at him.*

"I should tell you. My credit score is not where it needs to be. But I swear I'm never late with payments."

"Valentina." He handed me a pen. Heat rushed to my cheeks. Every time he said my name, the air filled with an electrical charge that slowly wrapped around my core and muted any logical thought. "Just sign."

Chapter Six
A Bit of Relief

Cole

I sat on a lounge chair and fired up my laptop. Of course, Bridget had tried to revoke my access to CCI, my own company. I closed my eyes, heat roiling in my belly. She never understood what it was I did. All she knew was that I managed our customers' data network. The how was never important to her.

I leaned back, and my gaze darted across the landscape. The morning sunlight glinted on puddles of rainwater across the terra-cotta tiles on the terrace. It'd be hot as hell later today, but for now, a breeze blew across the desert and into my backyard. Monsoon season had arrived early this year.

When the computer finished booting, I accessed the main server, using a ghost profile I'd created. In matter of minutes, I'd found my way to the personnel files and had Valentina's profile up on the screen. I rubbed the back of my neck. My heart had skipped a beat yesterday when she wrote CCI as her employer on the lease application. One way or another, Valentina was meant to be part of my world. If we hadn't met at Cafe Triste, we would've met at work, eventually.

I scanned the rest of her employee page. She was an information systems major with emphasis on data networks. She had a minor in astronomy, and she was bilingual. Good girl. Her transcripts showed she had a four-point-zero GPA. I smiled at the screen, turning my attention to the role tab. She'd been assigned to contracts and reporting. A good place to start, but she'd be a better fit in the development group. With her lists, I bet Valentina could project manage the heck out of anything.

Her salary was ridiculous, cringe worthy. Bridget and I had often gotten into it over what we each thought were fair wages. But as the CEO, I always had the final say. She didn't take long to correct the matter the minute the board kicked me out. No wonder Valentina didn't have enough money to pay off her debt and find decent housing.

"You're in a cheery mood this morning." Em set a basket of her signature puff-pastry apple pies on the table.

"I'm tackling the repairs in the cottage today." I eyed the small house across the courtyard.

After Valentina'd signed the lease last night, she'd taken two minutes flat to climb back into her little car and careen out of my driveway. I'd let her go. She'd be back. By my estimation, that'd be Sunday at the latest, which meant I had three days to get the house fixed. Hiring someone to patch up the wall and take care of the water damage would be easy, but Em was right—though I'd never admit that to her. This was a mess I needed to clean on my own.

Em pressed her lips in a half smile. "And the mail? I know you don't like me saying this, but there's a new envelope waiting for you."

"Yeah, I'll take a look." For once, the thought of

tackling divorce papers didn't make my stomach roll. I grabbed a mini puff and bit into it. The light sweetness of the apple and the spiciness of the cinnamon in the warm filling swirled in my mouth in a kind of dance. I didn't much care for sugary treats, but these pastries were hard to resist.

Sitting back on the lounge chair, I glanced at the cottage. Certain things in life were just that: irresistible…like Valentina's mouth. I licked gooey stuff off the pad of my thumb and adjusted the napkin over my crotch. What would it be like to kiss her lips?

I sat up. *Jesus, I can't go there. I'm not that kind of asshole.*

Having Valentina so close brought me peace. She had something that made me feel alive whenever I was around her. That was all I needed. For six months, I sat next to her in the coffeehouse, and that was enough. Yeah, we were neighbors now, and if I had to be honest, the way she looked at me sometimes made my blood boil. In a good way. But getting further involved with her would ruin what we had. *I* would ruin it.

Shit. I raked a hand through my hair and squeezed it into a fist. I had to figure out a way to keep my distance. Valentina didn't deserve to get caught up in all my bullshit. I didn't want to be the one to cause her more pain. She'd already been through a lot.

The usual flutter darted across my belly and chest. It was there every time I thought of her. Every time I saw desire in her eyes—not that she'd ever do anything about it. A smile pulled at the side of my mouth. I'd never seen anyone with that kind of self-control. Where did it come from? What was holding her back?

"You look like you're up to something." Em had

breakfast laid out on the table, enough for two people.

"What?" I laughed. "I don't know what you're talking about."

"You need to let her be. She seems like a good girl. A girl who's been through a lot." She clasped her hands together and eyed me over the rim of her glasses.

"I thought so too." I leaned forward, reaching for the coffee. "What do you think happened to her? She walks around like she's carrying a heavy armor. Like she was hurt bad."

"No." Em shook her head. "I'm not going to help you seduce her."

I choked on the hot liquid. Coughing, I grabbed the water goblet and sipped in between coughs. After I recovered, I swallowed and put up my index finger to make my point. "One. I don't need your help in that department. And two. I had already resolved to stay away from her. What kind of an asshole do you think I am?"

"The kind who's in pain. And would do anything for a bit of relief."

Sucker punch in the gut. I blew out air. "I'm not discussing this with you." Heat rushed to my cheeks. Maybe it was because of the accuracy of her statement or maybe because I was discussing sex with sixty-year-old Em.

She snorted as she placed a second setting across from me. "I've been clearing naked women out of your guest room for months now, and this is the thing that embarrasses you?" She poured more coffee in my cup.

"I'm not doing this." I threw the napkin on the table and leaned back, arms crossed. The woman could be impossible at times. "Who's this for?" She was going overboard with the table setting.

"Just think about it. You have other things to take care of first."

I had nothing to think about. Valentina needed a place to stay, and I happened to have one. Just that. I had no plans to seduce her. I needed her near me. That was it.

"The gate called ten minutes ago. Dom is on his way here."

"Actually, I've been downstairs for a while. Holy shit, these muffins are good." Dom's deep voice boomed as he came up the stone steps. He'd gone out the patio door in the living room and come up to find me on the terrace. "Man, I forgot how massive this place is." He went to hug Em first. His six-three frame towered over her, though she didn't seem to mind as she wrapped her arms around his waist, beaming. He squeezed her arm. "Is this asshole treating you right?"

"Don't they have barbers in New York?" Em reached up with both hands to grab the dark hair growing over his ears. "You need a haircut and a shave." She rubbed the stubble on his cheeks.

He chuckled. "The ladies don't seem to mind."

"I'm sure they don't." She shook her head. "Now that you're here, maybe you can talk some sense into this one. Now sit and eat. I have more muffins baking." She patted his belly and went back inside.

"I'll see what I can do," he called after her.

I stood and greeted him with a hug. "You made it, brother."

"Yeah. You finally got me out here. What's up with this fucking heat, huh?" He took the chair across from me, throwing a legal envelope on the table before loading up his plate with the frittata and fruit. "No time to beat around the bushes, man." He pointed at the papers. "It's Bridget's latest proposal. Read it."

Stomach churning, I took a deep calming breath and opened it. Bridget and I were married for ten months, but for whatever fucked-up reason, she didn't think walking away with half my assets was compensation enough. She wanted more. My muscles tensed as I glared at the document. She wanted my company, the one *I* built from the ground up. When she came to work for me, I was already a brand. Her job was to run the business while I focused on the stuff that really mattered to me—my people. What would be the point of being the boss if I didn't get to do what I really liked?

"It's been seven months." I focused on the writing in front of me. "Is it me, or is she all of the sudden in a hurry to finalize the terms of our divorce?" God, I was so sick and tired of this bullshit.

"This is the second proposal in the last two weeks. I'd say she's feeling motivated to end this."

I read on. The motion was loaded with legal jargon, but at the heart of it all, Bridget's voice was in there, terse and calculated, as if she had dictated the entire text to her lawyer. She was willing to waive her rights to most of the properties I owned, but she still wasn't letting up on the communications company. Why not? I read page after page, picturing her narrow face, her pursed lips.

The underlying tone to her words was hard to miss. She blamed me for the failure of our marriage. And she was probably right, but in no way did that justify what she did. If she wasn't happy in our marriage, all she had to do was ask for a damn divorce, not wait for me to find her in bed with our accountant. That spineless jerk. In the end, the thing that hurt the most, or rather, the *only* thing that hurt was her betrayal. We were partners. I thought she cared about CCI as much as I did. I was an idiot for not seeing that Bridget only cared about herself.

The question remained. Was I ready to give up my company in exchange for my freedom? Did I have the strength to start over, build a new company? I wasn't sure. I swallowed the lump in my throat and rubbed my eyes. My freedom was something only Bridget could give back. She'd won.

"How you doin', man?" Dom brought me back. "What're you gonna do?"

I grabbed the proposal and signed it. "Tell her I agree to her terms." The need to move on with my life had won over.

"Well, fuck me." He leaned forward, his dark eyebrows pinched together in a frown. "How about we give it another thirty days, hmm? That's how long they gave us to respond."

"I thought you wanted me to sign," I said.

"No. I wanted you to tell me what you wanted to do so I could give you advice. I'm your lawyer. Let me give you some fucking advice."

I laughed. I'd met Dom in college. A boy from Jersey, he was a no-fuss, no-bullshit kind of guy. Loyal. My kind of guy. Back when we first met, Dom didn't give a fuck about anything, which was why I'd been surprised when he'd decided to go to Columbia after college. But as it turned out, that was truly his calling. Up until I lured him to Arizona, he'd been one of the best lawyers in New York City. Probably because he didn't give a fuck.

"Advise away."

"I ran into Bridget yesterday during lunch. She was eating at the same restaurant as Nikki, by the way. I wonder if she knows about you two. Em tells me Nikki spent the night the other day. Again." He wiggled his eyebrows.

"Nikki and I are *not* a thing."

"Really? I mean, yeah, she's trouble, but man…" He blew out air. "She's something else."

"Not interested."

He shrugged. "If you say so. Anyway, Bridget and I talked for a while, and you know what? She seemed desperate."

"How do you mean?"

"She hit on me." He did a mock shiver and pointed a finger at me. "That woman is hiding something. I already hired an investigator. If she's got something fishy cooking, we're gonna find out."

"Fishy? Like what?" I bit the inside of my bottom lip, feeling a jolt through my body. Desperation was something Bridget didn't quite know how to handle. She was used to getting her way. Was the long wait finally getting to her?

"Dunno. All I know is that she's desperate."

"Okay, that might be good for us. We'll do it your way for now. Let me know if something turns up."

"Will do." He stood. "Hey. Wanna do drinks later this week?" he said as a way of saying good-bye.

"Sure. Come over any time."

"That's not what I meant." He placed his hands on his hips. "Come down from this ivory tower of yours.

Let's have a couple of shots like normal dudes, at a bar."

"Yeah, okay." He was right. A bit of normal would be good. I glanced at the cottage, wishing Valentina hadn't left yesterday.

"Let me know when you have time." He headed for the stone steps.

"I'm available every night." I followed behind to walk him out.

"Now I feel like an asshole." He spun to face me, raking a hand through his hair. "I'm gonna fix this for you, brother. You hear?"

I nodded. "Thanks. 'Preciate that."

"Let's do drinks tonight. Seven, no make it six."

"Done," I said.

"Done." He put his hand on my shoulder. "Stay. I can see myself out. I wanna see if those muffins are ready." He turned around and left the way he'd come in.

From day one, Bridget couldn't stand the sight of Dom. She used to say his personality made her dizzy. Dropping the f-bomb every three seconds was unprofessional and disrespectful in her mind. Maybe she was right. But Dom's lack of filter was what'd made me trust him in the first place. With him, I could always count on getting the truth, no sugar coating, no hidden agenda. If she hit on him, she had to be desperate. She wanted something bad. But what? What did she want that wasn't already on the settlement agreement?

I straddled the low stone wall, gazing at Valentina's house. Something I didn't recognize fluttered in my chest. How long had it been since the last time I felt anything?

My body stood at attention when tire tracks on the gravel came into focus. Why hadn't I noticed it before? That was her car in the side driveway. Taking two steps at a time, I rushed down. When I reached the cottage, the door and all the windows were wide open. My cock reacted immediately. Valentina was here.

A small speaker blaring out "She Looks So Perfect" sat on the kitchen counter. Next to it was a sheet of paper, one of her lists. I looked behind me before I peeked at it. According to the list, Valentina was moving in on Saturday. I rubbed the stubble on my face, smiling. Just like that, all the bad in my life got muted.

Yesterday, she hadn't been able to give me a move-in date. She said she had to talk it over with her mom. I had a feeling her mom wasn't too keen on Valentina and her son living on their own, which would explain why Valentina couldn't find an apartment. A recent grad with bad credit would need a cosigner. I'd be willing to bet her parents said no to that—easiest way to keep her and Max home.

But Valentina had already proven she deserved a place of her own. I wasn't sure why, but something gave me the impression she'd been trying for a long while to make up for her one slip six years back. Maybe it was her face when she told me about her son, Max. It'd sounded like a confession of sorts.

I'd assumed Max's dad wasn't in the picture. But now that I thought of it, she never really explained what was going on there. I should get the guy's name and do a background check. That kind of information could come in handy. I bet he walked off on her. What kind of a jerk gets a woman pregnant and then takes off? As if she didn't matter.

Going through the kitchen, I opened the cupboards. She had already moved in some dishes. Probably the stuff she had in her dorm. The fridge was also stocked with milk, fruit, and vegetables. And two bottles of bubbly wine. A champagne girl.

I followed her voice to the bathroom. She was in the shower, cleaning the rusted tile with a toothbrush. Who knew how long I'd stood there, watching her singing happily to a boy band song? How could she look this sexy wearing a pair of yoga pants and tank top while in the shower?

The day before she'd worn a gray pencil skirt with a navy-blue cropped top and high heels that kept me up all night. What would it be like to have those long legs wrapped around my waist? She was barefoot now. What would she look like covered in suds and nothing else? *What am I doing?* I wasn't an asshole, but that didn't make me a saint. I had to get out of here.

"Oh my God, you scared me." She turned to face me, her cheeks flushed.

"Good morning." I rubbed the back of my head, having found the decency to feel embarrassed for stalking her in her own home. "I'm sorry. The door was open, and I heard music. I…what're you listening to?"

"What? It's the top-fifty station."

"You mean the teen radio station." I strode to the kitchen under the pretense of turning off the music. Really, I just wanted to remove myself from the current scene. I reached for her device, but she blocked me, putting herself between the mobile and me. Okay, this wasn't an improvement. Now I had her within reach, and that gardenia smell of hers was wreaking havoc in my pants.

"It's still good music."

"You know those guys are like sixteen, right?"

Her laugh was light and carefree. "They *are* not."

"I didn't know you'd be here today." I changed the subject before she noticed I was jealous of a boy band.

"I wanted to get a jump start on the cleaning." She gave me a bright smile. "I'd like to be all settled in by Saturday. If that's okay?"

Right. Her list said so. I'd bet it would happen just as she planned. I should give that a try sometime. What would my list look like?

1. Go out for a run

2. Eat breakfast

3. Help Valentina clean the cottage

4. Take her back to my room

5. Kiss her gently until she begged me to undress her

6. Have sex

That was easy. Maybe there was something to be said for lists. I grinned at her. God, if she only knew my thoughts.

"Of course. What can I do to help?" I wanted to get the cleaning out of the way.

I turned to the wall and did a double take. She'd patched it up. A heavy weight lifted from my chest. The room was whole again. A stark white blotch showed where the hole had been, but the surface was smooth and ready to be painted over. I forced myself to exhale when a slow burn spread inside my lungs.

She walked around me and gave me a brush. "You could start painting. I'm still cleaning the water damage in the sink and tub."

"This is new."

"What is?" she asked, rosy cheeks and pouting lips. God.

I wrapped my hand around her wrist, and her breath hitched. "You accepting my help without complaint or turning to the door calculating your escape." I took the brush from her.

"I only have a couple of days to finish up." She yanked her arm, and her fingers slid through my grip.

"Right. Your list." I pointed to the counter.

Her face went from rosy to red. "Don't mock the list." Her dimple appeared again on the side of her mouth. I wanted to touch it. Kiss it.

"I'm not. See? I'm painting." I couldn't stop smiling. Giving this place a new purpose had been a good idea. Now all I had to do was keep my mind off Valentina. I could leave, but then what would I do with the rest of my day? I dipped the brush in the pan she had already set up and started cutting at the top, making sure the line was straight.

By the time Valentina joined me, I was rolling on the first coat of paint. She grabbed a roller and got to work on the opposite wall, inching her way toward me.

"What?" She slanted a glance at me.

"Just wondering." I shrugged. "I don't see a ring on your finger. What happened to Max's dad?"

Her eyes turned dark, and the lines around her mouth hardened. I'd hit a nerve. Her wince was like a kick in the nuts, but the need to know what'd happened made it impossible to feel sorry for asking.

"He got spooked when I told him I was pregnant." Her response was mechanical, as if she'd explain this small fact a million times. "I never heard from him again."

"Wow, an asshole of epic proportions."

She laughed, a deep laugh that warmed me to my core. She shrugged, skimmed the roller front and back on the paint pan, and turned to the wall.

"Was this your first year in college?" I knew she was twenty-four from her rental application, which meant she was nineteen when the asshole left her.

She puffed out her cheeks before she blew out air. "I finished the school year, but then I quit after Max was born. It wasn't fair for him, you know."

"But you went back to school."

She nodded, beaming. Max canceled out anything else that was bad in her life. "Yeah. My parents were willing to help out. I didn't really have a reason not to. And I had to finish. For Max."

"God. I can't imagine walking out on my kid."

"You mean, if *Wednesday* got pregnant, you'd marry her?" She raised an eyebrow, a cute wrinkle trimming the corner of her eye.

"Her name's not *Wednesday.*" I hated myself for letting Nikki invite herself to my house Tuesday night. The whole scene made me look like a womanizer. No doubt that was Em's intention when she "forgot" to get Nikki out of the house.

"Oh no. I got that." Her laughter was infectious.

"It's not what you think. At all."

"Well, I'm thinking you bring a different girl home every day. Em can't keep track of them, so she calls them by the day of the week instead. Is that right?"

"Okay. So it's exactly what you think. Or it was." This wasn't the time to explain how fucked up my life was right now. Nikki was a replacement for something, or someone, I couldn't have. Until now. "Anyway, she could never get pregnant."

She gasped, dropping the roller in the pan. I froze when she reached for my hand. Her smell was calming and exhilarating. She knocked my hand against the wall. I let it go limp, a burst of a laughter building up in my chest.

"Never say *never*. You'll jinx yourself."

"I'm sorry." I knocked on the wall. No reason to tempt the jinx gods.

"What makes you think it could never happen?"

"I never do it without a condom. So the chances of a baby are extremely slim. I mean, we'd be talking about a miracle baby here." She blushed at my words. Why in the world were we talking about sex? "But if for some reason it did happen, I would take responsibility for the baby. Marriage is not really for me. But I would definitely be there. All the way."

She looked down at her hands. I shouldn't be turned on right now. I closed the space between us and cradled her face to make her look at me. This close, her irises looked more chocolate than espresso. I never knew brown eyes could change colors.

"I'm not sorry for what I did. I would never be sorry for having Max." She swallowed her tears and quickly recovered.

"Is that why you try so hard?" My left hand brushed hers, and she wrapped her fingers around it. "Sweetheart, you have nothing to be sorry about."

Standing in the middle of the room, Valentina met my gaze, and everything else fell away, the loneliness and the pain. Tears brimmed her eyes again. I traced the wet trail down to the dimple forming near her lips. When she glanced down, the sunlight touched her face at an angle, adding to the glow on her cheekbones.

"I should go." She peered up at me, eyes slowly moving down to my mouth.

Yeah. That was the look. My chest hurt.

"I need to get home," she said.

"Valentina, you *are* home." I bent down and kissed her cupid's bow.

So much for staying away.

I meant only to comfort her. But she parted her lips slightly, and I couldn't resist taking what she offered. I covered her mouth with mine, and my heart pounded when she didn't reject me. The need she aroused in me was strong, painful. I wanted her more than I thought possible.

A quiet moan escaped her as she pressed her breasts against my chest and slipped her hand under my shirt. Her touch was like hot wax pouring over my skin. I buried my fingers in her soft hair and kissed her neck as I worked my way down to the front of her top, tasting sweat on her gardenia-scented skin.

"No," she whispered on the top of my head, pushed me gently, and stepped back.

And just like that, my entire to-do list fell to pieces. I nodded, stuffing my hands in my jean pockets, lungs fighting for air.

"Derek, you're my landlord. Remember? Plus, think of your girlfriend. How do you think this is going to make her feel?"

"Dammit, Valentina. She's not my girlfriend. You know that."

"Does she know that?"

"Yes. That's the deal." I inhaled to catch my breath. "They want to have fun. I'm their guy. If they want more, they need to move on."

"Is this supposed to make me wanna kiss you again?" She gave me a nervous laugh, shaking her head.

"I know you want to," I whispered. Her body still hummed the way mine did.

She swallowed hard. "What I want is irrelevant here. I can't. I'm here for Max. You can never be more than my landlord. If you don't think you can agree to these terms, tell me now. And I'll go to the next apartment on the list."

"Don't do that. Please." My mouth went dry, and legs weak. "We'll do it your way. Your rules."

"Promise me you won't do this again." Brows pulled in, she trained her gaze on me.

I bit my lower lip and nodded. She needed this as much as I did. "I promise." I took a step closer to her. A dimple appeared on her cheek, as if she was about to say something. "I won't kiss you again until you ask me." She let out a long breath, and the dimple disappeared.

Oh, sweetheart, I promise you will.

Chapter Seven
He's Not on the List

Valentina

It was a miracle I still had my clothes on.

God, I wanted his hands on me again. I still wasn't sure what'd happened. One minute we were painting, and the next he was kissing me. Really kissing me. Like out-of-breath, I-want-you-naked-now kind of kissing. I checked my top and pants again, smoothing out the fabric. Everything was in its place. *Wow.*

He reached for my hand, cheeks flushed, lips red and puffy. "Valentina—"

"Sorry. I'm…late." Annie, my best friend, stood in the threshold, brows furrowed.

The early afternoon sunlight came in through the doors and created a dusty halo around her straight dark hair. Her mouth fell open as her gaze darted from Cole, to me, and back to Cole. No doubt her mind was going a hundred miles a minute trying to figure out what she'd just walked into. She pursed her lips. Crap, she knew. And for some reason, she wasn't happy. Annie, who for the past six years had been on my case about going out on a date and *getting some*, as she'd put it.

"Um," I said to buy myself a few seconds and catch my breath. "No worries. Cole's been helping out." I winced a little at that. I had no right to call him that.

Cole? he mouthed with a slightly cocked eyebrow before the corner of his lips twitched into a smirk.

I wanted to tell him that a kiss didn't make us friends, but he didn't wait for an answer and turned to Annie instead. "Hi, I'm Derek Cole." He shook her hand.

"I know who you are," she said. "You own the strip mall where I work."

"Which one?" He inched closer to me, even though his attention was on my best friend. A glimmer of light slanted on his profile and his incredibly long eyelashes. I could stand here and watch him all day.

"Saigon Cafe on Swan," Annie said louder than necessary, and effectively snapped me out of my trance.

"I love that place. Their green papaya salad is amazing. You work there?"

"She owns the place," I said. "She's also *the* fashion blogger in all of Tucson." I put my arm around her. Annie and I had been best friends since kindergarten. She'd been there for me when I got pregnant and had to go back to live with my parents after my first year in college.

"And Max's godmother." She set her purse and several plastic bags on the kitchen counter. "Cute place you've got here." She turned to me. "Way better than that shaggy carpet with walls."

I gave her meaningful look. Cole didn't need to know there wasn't really another apartment on the list. What would I have done if he'd called my bluff?

Cole chuckled. "Still needs a bit of work, but we're getting there." He eyed the patched hole and the walls on either side of it, the ones we'd been painting for the last four hours. With his hands in his pockets, he turned to face me. His eyes bore into mine, as if he wanted to telepathically explain what'd happened, apologize.

I wanted to tell him we were past it. That as long as he didn't try it again, we'd be fine. But Annie's eyes were still on me. I'd already said my piece. I had to let it go.

He beat me to it. "Well, I'd hate to be a third wheel, and I can see you girls have a lot to talk about. I'll leave you to it."

"I'll see you later," I blurted out while I fumbled with the bags Annie had brought.

He shook his head once, biting the inside of his bottom lip. What did he expect? We kissed. So what? Annie, on the other hand, took pity on him—a rare occurrence. She always handled men with a firm hand. It was how she'd become so successful right after college. She never took crap from anyone.

"Hang on," she said. Her high heels scraped the terra-cotta tiles as she strutted to the kitchen. She dug through a bag and pulled out a Styrofoam container. "Green papaya salad." She leaned in and whispered, "Extra spicy. It's her favorite too."

As if he would care what I liked or didn't like.

"Thanks." He took the container and left, giving me a wink instead of a wave.

Annie and I stood silent in the kitchen for a whole minute. We hadn't done that since we were in grade school and were given detention for talking during a test.

She broke the silent first. "What the fuck, Valentina?"

"*What*?" I put my hands up.

"You didn't tell me you were living with *the* Derek

Cole."

"I'm not living with him. Just leasing his cottage." I eyed the front door. Why did it feel like I was living with him? I went to the sink and poured a glass of water. I was suddenly parched. "There's a difference there."

"Okay. Fine, I'll give you that. But what about the moment you were just having. Come on. You could cut the tension with a paintbrush." She pointed at the brush on the floor to make her point.

My laugh was something between a snort and a cough. "Nothing happened." I knew that'd be her next question.

"Shit. You kissed him. You did, didn't you?" She fished the food containers out of the bags.

I avoided her gaze and went to grab a couple of plates from the cupboard instead. The kitchen was the first thing I had unpacked when I arrived earlier. Annie piled the food up high on each dish, expertly working the chopsticks as if they were an extension of her hands.

"Technically, *he* kissed me," I said when she set a plate in front of me. I didn't have a dining table, so we just stood around the kitchen island.

"I'm not saying I'm not glad you finally decided to end your six-year drought. And I'm sure the all-powerful Derek Cole is a spectacular kisser."

Spectacular didn't begin to cover it. A warm current surged down my legs, so intense I had to lean on the counter for support and wait for it to pass.

"But, sweetie, you gotta start small. This guy will have you for a morning snack and then forget all about it by lunchtime." Without asking, she walked to the fridge and pulled out a bottle of bubbly I picked up at Basha's on my way in. She grabbed a couple of wineglasses and poured.

"I can take care of myself. It was just a kiss. We were both simply caught up in the moment." I stopped to inhale, hoping to take the defensive edge out of my tone and hide how all-consuming Cole's kiss had been, how his warm breath on my neck and the feel of his hard abs under my fingertips still burned white hot at my core. Heat rose to my cheeks, and my legs went weak again. Annie was right. I was so screwed.

"Caught up in the moment? You guys were painting. That's hardly an onset for romance."

"You know I don't have time for that kind of stuff. He knows where we stand now. It's done." I sipped from my wineglass and shoved a bite of the papaya salad in my mouth.

"Okay, sweetie." She shook her head, raising an eyebrow. This conversation was far from over. "Oh hey, I brought you some goodies." She bit into her spring roll.

Clothes. Her blog had really taken off in the last couple of years. So much so that local designers sent her free clothes in hopes of getting featured there. I usually ended up with those clothes. The catch? I had to provide headless Polaroids of me wearing the outfits for her page. She claimed it made the blog look more professional if she had her own models. Something told me she just wanted to give me the free clothes without hurting my pride.

"And since you're starting a hot new job on Monday, I decided to do a nine-to-five piece. I got some amazing stuff." She rummaged through the bag, brows furrowed. "There's a sequined miniskirt in here. You're just going to melt when you try it on. Wear it with that white tank I brought you last week." She waved the skirt in front of me. "Right?"

"Thanks." I put my arm around her, taking the clothes she offered. I never put up much of a fight. Free clothes trump pride. "Can we do the shots later, though? I'm all sweaty."

"Yeah. Sure. Hmm." She took a long swing of bubbly. "I also have a gig for you. There's a fund-raiser next Saturday. I need about ten girls to wear the dresses being auctioned that night. I'm featuring them on the blog…just trying to do something different, you know? Bring fashion to life." She wiggled her shoulders. "The Polaroids are getting a bit stale."

"Oh no," I said. "Headless Polaroids, I can handle. But a real-live thing. I'm sorry. You know I can't. Can't I just play bartender again? That was fun." I chuckled.

"Come on. This will be fun too. And I'll be with you the entire time. Hour tops. Pleeeease?"

"I'm sure you have other girls who're way more qualified." The idea of modeling clothes made my stomach queasy.

She looked away for a moment before she burst out laughing. "You're the only one who works for clothes. Everyone else wants money or their face on the landing page. I'm barely making money here." She gave me her sad puppy eyes. A look she only used on her mom and me.

"Okay," I said. Annie had done way more than put on a dress for me over the years. "One hour. And I'm not talking to anyone."

"Yeah, sure. I'll email you the details tomorrow."

She took one last bite of the spring roll and dumped the empty containers in a bag. "So when are you getting Max out here?"

"Next Saturday. I already signed him up for summer camp." I let out a giggle. It was finally happening for us. Max and I were going to be a family, on our own.

"Good for you, sweetie. But why not this week?"

"Mom thought it wouldn't be a good idea to have him here while I'm fixing up the place and moving."

She rolled her eyes. "I love your mom—you know that—but don't you think it's time she butt out?"

"She's just doing what's best for Max," I said dismissively, but I knew what she meant. In trying to make up for the lack of a *normal* family, Mom had become a zealous grandmother. Sometimes she'd go overboard protecting Max, but her heart was in the right place.

Nodding, she patted my arm. "Next Saturday will be here before you know it. You guys deserve this so much."

"It's all thanks to Cole, you know."

"You don't have to defend him to me." She gave me a knowing smile.

"I'm not. I'm well aware of who he is."

Of course, Annie was right about him too. For Christ's sake, his housekeeper referred to his girlfriend as *Wednesday*, and he didn't even bother to deny he had several women on rotation throughout the week. The image of the incredibly hot blonde strutting out of his bedroom yesterday was still stuck in my head, on auto repeat. I stuffed my hand in my hair. I was a morning snack, as Annie had said. Nothing more. I took care of my body, but I could never compete with a girl like that. She oozed sex and confidence, obviously something Cole was attracted to. I didn't have a chance in hell. Not that I wanted one.

If I had to be honest, though, I'd been curious about what it'd be like to kiss him. God, it was everything I thought it'd be. No, it was more, way more. His full lips were soft and strong. What if I'd let him keep going? Let him kiss my breasts. Wasn't that where he was headed when I stopped him? My heart raced at the thought, and goose bumps covered my arms. But none of that mattered.

As much as it pained me to say it, he wasn't on my list. He wasn't the goal. All I needed to do was stay strong and stay focus. Cole was just like any other guy who'd tried to get me to sleep with him. Maybe not exactly like the others. He was ridiculously hot with the abs and shoulders of a demigod. He could also break my heart into a million pieces. I barely survived the last time someone stomped on my heart. I couldn't go through that again.

Annie helped herself to some of my salad, squinting at me the way she did when she read my thoughts. She stopped chewing. "I've known you for a long time. If you say you can beat this, then you can."

"You talk about him like he actually wants me. He's just my landlord, and he knows that. I think he felt sorry for me." I took a long sip of my wine. "So you really know him? How?"

"Between the restaurant and the blog, I have to maintain a certain social life." She winked. "I've seen him around, heard things."

"Like what?" When she gave me a look, I added,

"He's my landlord. I need to know."

"I'm surprised your dad didn't do a background check on him."

"I may have omitted the specifics of where the cottage is located." I ducked my gaze, stuffing the last bite of egg roll in my mouth.

She shook her head and grinned. "I have to say I'm loving this new side of you. You must really want this."

"Just tell me what you know."

"Okay." She really wanted to tell me. "He has a lot of property all over the country, but he's been setting up roots here in Tucson, buying real estate here and there. My *entire* strip mall among others…parking lots and office spaces. But his real passion, as my sources tell me, is IT stuff. You know, like financial giants sending transactions over the internet." She drank from her glass.

"Financial transactions aren't sent through public access." I was beginning to doubt her sources.

She waved her hand in dismissal. To her it was all the same. "I wish you'd told me he was the guy you'd been having coffee with for the past six months. I would've done more digging."

"Seems to me you know plenty. What else?"

She laughed. "I thought you were the computer geek."

"What does that have to do with anything?"

"Valentina, CCI is his company. He's your boss's boss's boss's boss. I'm sure I skipped a few bosses in there."

"Crap. Why didn't you tell me?" Heat flushed to my cheeks, arms, and legs like warm water.

"I had no idea he was the same guy you were

rambling about. You never gave me a name."

"Because I didn't know it. What does this mean? Do you think he knows?" I placed my hand over my mouth.

She shrugged, shaking her head. Of course he knew. I put CCI as my employer on the lease application. Why didn't he say something?

"The real question, is how did *you* miss that bit of information? Maybe your head is not where it should be when it comes to your landlord."

"That's not true." Yeah, I was screwed.

"Now I see why you didn't mention this place until last night. You knew I'd try and talk you out of it."

"Enough about boys," I said. "How's your mom? Is she feeling better?"

"She's fine. Are you going to be okay?"

"Yeah." I nodded, looking out the window. On one side, I had a view of his incredible overlook terrace. On the opposite side, I had a green landscape and beyond that the beautiful Sonoran Desert against the backdrop of the Santa Catalina Mountains. "Why wouldn't I be?"

So what if Cole owned the company I worked for *and* my new home? As long as I stayed on my side of the lawn, we'd be fine.

"Don't fall for this guy."

"What?" The wine bubbles went up into my nose and made me cough. I cleared my throat a few times before I found my voice again. "Not me. You know that."

She knew my story with Max's dad better than anyone. She knew if I fell for the wrong guy again, I'd never recover.

"You sure?"

"Annie. He's not on the list. I promise I won't fall for him."

Chapter Eight
A Big, Huge Assumption

Valentina

The clicking of keyboards and hushed voices filled the office. Swallowing the giggle stuck in my throat, I took a sip of my latte and sat on my desk chair. My new-employee orientation was done. All I had to do was get through the rest of the day without making a fool of myself.

My assigned cube was at the far end on the third floor, in one of the many clusters of low-walled cubical offices in the massive warehouse-style building. Sixty-inch flat screens hung from the ceiling over the bobbing heads of the operations team in the middle of the room.

According to my tour guy from this morning, everyone had access to playrooms, napping quarters, and free breakfast and lunch on the second floor. For anyone staying past seven at night, the kitchen had lunch leftovers wrapped in individual servings. Coffee, pastries, and fruit were available all day in the various break rooms. Cole's priority was to take care of his people. His passion for the company touched every corner, and I found that I wanted to be part of all this more than I'd first thought.

Without meaning to, Cole now played a big role in my life. Because of him, I had a home and a job—a means to give Max the life he deserved. I touched my lips, feeling warm and tingly all over. *No.* I shook my head and ran a hand through my hair. If I wanted to thank the guy, I could bake him some cookies. More kissing was certainly not the answer, even if that was the only thing I could think of lately.

I squeezed my eyes shut against the flicker in my belly. When the moment passed, I turned my attention to the high pile of contracts I had to read. Grinning like a four-year-old in a candy shop, I grabbed the first three-inch binder and got started. On top of all the legal jargon, there were specific formulas to calculate and determine the level of our success. Just what I needed to get Cole out of my head. I wrote it all down in my notebook and worked out the examples provided in the text.

Hours later, my laptop screen flickered a couple of times before it went blank. Not the blue screen of death, but a black screen with a cursor that scurried across the bottom of the screen, leaving a text from a "DC" in its trail.

—How's your first day going?—

My head shot up toward the operations gallery, and my heart pumped hard. No one looked in my direction. I checked behind me. Nothing. For some reason, I thought of Cole. He was the owner and probably had all kinds of access and security clearance. I grinned at my screen as I typed a response.

—Is this where you tell me the answer is out there?—

—I could, but you already know that. Just curious how your day was going, is all.—

That sounded innocent enough, but I looked behind

me again anyway. I covered my mouth to stifle a giggle. An actual giggle. How did he do that? Two lines of text was all it took for him to chip away at my resolve to stay away from him.

—Cole?—

—I went by the coffee shop this morning. You weren't there. I miss seeing your face.—

—I have a real job now. Can't afford to sit around in coffee shops, waiting on you.—

—Is that what you were doing before?—

Shit. Did I just confess I went to Cafe Triste to see him?

—Heads up!—

My fingers touched the keyboard, but the screen cleared and Windows came back up. I sat back on my chair, brows furrowed. He was gone. I understood how he'd found me in the network. What I didn't understand was why.

"Hi, I'm Christopher." A man with big curly hair and a goatee came up from behind me.

"Hi, nice to meet you." I stood to shake his hand. According to the paperwork I was given this morning, this was my new boss.

"I'm sorry I didn't stop by earlier. It's been a crazy day."

"No worries. I've been keeping busy." I patted the tottering stack of contracts on my desk.

"Well, you can finish those later. Come on." He waved for me to follow.

I had no idea where we were going, but I grabbed my notebook and pen just in case. We strode to the opposite end of the building, where a glass-paneled office took up the entire width of the floor. Through the first door, we reached the receptionist area, where a woman my age sat and manned the phone.

"Is she ready for us?" Christopher asked, turning to me when the woman picked up the phone. "Bridget Cole is the president of the company. She likes to meet all new employees. She asked to see you. It'll be quick." He gave me a reassuring wink.

I nodded, surveying the office. Something about it screamed Cole. Why was he not here? Now that I thought about it, he spent most of his time at home.

"Go ahead." The receptionist led us into Bridget's office and closed the door behind us.

Christopher stopped fidgeting long enough to introduce me.

"It's a pleasure to meet you." I shook her cold and bony hand with my clammy one.

Bridget responded with a formal, curt nod. For someone who liked to meet her employees, she certainly didn't seem too interested in me. She leaned on her desk and hit the pager button on her phone.

"Still waiting on that coffee." She released the button and smoothed out her dark pantsuit before she faced Christopher. "Did you get those new usage reports squared away?" Her large, deep blue eyes trained on him so intently I shuffled closer to my boss. When he didn't answer right away, she pursed her lips into a thin line and blinked slowly, which accentuated the hollow of her cheekbones. She pushed a crispy blond ringlet away from her face, where it stayed suspended near her ear. Similar curls covered her entire head. All neatly pressed and hair-sprayed. Her makeup was in the same style, with perfectly penciled eyebrows and glossy dark-cherry lips.

"You got your body," she said. "Don't tell me you still can't do it."

Christopher peeked at me, his eyebrows pinched together. I figured I was the body she was referring to. He hadn't had time to walk me through the old reports, let alone the new ones. I understood his hesitation—the woman was terrifying.

"I should have the additional ten reports configured by the end of the week."

Shaking her head, she tightened her grip on the edge of the desk and gave him another slow blink. Her hair didn't move an inch except for the one ringlet, which she put away from her face again. "We've talked about this multiple times."

He did several quick, sharp nods. "We *will* have those configured by Friday."

"Oh good, you're back," she said over our heads. "I can't get this ridiculous machine to work."

The receptionist rushed to the espresso machine in the corner of the office where a butler's pantry was set up. She knocked a couple of shot glasses over as she rummaged through the cupboards. With every door she opened, she glanced our way, cheeks blotchy and shiny. I stepped toward her, but Christopher put out his hand at waist level to cut me off.

"Make it a quad," Bridget said.

A quad americano. Cole's coffee drink. My stomach did a quick somersault. *Bridget Cole*. Was she family or—

"Anything else?" Bridget asked Christopher, bringing me back.

"No, we're good." He hugged his binder to his chest. A smile touched his lips for a second.

"It was nice meeting you," I said.

She didn't look away from the computer as she typed. "Stay."

I turned to Christopher. Did she mean him or me?

He gave me a one-shoulder shrug and stepped forward. "You have—"

"Not you. Her." She kept her eyes on her screen.

"Okay. Come find me when you're done." *Good luck,* he mouthed before he spun and scurried out with the receptionist on his heels.

When he closed the door, Bridget looked away from her computer. My ears turned hot under her gaze. Yeah, no one could say no to this woman. In a screwed-up way, a part of me wanted to be like her.

"I was going through your employee profile this morning."

I nodded, gripping the back of the chair.

"When did you move into my cottage?"

"I'm sorry?" Holy shit. Her cottage? *She* built the cottage? Her eyes bored into mine. I couldn't stand it, so I focused on my shoes instead. My heart did pirouettes somewhere by my feet. Something big had happened in that house—the hole in the wall, the broken shower. Did she have anything to do with that? "Um. Cole leased the place to me last week."

"Cole? Well, that didn't take him long, did it?" She raised an eyebrow, gritting her teeth. "Are you sleeping with him?"

"No." My voice went up an octave. This wasn't how I wanted my first day on the job to go. I swallowed and hid a trembling hand behind my skirt. "I promise. This is a strictly professional arrangement."

She smiled at me, the hard lines around her mouth

gone. "You have nothing to be worry about. You probably didn't know Derek had no authority to lease the property. Not until our divorce has been settled and ownership of the property has been determined. Am I right?"

I gave her three quick nods. *Holy shit, Cole's married.*

"I like to take care of my employees. Don't worry. I won't kick you out onto the street." She laughed as if she'd told a really funny joke, and I wanted to crawl under the carpet and never come out. "I'd like to ask you for a small favor, though."

I exhaled. "Of course. Anything."

"I need you to sleep with my husband." She paused, and our gazes locked.

My stomach rolled before it dropped to the floor. I opened my mouth to speak, but the words didn't come out. *Holy shit. What?*

"That's just a suggestion, of course. Feel free to improvise. I figured you'd be a good distraction. I need you to convince Derek to sign the divorce papers before the end of the month."

My throat ached, thick and raw. "I'm sorry, but Cole…Mr. Cole and I are not. We're not. I mean, I don't think…" I swallowed and cleared my throat. "I mean, why would he listen to me?"

She let out a shrill laugh. "I'm sure you'll figure it out." She pursed her lips and dropped her gaze to my chest. "I'd hate to have to void your lease."

I crossed my arms, shuffling away from her. "We haven't…done anything." But that wasn't entirely true. This was insane, a joke.

"Let me know when it's done." She turned her

attention to the monitor.

What the hell was I supposed to do with this? I had no idea what was going on between Cole and Bridget. And I sure as hell had no right to meddle in Cole's private life. If he hadn't signed the divorce papers, there had to be a good reason for it. He helped me when I needed it most. I couldn't betray his trust. Of course, that would be assuming Bridget was right and I had the ability to convince Cole to sign his divorce papers before the end of the month, in two weeks to be exact. That was a big, no, a colossal assumption on her part.

This much was clear to me—Bridget Cole wasn't one for making empty threats. And she'd threatened to take away everything I'd worked so hard for. Max was coming home in three days. I couldn't lose it all before he got here. Shit.

"Are you going to stand there all day?" she asked, typing fast on her keyboard.

My body jerked at her words. "No. I'm sorry. I'll go now." By some miracle, my stiff legs carried me out of her office.

When I got back to my desk, Christopher was there. "What did she want? She's so intense, isn't she?"

"Just wanted to welcome me. That's all." I gave him a nervous laugh. "I thought you said I had nothing to worry about. She's scary." *Or more like freaking insane.*

"I didn't want to spook you." He sat on my desk, patting his forehead with the back of his hand. "But now that the worst part is over, we can get to work."

"Sure." I plastered a smile on. "If you show me the reports, I can start the programming for them."

"You just made my day." He jumped to his feet.

"I'll be right back with both, the old and new. I'm warning you, though. The new ones are all screwy. God, I miss Cole. He never would've agreed to any of this. It's like she wants us to fail," he mumbled as he stomped away.

I sat on my chair, heart pumping so hard all other noises around me were muted. What just happened? I ran both hands through my hair and swallowed my tears. The black screen appeared again. I think it was safe to assume that Cole could not only direct message me but also see me.

—*You haven't run out the door. Good.*—

—*I met our esteemed president. Any relation?*—

—*Sort of. Wife. Ex-wife, really.*—

I crossed my arms, back muscles painfully tight. I'd hoped he'd say she was lying about being married to him. I couldn't picture someone like Bridget with Cole. An odd arrangement for sure. Did he love her? Is that why he punched a hole through the wall?

—*You still there?*—

—*You know I am.*—

—*I gave that one away too soon, didn't I?*—

—*I have to get back to work.*—

—*Sure. I'll see you tonight.*—

The Windows screen came back on after his seemingly harmless good-bye. I stared at my computer, my mouth hanging open. Did he want to see me tonight? What did that mean? Shaking my head to chase the thoughts away, I grabbed a binder and placed it on my lap. How in the world was I supposed to convince Cole to sign his divorce papers?

He's going to hate me.

Diana A. Hicks

Chapter Nine
Just a Snack

Cole

"You've resorted to stalking the poor girl?" Em set a highball glass on the terrace retaining wall.

The afternoon was perfect for what I had planned. With a bit of luck, the weather would continue to cooperate for the rest of the night too. My stomach fluttered, a feeling that hadn't gone away since I kissed Valentina four days ago. Not seeing her all weekend had been pure torture, but I wanted to give her space. Except now I needed to apologize for not telling her about Bridget and explain the whole divorce bullshit. Was I hoping she'd also release me from my promise not to kiss her again? Hell yes, but one step at a time.

"I live here. How is this stalking?"

"Do you really think this is a good idea?"

Gravel crushing under the weight of car tires was music to my ears. "I wouldn't be doing it if I didn't think so." I leaned over the stairwell, craning my neck to get a better view of Valentina's private driveway. When I spotted her, I grabbed my drink and rushed to the nearest lounge chair. A minute later, Valentina strolled along the path, past the pool. She looked beyond sexy in a high-waist pencil skirt and a sheer silk top.

Taking a sip of my bourbon, I gave her a nonchalant wave when she looked my way. I could've sworn she was blushing, but from this distance it was hard to tell.

"Em, are we all set?"

"No."

"What?" I whipped around to face her. "I specifically remember being extra charming when I asked."

The woman stood her ground and gave me that look she reserved for when she didn't agree with my behavior. I was familiar with the look.

"Fine. I'll improvise," I said to her retreating form.

An hour later, I knocked on Valentina's door. She didn't answer right away, which had me wondering if she'd maybe fallen asleep. What a sight that would be. Valentina in bed, wearing something silky and translucent. The sudden rush of desire caught me off guard. I was here to explain myself, nothing more. Maybe this wasn't such a good idea.

"Hi," she said, out of breath, wiping her forehead with the back of her hand.

Instead of the nightie I'd hoped for, she wore a pair of yoga pants and a tank top. She looked just as hot, though. I felt like an asshole. She was still working on getting the cottage cleaned, and here I was concerned about nothing else but the heat pulsating in my pants.

"I'm sorry. I didn't mean to interrupt."

"Did you need something?"

I exhaled. She didn't send me away. "You up for a walk? I never got to show you the rest of the property."

A blush covered her cheeks, and the dimple on the side of her mouth appeared a few seconds before she spoke. "Let me just grab my shoes."

I leaned my shoulder on the threshold. If I went inside, I didn't think I could keep my promise to her. When she returned, she stopped a few feet away from me.

"Let's go." I urged her to go on but didn't get out of the way.

She squeezed through the small space between the frame and me, her shoulder brushing my chest. I inhaled and held my breath. Damn. There it was again. Past the desire, deep in my soul, was the peace I felt every time she was near. I needed that as I'd never needed anything else. And for the first time ever, I didn't know what to do to get what I wanted.

This was a game I'd never played. For whatever infuriating reason, Valentina couldn't make up her mind about me. She wanted me. That much was clear. But something held her back. Would she be this hesitant if she weren't practically living in my backyard? I took my time catching up to her. The view of her backside in those tight yoga pants made me slow my pace way down.

"Where are we going?" She turned to face me.

"This way." I gestured for her to follow the path behind the cottage. *Shameless* is what Em called it when I asked her to set up a picnic at the overlook a mile down the path. The view from the edge of the ravine was an aphrodisiac. "I owe you an explanation."

"You don't have to," she blurted out.

"I do." I searched her eyes. "I *am* married. A colossal mistake that I can't even begin to explain. All I can tell you is it'll be resolved in the next month or so."

She nodded. "Okay. You don't have to explain

yourself to me. It's not like I'm your girlfriend or anything."

"Right. You're not my girlfriend. I just didn't want you to think I was a cheater or anything." Great. I was rambling. This wasn't how it all played out in my head earlier today. Valentina had a way of unhinging me. "I signed the divorce papers the other day." Even if they hadn't been submitted yet, I was close to having my life back. I wanted her to know, though I hadn't figured out why. I pressed a hand to my chest and let out a breath, feeling light, lighter than I'd felt in months.

Her eyes snapped at me, wide and dark. She shook her head twice. "I have to admit the news took me by surprise. You certainly don't look or act married."

"I was only married for ten months. It wasn't that hard to get back into the swing of things." That came out all wrong. I wasn't helping my case here. What the hell? I usually did way better than this.

"Yeah, I got that." She laughed. Then she stopped in her tracks, her mouth slightly open.

God, I wanted to kiss those lips again.

Following her line of sight, I turned to see what'd made her halt like that, and did a double take. One, I hadn't realized we were already at the place. I'd lost track of time. And two, Em had lied. She'd done what I'd asked her to do—and then some.

We still had an hour of daylight, but Em had strung lights around the pergola and the paloverde at the edge of the ravine where old saguaros dotted the land and an earthy smell lingered in the air from last night's rain. On a coffee table next to a couple of Adirondack chairs, she'd left a cheese plate and a chilled bottle of champagne.

The dying sunrays burned bright in the horizon, turning the sky a light shade of pink and purple I'd only seen this deep in the Sonoran Desert. The tree behind us provided decent shade and kept the area a few degrees cooler.

"Is this for us?" She rewarded my efforts with a big smile featuring a dimple on each cheek.

Nodding, I silently thanked Em, the weather, and the desert gods. I gestured for her to take a seat, and she obliged. Her eyes fixed on the incredible view.

"You hungry?" I asked.

"Starving." Her voice was low and raspy. She stopped playing with the hem of her top and was more relaxed than she'd been when we first left her house.

I held her gaze. Suddenly, I was hungry for something other than cheese and wine. This incessant urge to touch her made me ache all over.

"Let me make you the perfect bite." I inched my chair closer to the bamboo table. The intimacy of sharing my favorite snack with Valentina was more revealing than telling her I was going through a divorce. I should be scared out of my wits, but instead I grinned like a moron and smeared fig spread on a piece of toasted french bread, layered on a bit of brie, and topped it with a slice of green apple.

Bracing an elbow on her knee, she took a plate and held it close to me. "Thank you," she said when I placed the bruschetta on it.

"Wait. It's not quite done yet. Savannah honey." I let the thick amber liquid ooze down from the honey spoon to create a zigzag pattern on the white flesh of the apple. "Mom sends me bottles of this stuff every month."

"Thanks." She licked her lips.

Our chairs were so close her flowery perfume taunted my senses. My heart picked up the pace, and I found myself wishing she felt the same way.

"What do you think?" I busied myself with the bottle of champagne. This would be easier if she'd already spent a night in my bed. But until then, I would have to suck it up. I kept my eyes locked on the horizon. Mostly to cool down.

To the west, far in the distance, ominous clouds hung low in the sky. The weather had promised no rain today, but that was the thing about monsoon rains. They could change direction at any time.

"Hmm." She fingered honey off her lip and licked the pad of her thumb. In my head, that sounded more like a moan.

Admittedly, I didn't bring Valentina here with the most of noble intentions in mind. I'd figured we'd eat, I'd apologize for not telling her about the divorce, and she'd reward me by releasing me from my promise not to kiss her. But what I had in mind now…

"Wow, that was delicious."

"Yeah." I offered her a glass of champagne. She took a sip and ran the tip of her tongue over her lips. *Jesus.* I had to get myself under control. "How do your parents feel about your current housing situation?"

"You mean, are they okay with me living in the backyard of a man who's notorious for seducing women?"

The bubbles went down the wrong way, and I coughed uncontrollably. "I was just wondering why they didn't cosign for you to get a real apartment or house?" I asked when I caught my breath.

"I didn't ask them to."

I'd assumed her parents didn't want to help her. But I was wrong. That was the kind of woman Valentina was. She didn't want to be handed things. She wanted to earn them. I smiled, and she returned the gesture. I should really leave her alone.

"Where did you get such a ridiculous idea about me? I don't *seduce* women." I crossed my arms, grinning. "How do I know you're not here to seduce me?" I teased.

Her breath hitched. She pressed a hand to her collarbone, coughed a few times, and drank from her glass, taking two big gulps to clear her throat. "Annie thinks you'll have me for a breakfast snack and forget about it before lunch."

"I have no idea what that means. But I'm guessing it's not good."

She shook her head. "I shouldn't've come here."

For a moment, I thought she was going to run off. Instead, she stood and walked to the edge of the overlook. The sun had set, giving way to the Tucson city lights below us, but she wasn't looking down. She was looking up.

Making a mental note to order a telescope, I refilled her almost-empty glass before joining her. "Do you think this is my big seduction game?" I offered her the champagne. When she took it, I leaned forward and whispered, "We're just having a snack."

Truth be told, I'd never gone past this point as far as seduction games go. Valentina's resolve was truly commendable. Lucky for me, her body hadn't gotten the memo yet. In that tight yoga top, her generous breasts told me what she wouldn't say. The harden peaks poked through the material, and she worked hard to keep her breaths even. But she couldn't help it. Every now and then she'd exhale, and her perfectly round mounds would rise and fall as she tried to keep her composure.

Hypnotized, I leaned forward. The promise I'd made said nothing about touching. I reached for her hand and wrapped my fingers around hers. Too much, too fast. This time she did take off. My mind raced, trying to figure out what to say to get her to stay.

She set her glass down and turned to me. "Thank you for the champagne, for everything. It was nice."

"Don't leave me." I placed my glass next to hers. Where did that come from? What I meant to say was "Don't leave yet."

I slanted a glance toward the dark sky, where gray clouds quickly rolled over our heads. A thunder roared and stopped her in her tracks. This was my chance. I closed the space between us in two strides and gripped her arm.

She spun, her eyes fixed on my hand. "Let me go. I made a mistake. I can't do this. I'm sorry," she mumbled.

Her gaze inched up from my arm to my face, and heat pulsed in my chest and my goddamn pants. The lust in her expression was clear. She wanted me.

"No," she said. This isn't who I am."

"What are you talking about? Relax. I'm not going to kiss you." I pulled her toward me until her breath brushed my cheek, and pressed my lips to her hair. "Valentina. Ask me. And put us both out of our misery."

Chapter Ten
The Wrong Guy Again

Valentina

Out of our misery? Did he want this as much as I did?

My heart had done a happy dance when he showed up at my door, looking all freaking hot and muscular, an hour after I'd come home. The man should not be allowed to wear jeans or white T-shirts. Or work out. Dammit.

I should've gone with my first instinct and hid in the bathroom until he left. But he'd seen me come in, so pretending I wasn't home would've been childish. And I still had that Bridget matter to deal with.

As I'd trod the hallway up to the door, I found myself asking what *Wednesday*, a.k.a. sex goddess, would do. How would she seduce Cole to sign the divorce papers? Well, for one, she probably wouldn't be caught dead opening the door to Derek Cole in her yoga pants and all sweaty. The thought had prompted me to run back to the bathroom and use a baby wipe to clean up a bit.

By the time I'd realized there was no way I could go through with it, I had already opened the door.

His piercing blue gaze undressed me, as if he didn't care I wasn't in designer jeans or sexy lingerie. That was his gift. He had the innate ability to make me feel like the most beautiful creature on Earth. How did he do that? Why'd he bother with me?

"Valentina." His voice brought me back, sending a burst of adrenaline down my legs and effectively killing the bit of buzz I had from the champagne.

I placed my hand on his chest to push him away, but instead, I slid my fingers down his front and stroked his sculpted abs, kneading every plane. A slow and delicious heat zipped over my skin as Cole ran the pad of his thumb over my arm, his hot and dark eyes on me. God, the man knew what he was doing. How he affected me.

The desire I'd suppressed for the last six years sprung to life and muted everything else. For a moment, I didn't care about Bridget's threat or that if I gave in, I'd be officially Monday. The most hated day of the week.

Kiss me now. Please.

Another thunderclap brought me to my senses before I voiced my thoughts. The moment had to be over. Or rather, I had to end it. I pushed at him. At least I thought I did. When I looked at my hand, I had his shirt in a tight grip. Ripples danced in my stomach as he covered my hand with his. That all-American-boy smile of his invited me in, intoxicating and infuriating.

After one more loud thunder, the clouds delivered on their promise. Rain pelted sideways, each cool drop extinguishing the heat gushing through my body. I clung to that feeling and tried again. This time I managed to put distance between us. Fuck Bridget. Doing what she'd asked wasn't as easy as sleeping with Cole. My feelings would get in the way, and I'd end up brokenhearted.

Cole rubbed the back of his neck. With both hands on his hips, he forced even breaths. My gaze fell on the patch of exposed skin just above the waist of his pants.

"You're incredibly hot, scorching really," I said.

That smile of his was back. He thought he'd won.

I pressed on. "But this?" I pointed at us. "This is a risk I can't take. It's not about me." The downpour muffled my words, but I had to say my piece. He had to understand why we couldn't be—Bridget's contract aside. I licked cool rainwater from my lips. "If I didn't have Max, yeah sure, no problem. I'd be your Monday Girl. Or whichever day is currently available on your weekly rotation. But that's not the case. You think you want me because I'm refusing you. You really don't…want me. How could you? You barely know me." The realization of how true my words filled my heart with icy sorrow.

"I know you're brave and determined." He thought for a moment, frowning as if he had finally realized the motivation behind my refusal. Max. "If I could give you more, I would."

"I'm not asking for anything." I waved in the general direction of the path we'd taken to get here. I'd lost our home before Max even arrived. But I couldn't do this. I couldn't get caught in the middle of whatever messed-up game Cole and Bridget had going on. One, this wasn't who I was, who I wanted Max to see in me. And two, I couldn't fall for the wrong guy again. In all this, I had way more to lose than Cole. Why did I let him get this close?

I took one last glance at the city lights and the magnificent desert landscape around us. "Good-bye,

Derek."

I turned and started up the trail, taking long strides. That wasn't running away, right? After five minutes, I was sure he wasn't following me. When I reached the cottage, I went straight into the kitchen, grabbed Annie's bagful of new clothes, and headed out again. Space was what I needed. I didn't trust myself to be this close to Cole and not run out and beg him to kiss me. To finally bring me some relief from this need I had for him.

Gravel crunched under my soggy sneakers as I made my way to my car. I climbed into it and drove off. My tires spun as they fought to find their grip. Just like the thoughts in my head—what I wanted, what I had to do, what he made me feel. Nothing made sense.

Half an hour later, I found myself in Annie's restaurant on Swan Road. I stood two steps inside the trendy cafe-style restaurant. Water pooled at my feet. The horror-stricken look on her face when she spotted me did me in. I burst into tears, with loud sobs, snotty nose…the works. Luckily, Mondays were slow, and the place wasn't crowded.

"Oh, sweetie, what happened?" She ushered me to her office in the back corner of the dining room, muttering a few words in Vietnamese over her shoulder.

I had no idea what she'd said. My Vietnamese was limited to her menu items.

She turned back to me. "Let me guess…Cole."

I nodded. "We didn't get to do our Polaroids over the weekend. I thought you might want to work on it now."

"We'll get to that later. But you know you don't need an excuse to come see me. Did he—"

A single knock on the door saved me from whatever string of questions she had lined up for me. She sidestepped her desk and opened the door. "*Bún riêu*?" she asked when she returned.

With a nod, I scooted my chair closer to the desk and let the steamy crab-and-tomato soup warm me up. Gingerly, she tossed sprouts, extra minced peppers, and cilantro in the broth. I grabbed the chopsticks she offered and started with the noodles. Soul food.

While I ate, she busied herself with the papers on her desk, eyes darting to me every now and then. I focused on the task in front of me and shoved small bites in my mouth in hopes the soup would numb this tightness in my chest.

When I finished, I blew out air and met her gaze. "I lied. I want him."

"Of course you do, sweetie. What're you gonna do now?"

"Stay away?"

She gave me a naughty grin. "Did he try something?"

I nodded, raising an eyebrow.

"That good, huh?"

"You have no idea." I shuddered at the memory of his hands on me.

"Well, I hate to say it, but he might change his mind after Max comes to live with you."

"I thought about that. You may be right. That's if we're there long enough."

"What do you mean?" Lines appeared across her forehead.

I couldn't stand the pity in her eyes. It was the same look she had when I first told her I was pregnant.

As if she wanted to make everything better but didn't know how.

"Oh." She slapped her hand on the desk. "I almost forgot. I did a little digging. He's married."

"I know." I sat back on the chair and covered my face with my hands.

"And he's going through a nasty divorce." Her breath hitched. "Omigod, you slept with him."

My head snapped up. "What? No. Though I strongly considered it."

She blew out air and shook her head. "Apparently, the wife wants to keep his company. Can you believe that? Some women just have ovaries the size of Pluto."

"Wait. What?"

"You know what I mean." She shrugged.

"No. The other thing. She wants his company?"

"That's what I heard. You met her? What's she like?"

I gripped both chopsticks in one hand and made a stabbing motion. "Scary?" Truth was, she was strong, full of confidence, perfect. In short, Cole's type.

"Another reason not to get involved. I'm telling ya—men are trouble. Even when they're not married." Shoulders slumped, she reached out and squeezed my fingers. "Just stay strong, and all this will blow over. Focus on Max. Men like Cole, they tire quickly."

"Do I want him to get tired?"

"Yes." She squinted at me. "There's more. Tell me."

I shifted uncomfortably in my chair. "His wife knows I'm living in the cottage…her cottage."

Annie covered her mouth, eyes wide. With a nod, she urged me to continue. "And she wants me to get him to sign the divorce papers. Apparently, sleeping with him will do the trick. As if it were that easy." I snorted and smoothed my hair away from my face. My cheeks felt sticky from the running mascara.

"Right. So she can keep the company." She stood and paced her office a couple of times.

"That would be my guess. She's in a hurry too. I have two weeks to get it done."

She sat at the edge of her seat, picking sprouts off my bowl and eating them. "You're not going through with this, are you?"

"Of course not." No need to mention that earlier today I had every intention to… I grimaced. *Stop it. Don't think about that.*

"You need to tell him. Tell him what Bridget asked you to do. Why would she even ask you?"

"She threatened to kick me out of *her cottage*."

She closed her eyes, pinching her nose. It was nice to know someone was on my side. "You need to tell him."

"Okay," I said with renewed fortitude that, honestly, I didn't feel. "You wanna do the pics? I'm sure my face is a mess, but…" I needed to do something to keep my mind off Cole.

"Yeah, let me grab my camera."

While I waited, I dug through the bag and pulled out the sequined skirt. No doubt Annie already wrote a great piece on how to wear it. I pulled my pants off and slipped into the skirt. It was comfortable and sexy. If Cole could see me in it… A pretty outfit wouldn't make him love me, but the idea he might be in as much pain from unrealized desire as I was made me feel better.

"I was thinking." Annie closed the office door

behind her. "Instead of doing full-body shots, I want to do close-ups. Let's start with the legs." She sighed. "Are you sure you're up for this tonight?"

"It's better than sitting at home thinking about Cole and how cozy he must be in his bed made of gold."

"That sounds uncomfortable." She laughed. "Some people have way too much money."

"I like that he earned his money."

"Wait. I thought we were hating on him."

"No. We are." I stood in front of her as she kneeled to angle the camera, aiming at my thigh. I dipped my chin and pictured Cole's long fingers brushing the inside of my knee.

"You're thinking about him," she said, her face flush against her camera.

"Am not."

"The goose bumps on your legs say otherwise." She peered up at me. "Just clear your mind."

"Okay."

"Oh and hey. Some good news. I found a model for the fund-raiser on Saturday. You're off the hook."

"Thanks. I really don't have time for parties right now. Sorry." I took a lungful, making a mental list of everything I still needed to finish before the weekend. Or trying.

Relax. I'm not going to kiss you. Cole's words echoed in my head.

Annie was right. Cole would lose interest as soon as he realized that whatever picture he'd conjured in his mind about me was incomplete. I wasn't like his other weekday girls. I was a mom. My feelings for him didn't matter. Max was the only priority. I had room for nothing else, not when I was so close to delivering on my promise to him. I could finally be the mom Max needed. Throwing that away over a hot magnate with amazing abs would be beyond selfish of me.

"Do you think he'll hate me?" I had to stay away from him, but that didn't mean I wanted him to hate me over this thing with his wife.

Annie wrapped her arm around my waist and shimmied a little, which got a small chuckle out of me. "I don't know. But why would he? This isn't your fault. Just tell him before his wife does, twists things around, and Cole kicks *you* out."

Chapter Eleven
The Family Life

Cole

"You were right. Is that what you want me to say?" I asked Em.

"Excuse me, sir."

"Don't 'sir' me. You know what I'm talking about." I slumped into the lounge chair by the pool.

The swim had helped my mood some, but Em's furtive glances at the cottage reminded me of the last night I'd spent with Valentina. Trying to seduce her with expensive champagne and stupid cheese wasn't one of my best ideas. It was quite possibly one of the worst.

"I've noticed she's kept to herself all week."

Had it only been a week? I couldn't tell. The days were blending into each other again. The last seven days had felt like one long-ass day. Em placed a highball glass on the small table next to me—the bourbon I'd asked for two hours ago. She'd taken to refusing me alcohol before noon. Sure, I could've gone inside and gotten my own damn drink. But not so deep down, I knew she was right. Again.

"She thinks I'm an asshole." I took a long swig of the bourbon and soda water. "I'm staying away from her. For real, this time."

"I didn't know she had a son."

"Yeah. I forgot to tell you." I rubbed my face.

She glanced up. Her smile went from a small tug on the side of her mouth to a full-on grin. My heartbeat picked up the pace. For a moment, I hoped Valentina had reconsidered and was on her way to me to apologize. I turned slowly in my chair.

"Now that you're in good company, I'll go back to the kitchen and make some lunch." On her way out, she stopped to pet Pirate.

The stupid cat was back, limp and all. He padded his way around the pool and casually jumped on my lap. As if he hadn't been gone all week.

"Where the hell have you been?"

His response was a long purr as he readjusted his weight to sit high on my chest. I scratched him behind the ear while I examined his twisted paw.

"Some pet you are."

"Is that your cat?" The new voice took me by surprise. My house was as close to a fortress as it could get. No one got in unless they had my permission. The boy looked at me intently with eyes I'd gotten to know very well in the last couple of weeks. This had to be Max.

"No, he's not my cat." I didn't want to make friends with the kid. Staying away from Valentina meant staying away from Max too. Besides, I didn't like kids much. "I don't even like cats."

"Are you sure?"

"Sure of what? Of course, I don't like cats."

"He looks like he belongs to you." The boy was inquisitive and to the point. He was smart and pragmatic. Like his mom.

"He just lives here, okay? He doesn't belong to anyone."

The boy reached for Pirate's hurt paw. Pirate rubbed his head against Max's hand, making him squeal. "I love him. Can I hold him?"

"Why are you asking me?" I shrugged.

Max lifted Pirate off me, and the damn cat let him. The traitor. "What happened to his paw?"

"I don't know. He started coming around less than a year ago. His paw was already like that."

"Maybe he was looking for food."

"Yeah, I think so." I leaned forward to touch Pirate's paw. "At first he wouldn't let me get near him. It took me days to earn his trust. Or rather, to figure out he liked canned tuna. He's been here ever since. Comes and goes as he pleases." Somehow, we were having a conversation now.

"He's the best cat ever. What's his name?"

"I call him Pirate because of the black spot on his face and, well, the paw."

"And because he's so fluffy." Max squeezed the cat tight. Even threw in a shimmy at the end.

Pirate, on the other hand, was dead weight in the kid's arms. Maybe he was the worst pet because I was a bad human companion. Great.

"How about you, kid? Do you have a name? How did you get through my security?"

He laughed, looking like a smaller, younger version of Valentina. "I'm just a human kid. I can't get through all those policemen."

"They're security guards." I furrowed my brows at him. He didn't care.

"My mom brought me here. In her car." He pointed

toward Valentina's private driveway, pushing brown, wavy hair away from his eyes.

"And what's your name?" I was hoping to intimidate him with a string of questions.

"I'm Maximiliano Andres de Cordoba." The kid was hilarious. And so serious for a five-year-old.

"Wow. That's quite a name. Can I call you Max?"

"Sure." He shrugged. "What's your name?"

"Derek Weston Cole," I said, but my answer lacked his conviction.

"Max." Valentina's voice carried across the yard.

"What the what?" He jerked to his feet.

Pirate dropped to the lawn and ran for it. By the time I rose from my chair, the cat was already inside the house.

"That's my mom. I have to go."

He took off without saying good-bye or asking why I was here, which led me to believe his mom had talked to him about me. The thought brought a warm feeling to my chest. With a sigh, I picked up a towel from the rack behind me and dried my hair. If I hurried, I could have lunch with Pirate. He always ate in the kitchen with Em while she cooked.

The giggles stopped me in my tracks. Coming down the path, all legs and hair, was Valentina, with a smile I hadn't seen before. My heart squeezed tight, and I rubbed my chest to ease the ache. Max had his arm wrapped around her hip. He was tall for his age, but he looked small next to her. They made quite a pair—same dark, wavy hair and brown eyes. I sat back on the chair and took a long sip of bourbon, feeling a kind of peace I hadn't felt since I kissed Valentina.

"Good afternoon," she said from a distance. She'd

stopped at the small patch of grass on the other side of the pool.

"He's the friend I told you about." Max waved excitedly. "He lives with Pirate."

I chuckled. "The cat lives with me. Not the other way around."

He nodded. "Do you want to play baseball with us?"

Valentina's hand shot out to stop him from inviting me to their game. She turned to me and mouthed an apology. *Sorry.*

Oh, sweetheart, say it. Say you're sorry for sending me away.

"Max, I'm sure Mr. Cole has many things to do. Let's just play on our own, okay?"

I sat down, made myself comfortable, and watched them play. Em returned, carting a lunch big enough to feed a small country. Pirate trailed behind her as if wrapping up a conversation they hadn't finished in the kitchen. She parked the cart next to the towel rack and proceeded to set the table. I hadn't told her I was ready to eat, and she knew I never ate by the pool. What was she up to?

Across the lawn, Valentina and Max had switched to playing catch. She had a good arm and had plenty of advice to give to Max.

"Sounds like she knows a lot about baseball." Em piled sandwiches on a plate. She suppressed a smile as she added some PB&J sandwiches.

I almost wanted to apologize to Valentina for Em playing the matchmaker, except Valentina hadn't notice the lunch feast Em was working on. Max had her undivided attention.

"You used to play baseball, right?"

I finished my drink in one swig. "That was a long time ago."

When I set the glass down, Em replaced it with a water goblet. I downed that too, keeping my eyes on Max's glove. He had it tilted too low. A ball with more speed would easily bounce off his hand and hit him in the face. Bloody noses were something I was familiar with.

Before I could think about what I was doing, I dashed down the path along the side of the pool and headed toward them. Valentina's eyes got bigger than normal, and her lips parted. She looked spooked. When was the last time she saw a shirtless guy? Max, on the other hand, was grinning at me, ready to welcome me to their game.

"Okay, kid. Let me show you a trick."

"Excuse me." Valentina wedged herself between Max and me while keeping her hands away from me, working hard to keep her breathing steady. "I think we're doing just fine."

I took the ball and glove from her. She reached for it, but I kept it at arm's length. "Let me just show him. I'll be fast." I winked at her.

She crossed her arms but didn't send me away. Good. Progress. I turned my attention to Max. "You gotta charge the ball. Don't wait for it to come to you. Step and catch. Got it?" I showed him the motion. From the corner of my eye, I caught Valentina covering up a grin. "That's also a good life philosophy." I raised an eyebrow at her.

"I'm sure you think it is."

All my life I've never been afraid to take a step and

reach for my goals. For the past few months, I'd been afraid to move forward, to follow my own advice, until Valentina reminded me what fighting for crazy dreams looked like.

"You got it?" I asked Max. "Let's try a few throws." Valentina's glove was small on me, but I shoved my hand in it as best I could. I gave it a few squeezes before I showed Max the ball. "Heads up." I threw a pop fly. He waited too long. By the time he charged, the ball had hit the grass.

"I almost had it," he said.

"You gotta get under it." Valentina picked up the ball and tossed it to him. Then she spun to face me. "He's afraid of the ball."

"Okay, Max, let's try it without the glove."

"I don't think so. The skin will come off my hands."

Valentina laughed, and I found myself chuckling along with her. The fluttering in my stomach returned with renewed vigor. And like a drug addict, I succumbed to the high.

" 'Kay. Can you show me?" Max asked, and effectively blocked all the fantasies swirling around in my mind.

"Throw it back," I said.

He did. Jeez, the kid had an arm on him.

Valentina beamed, scooting closer to me. "It hurts, doesn't it?"

"Ouch." I flick my wrist before I pitched the ball again. "Don't wait for it," I called out.

When he caught it, he jumped high and pumped the air. "Mom, did you see that? I did it."

We kept at it for more than an hour, until Max

dropped to the ground and announced he needed a break. "I'm tired."

"What? Come on. We just got started." I was fired up. It'd been too long since I played ball. But the kid didn't budge. "Fine. How about some lunch?"

"No, we don't want to impose." Valentina was quick to respond, as if she'd been waiting for the invitation to come just so she could turn me down. Again.

"Impose?" I eyed the feast Em had laid out. "Look at that. Are you really going to let all that food go to waste?"

"Please, Mom. Can we have some watermelon?" Max asked.

She couldn't say no to him. What would it take for her to stop saying no to herself? Last week, she made me understand why she couldn't be with me. All this was for Max. How long before she understood she mattered too?

"Are you sure this is okay?" she asked me.

I nodded, offering her my arm. To my surprise, she took it and allowed me to escort them to the other side of the pool. I didn't think we were ready to call this progress, but it was something. Her hand on my arm sent goose bumps up my shoulder and down my spine. Taking a big risk, I placed my right hand over hers. She playfully bumped her shoulder against me, her eyes soft and bright. That was different. I'd gotten all kinds of looks from women. Gratitude wasn't one of them.

Max reached the table first and quickly started working on the bowlful of watermelon pieces. This prompted Valentina to leave my side to help him with a plate. When I joined them, she had a plate loaded with sandwiches, fruit, and veggies ready for me.

"Thank you," I said. "You didn't have to serve me."

"Please. It's the least I can do." She gestured for me to sit. "Do you always eat PB&J sandwiches for lunch?"

I chuckled. "Never. This was Em's idea."

"I'll make sure and thank her. Thank you for the baseball lessons." She got another plate. "Do you coach or something?"

"No. I played in college."

"Oh. Was that like a long time ago?" She lowered her eyes.

I liked the implication of her question. "I'm twenty-eight, if that's what you're asking. Do I look that old?"

Her laugh, the one that made everything around us fall away, floated through the air again. "Not at all," she said, cheeks red. "It's just that you've accomplished a lot in such a short amount of time. I wasn't sure."

"Are you impressed?" I leaned forward to catch her gaze.

"Is one compliment not enough?" She sat back in her chair and stared at me.

I shot a quick glance to Max, who was still digging through the watermelon bowl. "Seems that's all I can get these days. Or have you changed your mind?"

Her breath hitched. "Max. Don't eat from the serving bowl. Let me fix you a plate."

Max nodded with big chipmunk cheeks. "Yes, please." Red liquid oozed from the side of his mouth.

She faced me again. "I can't look."

"What's wrong?" I took a big piece of watermelon

and stuffed it in my mouth. She looked away, stifling a giggle.

"That is disgusting." Max burst out laughing.

"This is how you eat watermelon." The juice touched my lips. I leaned over and pressed my mouth to her neck.

"Hey."

"Eww. Gross." Max walked over and planted kisses on her face, leaving sticky stuff all over her.

"Oh no, Max. We made a mess. You know what she needs?"

The idea struck him right away, but he was too excited to verbalize it. He jumped in place, pointing at the pool, eyes darting from Valentina back to the shimmering water. "She…she needs a bath," he finally said in a voice that was half squeal.

Valentina left the chair with incredible speed. It was a guy thing. She fled; I had to chase her. Taking three long strides, I blocked her before she reached the path that led to her cottage. I picked her up and threw her over my shoulder.

"Do it." Max egged me on.

"You little rascal." Valentina's fake anger made Max titter even harder.

She pushed against my bare back, arms locked against my shoulders. I was losing her. My hands slid up her legs, those long legs, and her backside. God, she felt good. I tightened my grip on her. Her face was only inches from mine, and her breasts gently pressed against my chest. Her proximity was too much for me to bear. Jumping in the pool was more than a good idea now. It was a necessity. I let the warm sensation linger another couple of seconds. Then I walked us straight into the water.

When we reached the bottom, my hands went to her hips, and she didn't push me away. I kicked and took her with me back to the surface. She looked good wet, laughing, and free of her usual armor."

"You are so grounded." She swam to the edge.

"How am I grounded? He started-ed it." Max pointed an accusatory finger at me. The little jerk. If he hadn't been here, I never would've done this.

"You should get out of those wet clothes," I said. I couldn't remember the last time I had this much fun.

"Does that ever work for you?"

"Every time." I swam toward her, but she jumped out of the pool before I reached her.

"Okay. You've had enough to eat," she said to Max. "Let's go back inside." She started down the path, pushing wet tresses away from her face and tugging at her soaked clothes.

Max waved before he bolted toward the house. I stayed in the water, mesmerized by the sight of Valentina. The pool was too quiet without them. A suffocating silence. I pushed against the wall and let my body float aimlessly.

So this was it? This was the family life Valentina was crying over the day we met? All her efforts, her crazy rules, everything made sense now.

How the hell was I supposed to stay away from her?

Chapter Twelve
My Cole Problem

Valentina

I rushed into the house, dripping wet, blood thrumming in my ears.

Max plopped himself on the couch in front of the flat screen to finish the rest of his PB&J sandwich that seemed to be stuck to his hand now. "That was epic," he squealed.

"Yeah, it was." I took off my shoes at the door. Who would've thought? Gorgeous Cole was also fun. "Can you watch a movie while I clean up?"

"Sure," he said, already engrossed in his dinosaur movie.

I went straight to the bathroom and locked the door behind me. A shower seemed like a good idea right about now—to cool off more than anything else. My body still hummed, an aftershock of Cole's touch. I couldn't believe how much my body reacted to everything and anything he did to me. And who could blame me? He looked incredibly hot in swim trunks, hair wet, and steely muscles all shiny. My heart, and part of my resolve to stay away from him, melted when he played catch with Max.

Dammit. I put the toilet seat down, sat, and buried my face in my hands. This was really getting out of control. I had hours to warn him about Bridget, and the thought never even occurred to me. My brain turned to mush the second he left his lounge chair and sauntered across the lawn with no shirt on.

Worst part was I was running out of time. Yesterday Bridget had come over to my desk and asked if *it* had been done. I'd almost told her I had no intention of playing her stupid game, but the woman was terrifying and I didn't want to cause a scene at work. I was still the noob…though probably not for long. With all the changes going on in the office, I wouldn't be surprised if CCI got dismantled and sold by the pound before the end of the year. Even my boss, Christopher, was worried. He had a lot more insight into the goings-on of the company. If he was updating his resume, he had a good reason for it.

I stuffed a hand in my wet hair and blew out air. Cole didn't deserve this. Christopher had mentioned many times how hard Cole had worked to make CCI successful, to take care of everyone working for him. CCI was his legacy. Why did Bridget want to take that away from him? Out of spite? She didn't seem the type. Money? Maybe. But she was married to Cole. How much more money could she need?

This couldn't wait any longer. I stood. My stomach muscles tightened, and a flutter flushed across my chest. I had to tell him—today. If he got mad at me, hated me over it, so be it. Placing both hands on my hips, I faced the woman in the mirror. Oh no. My sheer top was completely see through. Every curve of my breasts was visible, including my hardened nipples. *Cole saw me like this!* My cheeks burned hot. I winced, pressing cold fingers on my face to make the red go away. Maybe he didn't notice. But what about the dark stare he shot me when I jumped out of the pool? The blue of his irises was barely visible. He saw me, all right.

I reached in the shower stall and ran the hot water. So what if he saw me? I didn't care. *Dammit. I did care.* I loved that he wanted me so much. The desire on his face every time we were near had become a sort of drug to me. I craved it, and it scared the hell out of me, though that didn't stop me from wanting him more than I ever thought I could ever want someone. Not that I had much experience in that department. The one time I thought I'd fallen in love, it ended quickly—and painfully. My chin trembled, and tears burned my eyes. I wiped my face with the back of my hand. I was done crying over that.

I peeled off my top and pulled it over my head. The sheer bra underneath was like tissue paper stuck to my skin. I took off my shorts and underwear and dropped everything in the sink. Was Cole different? Or were my feelings for him strictly lust related?

Stop that. Don't even go there. Damn. Too late. I was already thinking about it.

I got in the shower and leaned on the tiled wall. Hot water trickled down my front. My breathing was uneven again just thinking of Cole and me in the pool, our bodies intertwined, the way I'd been able to touch every plane of his naked back. I'd been grateful for the unexpected dip. Honestly, I didn't think he'd do it. But if he hadn't jumped in the pool, who knew what I would've done… Beg him to kiss me? The intense need Cole had awakened in me tortured me day and night.

What if I let him in? Just once. Closing my eyes, I

rested the side of my head on the wall and ran the puff across my belly to make a rich lather. My hand wandered lower—

The shower spray turned to icy pricks, and my eyes flew open. Jeez, even my water heater knew this was a bad idea. I rushed out of the shower and killed the water.

Damn you, Cole.

Still shivering, I wrapped myself in a towel and leaned on the sink, raking a hand through my hair. All these years, I thought this side of me was done. Between my broken heart and childbirth, I'd convinced myself I would never love again. Never want anyone again. I was wrong.

I wanted to be with Cole.

If he could make me feel like this when he wasn't even in the room… My knees went weak at the thought of what it'd be like if he were here. I'd crossed the threshold. How could I refuse him now that I knew how much I wanted him? I dropped my head in my hands, taking deep breaths. *No. Focus.* All I had to do was stay out of his way.

Next time Max and I went out to the yard, if Cole was half-naked by the pool, I'd run. As fast as I could. In the opposite direction.

Yes. That was it. I looked around for something to write on. I should definitely make a list of what to do to ensure plenty of space and dry clothes were between us next time. A list was the solution to my Cole problem.

A bang on the door brought me back. "Mom? Are you in there?"

"What is it, buddy?"

"Aunt Annie is on the phone. She wants to talk to

you."

"Tell her I'll call her back in a minute. I need to get dressed, okay?"

On the other side of the door, Max kept talking to Annie, not giving her my message. I donned my bathrobe and opened the door. He followed me into my bedroom. Crap. He was telling her about the incident with Cole.

"Okay. I can take it from here." I reached for the phone. But he turned away from me, his hand out to keep me at a distance.

His plan was to entertain her until I was ready. Fine. I was too late to stop him anyway. He'd already told her about the pool dip. From the chest of drawers, I grabbed a pair of yoga pants and a top, skipping the bra. The twins needed the rest of the day off. When I was dressed, I waved Max over to the bed. He talked so fast I seriously doubted Annie understood what he was talking about.

"Okay, bye," he said into the speaker before he went back to his movie.

"Wow, that was an earful," Annie said. "Sounds like he's having an awesome time with your hot landlord."

"How're you doing today?" I ignored her comment. I wasn't ready to discuss Cole and our little episode by the pool.

"Great. And I would very much like to hear *your* version of the pool dip. But for now, you're off the hook."

"Thanks." I glanced at my phone. I was never off the hook with Annie.

"I need a huge favor. Tonight."

"Tonight? What's going on?"

"The fund-raiser I told you about last week, remember? I need you to wear one of the dresses."

"I thought you'd found someone else. I don't have anyone to watch Max."

"Come on. One of my models bailed. And I already committed to this event. The dresses are being auctioned, and I have the exclusive. It's a huge deal for my blog. And don't worry about Max. Mom says she can spend the night and watch him. She hasn't seen him in ages. Be a friend, pleeeease."

"I don't know."

She let out a heavy sigh. "The other model was getting two hundred dollars. Money's yours if you want." Silence. Then a sigh. More loud sighing. "Okay. So I have free childcare, a stunning dress for you to wear for the night, and two hundred dollars. Why are you saying no?" Did she stomp her foot?

"I'm not." I plopped myself on the bed.

"What? Yes, you are."

"I just don't feel like going to a party. It's always so awkward, feeling like I have to talk to people." I lay down and closed my eyes. The thought of going to a party tonight made me feel tired.

"You are not required to talk to anyone. In fact, I think it's better. It gives the dress a certain allure." She laughed at her own joke. "Come on. What time should we come by?"

"Fine. Max goes to bed around seven. So anytime after that."

"Great. We'll be there at six sharp. Wash your hair and roll it. I'll help you with the updo and makeup." She was all business now.

119

"Annie, two hours tops. And I said seven, not six."

"Sure. Done. The auction ends at midnight. We'll need to return the dresses then. Bring a backup outfit. See you in a few hours." She hung up before I could ask her anything else.

I dropped the phone next to me and scooted up onto the pillows. I stared at the ceiling until Max came looking for me, munching on his sandwich. "Can you finish that already?"

"Okay. Okay." He shoved the whole thing in his mouth.

"I didn't mean… Forget it. Do you want to take a nap with me?"

"Yeah." He jumped in and got under the covers.

"Aunt Annie and I are going to a dinner tonight. Mrs. Hwang will stay with you until I get back. Deal?"

"Can I come?" His eyelids were already droopy.

"It's for adults only. But you and I can have pizza tomorrow. How about that?"

"If I behave and brush my teeth, can I have a lollipop with my pizza?" He cuddled next to me. He was making me sleepy too.

"Sure, why not."

"Mom?"

"Yes?"

"I had the best time with my new friend. I wished all weekends were like this one."

Wouldn't it be nice if every weekend could be like this? Minus the frustrating sexual tension, of course. I could definitely do with less of that. But what would happen when Cole decided he was done with us? I squeezed my eyes shut. I could handle a broken heart, but the thought of Max getting hurt was too much for me.

"Can we stay here forever?"

"We can't. When our lease is over, we'll need to find a different house."

"I like this house."

"But it's not ours. This is temporary. Do you understand that?"

He didn't answer. His little face was fully relaxed as he drifted off to sleep. I cleaned grape jelly off his cheek and hugged him close. Stroking his hair, I glanced at my watch. I still had a couple of hours before I had to get ready for Annie's fancy party. My pulse picked up the pace. Time to find out how temporary our living arrangements were. I grabbed the phone off the bed and hit one on the speed dial for the main house.

Em answered before the second ring. "Hello, Valentina."

"Hello." I sat up, furrowing my brows. How did she know it was me? Oh right, Em knew this number. "Hi, Em. Thank you so much for lunch."

"It was my pleasure, dear. How can I help you?"

"Is Cole around?" I felt like a kid asking if my friend could come out and play.

"You just missed him. He has an engagement tonight. He left early, but you can reach him on his mobile if it's urgent."

"No. That's fine. I'll just talk to him tomorrow. Thanks." I hung up and let my head fall back. I was off the hook for tonight.

Chapter Thirteen
The Shindig

Cole

"Remind me again why we're here?" I asked Dom, leaning against the bar, tapping my fingers on the counter as the laser lights of the venue shone on the floor in front of us, reflecting the letters *DCF*. Women dressed in intricate lingerie did a hypnotic dance on small platforms at various spots throughout the warehouse-size gallery. Their moves were synchronized to the club music and repeated every eight beats, the same beat they did for all my events.

A blast of vanilla-scented air rushed in from somewhere above our heads. The extra oxygen was the only thing keeping me awake tonight. An acrobat slowly dropped from the twenty-foot ceiling and offered me a shot of vodka. I shook my head for what had to be the fifth time in the last hour. Three other girls dressed in full-body leotards were suspended around the room, spinning next to expensive art. Art that was part of the silent auction.

"It'll help with your divorce. You know, show the judge you care and shit." Dom took a shot from the acrobat. Her overly made-up eyes lingered on his face as he drank more than the usual two ounces. "Plus, the Derek Cole Foundation is hosting this shindig."

"God, I feel like a five-year-old putting my name on things." I pinched my nose, feeling drained. Maybe we needed to pump more oxygen in the air.

"It makes the foundation sound personable." He tore his eyes away from the swirling woman overhead to look at me. "It's cool you're helping kids. You're all right, man."

Ironically, the fund-raiser to help orphans had more to do with decadence than with children. According to Nikki, my event planner, sex, booze, and half-naked women triggered men to spend a shitload of money on art. The faces of hungry and neglected children made people, men and women alike, run for the hills.

The Derek Cole Foundation should really be called the Em Foundation, though. Em was the one who came up with the idea in the first place. And then put me in touch with the orphanage where she'd spent most of her childhood years. At the time, the agency had been in trouble due to their sizable debt. The interests were slowly putting them out of business. Being the asshole that I was, I'd been bitching to Em about the amount of taxes I had to pay now that CCI was making money. That was when she'd suggested I put that money to good use and stick it to Uncle Sam. It was a match made in heaven.

I looked at my watch again, my eyes lingering on the second hand. I swear for every other tick, it went back three.

"You miss the simple days, huh? Refurbishing routers in your mom's basement, making pennies on the dollar."

"I don't miss that. I'm proud of what I've done. Just wish I could be doing more of it, you know."

"We'll get there, man." He pulled his head back, mouth wide open.

"Stop drinking my booze."

"I can't seem to say no to her." He smiled at the acrobat, who was now several feet over our heads, spinning with one long leg touching the back of her head.

"You said you'd heard from the investigator. Anything that can get me my company back?"

"Not exactly." He frowned. "Yesterday Bridget flew to Vegas. Burned several hundred thousand dollars on a single blackjack table. But nothing to make the board of directors change their minds about letting you back in."

"That would be par for the course," I said. Bridget had a thing for gambling, so much so that we spent our honeymoon in Monte Carlo. Never saw the outside of the casinos there. She gambled the night away while I sat at the bar, not having sex.

"You're right. She's been doing this for some time now. Expensive habit."

I shrugged. "I don't care what she does with her money." Damn. I braced my arms on the bar, stomach clenching. After my talk with Dom last week, I'd figured all this would be sorted out quickly. No such luck.

"True. But that got me thinking about her financials. I thought I'd sniff around there a bit. I'm telling you—she's hiding something."

"Are you sure you want to waste your time with this?" All this waiting seemed pointless. My choices remained the same. My company or my freedom.

"We still have two weeks. I'm gonna keep at it

until the clock runs down." His eyes had turned obsidian with determination.

This was why I'd hired him as my lawyer. I was too close to it all and couldn't see the big picture. Not that I loved Bridget. Truth was, after all that'd happened, I finally had come to understand that I never loved her. The marriage had been her idea, after all. I just went along with it, thinking it was the best thing for CCI. Somehow it made sense to be married to the woman who ran my company.

After all the nasty business of her cheating on me, I realized I wasn't mad at her because I loved her. I was pissed because now my baby would suffer. CCI was why I'd stepped down without challenging the board, why I'd let the settlement drag on for so long. It was my legacy, and so many people depended on its success. But now I needed my freedom more than anything. I needed the ability to give myself to someone if that was what I goddamn wanted to do. Assuming there was a someone and that someone felt the same way about me. Chest tight, I ran a hand through my hair, almost smelling gardenias in the air.

"Incoming." Dom elbowed me in the ribs. "Something in Nikki's eyes tells me there's more to her than fancy dresses and catwalks."

"I know." I nodded and looked at my watch. Ten more minutes before I could go home and have some peace and quiet. Or maybe take another dip in the pool. Clothing optional this time.

"Nikki, how you doin'?" Dom greeted her first, drooling over her white dress set against slightly tan skin.

No matter what he said about Nikki, he'd always

had a soft spot for her. She definitely had a way with men, including me. A woman like her could have any guy she wanted. Why did she bother with me? Underneath all that sex-goddess game, she was a smart and calculating woman. Surely, she understood I couldn't give her what she wanted.

"Aging. Waiting for your friend here to call me or DM me or something." Nikki, or *Wednesday*, as Em called her, kissed Dom on both cheeks. He enjoyed every bit of it. She spun and wrapped her arms around my neck. "I've been playing hard to get, but it's been too long since the last time I saw you. You're breaking my heart, darling." She had a raspy voice, like something out of a forties movie.

"I never said I'd call you back." I peeled her arms from around me and pushed her knee away from my crotch. She knew exactly how to get my attention.

"A girl can dream." She purred in my ear, her breasts pressed against my side.

"Well, before this gets awkward, I'm gonna go see if I can get her number." Dom pointed up, wiggling his eyebrows.

I laughed. "Good luck. And thanks."

"Just doing my job."

"Would you at least buy me a drink?" Nikki said, pouting. "You haven't told me what you think of the party. We already beat last year's record."

"I've never seen a benefit quite like this one. Thank you." I turned my back to her and waved the bartender over after he finished pouring a couple of beers.

"What can I get you, Mr. Cole?"

"Bourbon and soda. And for the lady…" I gestured for her to order her drink. For the life of me, I couldn't remember what she was drinking the night I brought her home.

"Martini, two olives." Tears pooled in her eyes. The bartender leaned forward, palm extended as if offering her help. She rewarded his efforts with a sweet smile before turning to me. "We've been on five dates, and you still can't remember my drink? You really *are* breaking my heart."

She was done playing games and went for the kill, cupping me with her right hand as her glossy lips came up to kiss me. She was good. Beautiful. But I just wasn't feeling it with her anymore. I gripped both her wrists and gently planted her two feet away from me. She frowned, fake unshed tears gone.

I laughed. "You knew what you were getting into from the beginning."

"After our last talk, I thought maybe you'd be of a mind to reconsider our arrangement. I'm not asking for marriage, Derek. Just a little exclusivity. You can't really be done with relationships."

"I tried the monogamy thing for ten whole months. It didn't bode well for me. So yeah, I'm done." Right now, the only relationship I was interested in was the one with my bourbon.

The bartender set the two drinks in front of us. "Martini, two olives. And a bourbon."

"Thank you," I said, and almost spilled both drinks on Nikki.

Looking like she stepped out of the *Casablanca* movie, Valentina stood by the entrance. My heart pounded so hard I couldn't hear, or maybe the entire room had gone quiet at the sight of her. She wore a red floor-length gown that tightly held her breasts in place and loosely hugged her waist and hips in a silky fabric. The color complimented her brown skin and dark hair. She was stunning and sexy as heck. And it looked as though she was waiting for someone. I stepped forward, a slow burn spreading from my stomach up to my chest. If she was here with a guy, he wasn't staying.

I scanned the room for a security guard. Where the hell were they? With a bright smile I'd only seen her bestow on Max, she glanced over her shoulder to someone by the door. But the entrance was dark, and I couldn't see who it was. She turned around, giving me a full view of the back of the dress. My gaze lingered on bare shoulders, followed the silky path down to the dip of her waist, and settled on her shapely backside.

I gripped the bar. My gaze darted from the front door to Valentina. After what seemed like hours, Annie strolled through the threshold.

"Oh good. Annie's here with her models." Nikki sipped from her drink and set the glass on the counter.

Small world. That had to be it. Valentina was here with Annie. All tension released from my body, and I let out a long breath. "Mark," I called out to the bartender. I didn't have time to wait my turn. He dropped what he was doing and rushed to my side of the bar. "Two glasses of champagne, please. And send the rest of the bottle to my tent."

"Right away, sir."

The image of Valentina in her white shorts and oh-so-translucent, wet white top was tattooed in my mind every time I closed my eyes. There she was, furious and beautiful. I'd spent most of the afternoon thinking of how I could invite myself over to her place, maybe finish what we'd started in the pool. In the end, I'd come to my senses and met Dom for drinks instead. I needed distance between us. But now she was here. Of all places, she'd walked into my shindig.

My world. My rules.

A snorting sound reminded me Nikki was still by my side. "I'm sorry, Nikki. My date's here."

She gave me a brilliant smile that made her look younger, and for a moment she didn't look like herself. Closing the space between us again, she squinted at me.

"What?" I asked.

"Well, I'll be damn, Derek Cole. You're in love," she said. Her signature honey-laced voice was gone. "That explains everything."

I shook my head. "*What*?" Grabbing the two glasses of champagne, I set out to meet Valentina before someone else got to her first.

"Like I said." Nikki's voice faded into the background.

Chapter Fourteen
Ask Me

Valentina

"Fuck."

"Valentina, language." Annie gave me a fake admonishing look. "What are we looking at?"

"He's here. Why didn't you tell me he'd be here?" And looking ridiculously hot in a tux. I smoothed out my dress and ignored the flutters in my belly.

"Well, of course, he's here. This is the event of the summer. Do you think he spends his days sitting around his house, waiting for the right moment to pounce on you in the shower?"

I cringed. Heat rose to my cheeks.

She laughed. "Please. Like the thought hasn't crossed your mind."

"Annie."

"Omigod, it has." She placed a hand over her mouth, eyes twinkling. "Oh, he's coming this way."

"Let's go somewhere else." I pulled her arm, but she dug her heels in and wouldn't budge. "He's bad for me, remember?" I stomped my foot, my high heels scraping the colored concrete.

"Well, I don't know. He kind of passed the Max test, didn't he?" She waved at him. "Not to mention you two have a conversation pending. I know you haven't told him," she whispered to me.

"It's been a busy week. I didn't have time."

"Well, here's your chance." She raised an eyebrow. She was right.

"I thought that was you, Valentina." Cole's voice was pure sex when he said my name.

I whipped around to face the music, so to speak. "Hi."

"Champagne? I noticed you liked the Veuve Clicquot the other night," he said, his tone full of meaning.

Annie took the glass he offered her. I eyed his hand, and desire pooled between my legs. Clearing my throat, I accepted the champagne and took a long sip. "Thank you."

Annie met my gaze, lips pinched together. "Well, Nikki and I have work to do. Play nice. And don't forget at ten you have to show the dress in the auction room." She was gone before I could beg her not to leave me alone with Derek Cole.

"So your girlfriend is also your event planner?" The words left my lips before I could stop them. I kicked myself for asking. I hadn't meant it to come out so catty.

"She's only my event planner." He flashed me a knee-weakening grin. "That's an amazing dress."

"Thanks, but it's not mine. It's on the auction list for tonight."

"What a pity," he whispered, and my heart did a somersault that made my chest hurt. "I can't imagine anyone wearing it better than you." He met my gaze and held it. This close, his hot blue eyes sparkled under the laser lights. "Up until now I'd been wondering how

I was going to make it through the night. And now you're here." He rubbed the back of his neck in that sexy way that was so familiar now. "Dance with me."

"I'm not here to entertain you." I tried to sound insulted. But the truth was, he already had me under his spell. The room itself wasn't helping. Everything around us hinted at forbidden things and sex. In short, Cole.

"Okay." He put his hands up in surrender. "I am your host, though. At least let me show you around."

"You can show me where the auction room is." I squeezed my thighs together.

Lines appeared between his brows as he bit the inside of his lower lip and his eyes settled on my dress for a split second. The dress was crazy hot with the power to make me feel sexy, make me think I could have a guy like Cole.

"Right," he said. "How about a drink first? Then I'll take you anywhere you want."

Okay, that was harmless enough. We were in a public place. I couldn't do anything stupid, like throw myself at him. Besides, we had a conversation pending.

He read the indecisiveness on my face. "Come on. We've had coffee before. This is pretty much the same thing."

I laughed. "By your definition, I've had coffee with countless strangers."

"That's not—" He rubbed his clean-shaven cheek.

I glanced at his long fingers. "I can do a drink," I blurted out.

He eyed the door by the stage as he considered something. "I think you'll like the VIP gallery, but maybe later." He ushered me to the bar in the middle of the room, where a cocktail was already waiting for him.

Being this close to him was torture—delicious torture, but torture nonetheless. I took another sip of champagne to calm my nerves. When I emptied the glass, he set it on the bar. The bartender promptly filled the flute and placed it in front of me.

"Thanks again for lunch today," I said.

"It was my pleasure." He closed the space between us. The smell of his cologne made my knees buckle. He cleared his throat.

"I have something to tell—"

"Hey, there you are." Annie wedged herself between Cole and me. "Nikki wants to talk to us before the auction." She looped her arm around mine and escorted me to the auction room. Away from Cole. Jeez, that was close.

I'll see you later, I mouthed to a scolding Cole. With both hands in his pockets, he looked like a real-life James Bond.

"Annie, I swear your parties are getting weirder and weirder. What exactly am I supposed to do in this auction room? You have to admit it sounds kinky." I eyed the two girls in lingerie dancing on either side of the entrance to the room.

"Get your head out of the gutter for a minute. All you have to do is hold your number at waist level and strut up and down the catwalk. People eat this stuff up."

"And you don't think that's weird?"

"Relax. It's mostly women. See?" She ushered me inside. She was right. The room was full of women ready to spend their money.

I smoothed out the expensive fabric again. "How much is this gown, anyway?"

"Five grand. Try not to spill on it." She waved at Nikki, or *Wednesday*, who stood in the back, talking to the other models.

Crap. Just what I needed—Cole's sex goddess telling me what to do. I rubbed my cheek. Maybe not all was bad. Surrounded by beautiful women, I would easily blend into the background. "Let's just get this over with."

Nikki gave us quick instructions on what to do and where to go and had us line up behind her as she readied herself to announce the start of the auction. Wishing I had finished the second glass of champagne, I stood in the middle of the miniature runway Nikki had set up. My legs felt shaky. Oddly enough, for the first time today the nerves and butterflies had nothing to do with Cole.

When it was time, I took a deep breath and sauntered down to the spot Nikki had indicated. I stopped, and my stomach dropped. Cole was leaning on the doorframe with both hands in his pockets. I ignored him, but it didn't matter. His dark stare stayed trained on me. Every time he adjusted the sleeves of his tuxedo jacket, the hair on the nape of my neck tingled.

So much for blending in.

"Chin up," Nikki said under her breath while she smoothed the straps on my dress. "And let me see those pearly whites. Don't worry. I won't let him do anything stupid. You're up."

I counted to ten, as I'd been told to do—longest ten seconds ever. I focused on Annie standing in the back as I strutted down the catwalk. Again, exactly as Nikki had instructed. She certainly knew how to entice. No doubt she could have anyone she wanted. When our gazes met, she put her chin in the air, gesturing for me to do the same. Okay, maybe this wasn't so bad. How did she do that? My muscles relaxed some when I joined the other models toward the back of the stage, but the knot in my stomach didn't go away completely, not with Cole's gaze still on me.

As I watched the rest of the models do their catwalk, I breathed a little easier. When the bidding started, Cole left his post by the door and made his way to Nikki, who stared at him, eyes wide and mouth slightly open. He wasn't supposed to be here. Hot looks aside, he stood out in a roomful of women. What was he up to?

I was third in line, so I had to wait while the other gowns were bid on. Both dresses sold for a couple of thousand dollars over their retail price. This was good news for both the foundation and Annie. Next, it was my turn. Doing my best not to fidget while the women eyed the dress up and down, I stood on the marked spot while the bids came in. Nikki started high, at four thousand. She pursed her lips as she ignored Cole whispering in her ear. A woman dressed in a beaded tuxedo jumpsuit raised her hand.

A nanosecond later, Cole raised his hand. "Five thousand."

Nikki looked down, but I could've sworn she rolled her eyes. "Do I have fifty-five hundred, Katie?"

Tuxedo Jumpsuit, Katie, nodded.

"Six thousand," Cole said.

Nikki leaned over and whispered something to him. He simply shrugged.

"Sixty-five hundred." Katie chuckled, thoroughly amused.

The rest of the room rumbled as the other women laughed and commented. My cheeks flushed. Was he doing this because of me? Could people tell he was staring at me?

His expression didn't change, but he was done playing games. "Fifteen thousand."

For a moment, Nikki touched the bridge of her nose. She peeked at Katie, who shook her head once. "Going once, going twice. Sold to our gracious host."

An excruciating hour later, the live auction was over and Annie released me from duty.

"Let me find out where you can change out of your fifteen-k gown." She shook her head. "Go have a drink. But don't go too far."

I nodded and trudged back to the bar, feeling drained now that all the adrenaline had left me.

Cole greeted me with a wolfish grin and a glass of champagne. "Dance with me."

"What was that all about?" I took the glass from him. I really needed a drink.

"Dance with me."

"Why? Because you paid an insane amount of money for this gown?"

He smiled, his usual scorching-hot, sure-of-himself smile. "No. Because you want to."

I glanced at the clock over the bar. It was fifteen minutes to midnight. We had a little bit of time, and he was right. I really did want to dance with him. And he had to know about Bridget's plans. I nodded. He took my glass and handed it to the bartender. He ushered me to the dance area by the stage, on the opposite side of the warehouse, but we didn't stay there. We strolled through the double doors on the side of the stage. A bouncer with massive arms stood at attention as we approached him. His eyes dropped to my wrist.

He started to say something, but Cole put up his hand. "She's with me."

The man nodded and let us through. This was life with Cole—an all-access pass. My heart pounded hard as I followed with fickle steps. The next room was a different world, and it screamed sex a bit louder. Instead of tables, there were resort pool tents along the wall. No DJ here, but an actual band playing jazzy tunes. When we reached the dance floor, he turned me once and brought me close to him. Of course, the man could dance.

"This place is incredible," I said, aware of how close my lips were to his neck. I wanted to kiss him on the lips…to hell with Bridget and the stupid promise he made of not kissing me until I asked.

"Did Max get grounded today?"

What? The mention of Max diffused the sexual tension building up inside me, the ache between my legs. Was he doing this on purpose?

"No. After all, it wasn't his fault. You were the one who threw me in the pool."

He laughed. His deep, smooth-as-honey laugh. "Technically, I jumped in. You just happened to be on me." His thumb slid under the line of my breast, sending a current of electricity down my back.

"Is there a place where we can sit for a bit?" Better to get our conversation over with.

He pressed his lips together and nodded. "Of course, I have a private tent in the other room."

My intent hadn't been to act so mysterious. But if he wanted to yell or throw me out after we spoke, I didn't want all these people ogling us.

The VIP of the VIP room in yet another section in the ginormous warehouse was smaller and more intimate than the last two. At the far end of the room, a violinist played an old tango I knew well, "Mano a Mano." The sensual and melancholic melody added to the decadent setting of the place. Probably the reason Cole didn't want to bring me here.

His tent was cozy, all done in white leather furnishings and infused with a faint scent of vanilla. Under the shimmer of the small chandelier overhead, my dress looked scarlet red. I swallowed and smoothed out the fabric around my waist. This was the worst place to tell him about his ex's plans. I plumped myself on the sofa, and a few pillows dropped to the floor.

"Oh, sorry." I bent to pick them up.

"Leave it." Cole caught my hand. He unbuttoned his tuxedo jacket and sat.

Out of habit, or cowardice, I inched over to my left to make room. He gave me a bright smile that said *nice try*. "Make up your mind, Valentina. I can't take this any longer."

A hot puddle of unrealized desire, I melted a little every time he said my name. I squeezed my legs together and scooted some more. This sofa wasn't big enough for the two of us. "I don't know what you mean."

"Do you want to kiss me or not?" He slid across the cushion, closing the space between us. "Ask me."

I adjusted my weight on the seat. He tightened his hold on my fingers. God, even if I had wanted to flee, I didn't think my legs would respond. Cocking his head, he rubbed his thumb across the inside of my wrist where my pulse was visible.

"I want you." The words left my lips of their own accord. I had meant to say something else, but for the life of me, I couldn't remember what.

"Close enough, sweetheart." Cupping the nape of my neck, he took my mouth with a longing that sent a wave of adrenaline from my core to my toes. Heat pulsed between my thighs as the tip of his tongue teased mine. I leaned in and sucked gently. I might not get another chance to taste him.

He eased me back on the sofa, and I landed on a bed of soft and silky decorative pillows. A groan escaped his lips, making my nerves dissolve. Did he want me as much as I wanted him? The knowledge that he might fueled the daring side of me. My hand trembled as I slipped it inside his jacket and kneaded the hard muscles under his shirt. I pulled on it, my fingers itching to touch his skin.

Eyes closed, he dropped his chin to his chest. "You are so beautiful." He planted hot kisses on my neck and the hard nipples trapped under my dress.

Earlier tonight, the gown had fit me perfectly, but now it felt tight and in the way. Cole must've read my thoughts because he reached behind me and pulled on the zipper, just enough to free my breasts.

His mouth found my taut nipple just as the dress slid down an inch. I moaned against his temple. One night, all I needed was one night to feel alive again. Tomorrow he'd hate me, but for now, he was here and he wanted me. I didn't stop him when he pushed my skirt up and rubbed my legs on the way up. I was completely at his mercy. He squeezed my butt cheek. God, I needed more than that, but I didn't know how to ask.

His eyes bore into mine. "Tell me what you want. How far?"

How far I wanted to go? I needed him. No more waiting. I sighed, let one knee fall to the side, and guided his hand from my hip to below my navel and farther down. The heat from his hand brought a new wave of sensation. I pushed on his wrist. He bit his lip, pressing his forehead to mine, sending goose bumps down my neck.

"Please." I was so hot for him I couldn't wait.

He nodded as his fingers tapped my entrance. Something in his eyes told me he'd do anything I asked. My mounting need responded to his jagged and warm breath against the valley between my breasts. Having a beautiful man like Cole wanting me was pure ecstasy. And I found I didn't have the will to turn him down anymore.

"Oh, sweetheart, you have no idea what you do to me." His fingers went deeper inside me, and I buried one hand in his soft hair and brought his lips to mine with the other. "I only wished you'd let me in somewhere less crowded." He captured my mouth again.

His words didn't register. What did he mean? Oh crap, we were still at the party. I turned toward the entrance of the tent, but he had already lowered the curtains. I had no idea when he'd had time or a free hand to do that.

"Now I'm going to have to wait my turn." He thumbed circles around the apex of my sex, sending an electric current down my legs.

Everything around me went quiet as the hum below

my navel grew bigger and bigger. I kissed him again. Desire had turned to heat, and the heat to a glorious ache. Fully in tuned with what I needed, he slid his fingers out and then in; his thumb never ceased its torture. Each time he reached deeper and deeper, until I clutched his shoulders and found my release. His mouth crushed mine and muffled my cry.

"Let's get out of here," he whispered, out of breath, sending small waves of pleasure to where his hand still rested.

Chapter Fifteen
If One Night Is All We Have

Cole

"Of all the places you could've said yes, why did it have to be here?" I held Valentina's hand in a tight grip as I pulled her behind me toward the general admissions room.

"I didn't exactly plan it." She struggled to catch her breath. "Wait." She yanked her arm back. My stomach dropped. Had she changed her mind? "I have to return the gown."

I spun to look at her. God, she really did look beautiful in that dress. "Don't worry about it. You can return it to me later." I grinned at her. She blushed, and my cock stood at attention.

Shit, we're not going to make it home.

"Text your friend and tell her I'm taking you home." I signaled for the valet to call for my car.

For once, she didn't question my intentions or high-handedness. Instead, she texted Annie while she kept her body next to mine.

While we waited for my car, Valentina cuddled up next to me and shivered.

"Are you seriously cold?" I shrugged out of my tuxedo jacket and draped it over her shoulders.

"There's definitely a chill in the air."

I hugged her close, glad for an excuse to keep my hands on her. When the car arrived, we climbed in the back seat of the SUV, where our driver had a couple of bottles of water waiting for us.

"Drink." I handed her a bottle.

"Make up your mind. Do you want me drunk or sober?" she teased.

"Drunk before, sober now." I planted a chaste kiss on her cheek, though I wanted to do way more than that.

"Going home, Mr. Cole?" the driver asked.

I gave him a look that said he had to work on his timing. "Yes, Jose. We're going home. Is the escort ready?"

"Just about. They're wrapping up staging."

"Thanks." I turned my attention to Valentina and placed my hand over hers. I didn't trust myself to get any closer.

"Like a police escort?" she asked.

"Nikki's idea. Traffic during events like this one can be impossible. They'll get us out of here fast."

She blushed, and my cock pushed on my zipper. *Jesus.* I took a deep calming breath. Valentina knew why I was in a rush to get home, but I didn't want to do or say anything to scare her off or make her change her mind. She squeezed my fingers, sliding her thumb across my palm. She might as well have been stroking me, the way my body reacted. Forcing myself to take even breaths, I slanted a glance at her. She gazed out the window, though everything around us was pitch black. Did she not realize what she was doing?

The electric charge in the air echoed against my chest. I snuck a peek at Jose and made a mental note to get a car with a divider. Or maybe just drive myself next time. Scratch that. What kind of an asshole pulls over to the side of the road for a quickie, especially for the first time with someone like Valentina.

She continued her torture on my hand, completely unaware of how her nerves fueled my desire for her. I adjusted my weight on the seat, pants tight, cock in sheer agony.

"Jose." I turned to the driver.

"Yes, sir. That's them now." The emergency siren blared a couple of times to get cars out of the way and let us through. A minute later, our SUV rolled forward. About goddamn time.

Valentina turned to me and smiled. I inched a little closer, and she leaned forward.

"I never asked you how the cottage is working out for you." Anything to get my mind off the tightness in my trousers.

She cleared her throat. "It's great."

The SUV flew down Skyline Drive. Valentina rolled down her window and exhaled before facing me. "I never thanked you for helping me that day."

I shook my head. "You did." I paused when she sat a little straighter. "I mean, please don't think I offered you the cottage just so I could…you know."

The police car lights flashed ahead of us. A red glow shone on her hair and bare shoulders as she shifted in her seat again and leaned closer to me. Her cleavage made me forget my words. I wanted to kiss her, caress her the way I had back at the fund-raiser. I touched my forehead to hers, and she squeezed my hand—it might as well be my heart.

"I don't think that at all," she whispered.

I ran my fingers down her cheek. Only a few weeks had gone by since she walked into my life, but I felt as if I'd waited a lifetime for her, for this. Putting a finger below her chin, I lifted her lips up to mine. I couldn't wait any more.

She shot a glance to Jose before she turned her attention to me. "There's something I should tell you."

I gripped her hand. Right now, Jose was my least favorite person. No. This wasn't his fault. This was on me and my poor planning. "What is it?"

She peeked at Jose again. "Umm. Let's wait until we get home."

By the time I opened the door to the house, the urgent need that assaulted us back at the party had subsided to a manageable level. *Thank God.* Valentina deserved more than a quick tumble. She never said it, but I was sure the last time she had sex was when Max was conceived. Or right around that time. Either way, it'd been a long time for her.

She whipped around in the middle of the great room when I threw the deadbolt, her eyes big on me. I caught up to her before she decided to run out the back door.

"Are you hungry?" I held her by the waist tighter than I intended to. She gave me a weak nod. And I got the impression she didn't have the ability to say no to me tonight. I felt the same way, and it terrified me.

In the kitchen, we found more champagne, a cheese platter layered with fruits and nuts, and a plate of macarons. I cursed under my breath. Valentina knew I didn't know she'd be at the party. Had she already guessed this midnight snack was meant for my guest for the night?

Hiding a smile behind her index finger, she sauntered around the island, the way she had done back at the live auction. Her other hand trailed along the edge of the granite countertop. Confidence looked good on her. "Okay."

"Okay, what?" I tapped my fingers on the cold stone. I was losing control.

"What happens if I eat the cheese and drink the wine?" she asked in a husky and playful voice. "Do I officially become *Saturday*?"

Sexy and confident, a lethal combination. God, I was enjoying this side of her.

"Don't say that." I raked my hand through my hair to buy some time. I couldn't think straight. Her words from earlier tonight flashed in my mind. *I want you.* She was here and ready, and now a stupid cheese platter might ruin my plans. "Em knows I get hungry after a night out." Not smooth or convincing at all.

She raised an eyebrow to tell me she wasn't buying it.

"I'm sorry."

"Don't be. I know who you are. I know you can't love me. We're worlds apart. But I don't care. Not tonight. I want you." Her voice was low and hoarse. "One night. That's all we have."

Valentina and her rules. But she was here. And that was progress. I had all night to prove to her that one night wouldn't be enough. At least not for me. I prowled around the counter. She almost took a step back, but she caught herself and stood her ground instead, daring me.

"So you're telling me…" With my hand on her waist, I thumbed the silky fabric below her navel. "That tomorrow…" I leaned closer, and our breaths filled the small space between our mouths. "This won't have any effect on you?"

She sighed, nodding a yes.

"Yes, it will?"

"Yes, that's what I'm telling you." She gripped the edge of the granite, her chin in the air.

It wasn't a dare. She believed her own words. "Okay. We'll do it your way." I grabbed the bottle and her hand. "Your rules. If one night is all we have, then let's make it count. Get the macarons."

"Where are we going?" She laughed as she snatched the plateful of sweets.

"I want to show you something." I waited by the patio door. "You're into astronomy, right?"

"Yes. How'd you know that?" Her gaze flicked to mine.

"You work for me, remember?"

She gave me an inquisitive glance before we dashed outside and followed the path up to the terrace. At the foot of the stairs, I took her elbow and helped her up the stone steps that led to the back door of my bedroom. The view from up here never failed to take my breath away. I hoped it would do the same for her.

She let out a long sigh when we reached the top. "Oh, wow. I always wondered what was up here."

"It's my bedroom." I pointed toward the french doors, wide open with sheer curtains dancing in the warm breeze.

"Oh. I didn't…" She cleared her throat. Was she losing her nerve? "I didn't know that." She held my gaze for a moment. Heat slowly reached every fiber in me.

147

The smell of wet dirt and gardenias lingered in the air. Clouds swiftly brushed past us, giving way to a bright sky. A perfect night for stargazing, except I couldn't stop looking at Valentina. We unloaded our loot on a nearby table, and I ushered her toward the telescope set at the far end. She hesitantly ran her hands over the device before she peeked through the lens. When the tech came to install it yesterday, I never dreamed I'd get to show it to her so soon.

"I can see Saturn." She glanced at me over her shoulder. "Wait, that can't be. Right?" I couldn't keep my eyes off her and that dress clinging to her shapely backside. "This is incredible. No wonder there's always naked women prancing around in your house. I have to admit I'm fighting the urge to take my clothes off right now." She donned one of her two-dimple smiles before she turned her attention back to the stars.

The gleam in her eyes was something new. Was she teasing me? I hoped she wasn't kidding about the getting-naked part. I wanted her so badly I couldn't breathe.

I took her waist from behind and whispered in her ear. "I never bring anyone up here. But I'm glad it's having this effect on you. Never fight the urge to get naked in front of me." I spun her and kissed the mounds standing proudly over the top of her dress.

She wedged her hand between us. "Why did you bring me up here?"

"I wanted to show you the stars."

Her eyes filled with tears. "Wait."

"No more waiting, sweetheart." My heart slowed down to a painful beat when she stepped back.

"There's something you should know." She

smoothed out the fabric of her dress, taking a deep breath. "Last week, Bridget…your wife."

My chest tightened, and I backed away from her. "What about her?"

"She asked me for a favor. She…" Valentina peered upward, as if she couldn't find the words, and my heart spun wildly. "She asked me to convince you to sign the divorce papers before the end of the month."

I sat on the low wall and swallowed the lump in my throat. The stir in my chest turned into small blades, cutting me deep. "That's why you're here."

"Yes," she said. My gaze snapped to her. "I mean, no. Yeah, I considered it for a moment, but only because she threatened to kick me out of my home, void the contract." She rubbed the creases across her forehead.

I fisted my hands, released them, and buried my face in them. "Just go. We're done here."

"Cole. Please." Her voice quavered as she planted herself in front of me. "I would never betray you. I panicked. She can be so scary. I couldn't say no. But I swear I never would've tried to trick you into doing something you don't want." She tunneled her fingers through my hair and pressed her lips to my temple.

I swallowed, not daring to move. If I did…

"I need this."

The scent of her perfume diffused the slow burn in my stomach. I groaned, and my hands skimmed over her hips and waist. I leaned back and pulled her between my legs. Her breath on my face reminded me of our first kiss, the same day I signed the divorce papers, the same day Dom asked me to hold off just a bit longer. Truth was, I would've done anything she asked.

"Why are you here?" I buried my face in her neck, and her swelling breasts touched the line of my jaw. I closed my eyes and focused on the beat of her heart.

"Because I want you. Even if it's just for one night."

I exhaled. "Why tell me about Bridget's plans, then?" I gripped her waist and met her gaze. I needed to believe her words, believe she'd never do anything to hurt me.

"I didn't want anything hanging over our heads tonight." She sighed. "You've done so much for us. You deserve the truth. You deserve to be happy."

Her blush sent a sudden surge of desire from my erection down to my toes. Bridget's sorry attempt to turn Valentina against me hadn't worked. Valentina was here for me. She wanted *me.*

"Say it."

She relaxed against me. "I want to be with you."

Goose bumps danced across her skin when I held her closer and blew out air. I nibbled along the edge of the low neckline of her dress, aching for more of her, but the fabric wouldn't budge. I reached behind her and took my time pulling down the zipper, my eyes never leaving hers. If she wanted out, she had to say it now. Head tilted down, she licked her lips. I ran a hand over her exposed back, all that smooth skin, until I reached the top of the gown and released it from her shoulders. She sighed again. A generous breast dropped into my hand. I squeezed and tugged before I captured the peak with my mouth. She rewarded me with a sexy moan as she dropped her head back to give me better access. Desire pulsed hard through me. If anticipation could kill…

"It's been a long while for me," she whispered, out of breath.

"I know. We'll take it slow." *It's been a while for me too.* I couldn't remember the last time I had sex while sober. Or the last time I needed someone this bad. I kissed her lips softly until she melted into me. Cupping both mounds again, I pinched her nipples.

She sucked in a breath and pressed her legs together. I filed the small details away. I'd have to do more of that later.

Red grooves covered her chest where the dress had cinched her all night. I rubbed my thumbs over her skin to soothe it. Mesmerized, I watched as her breasts heaved in my hands. God, these beauties were more gorgeous than I'd imagined. I tongued a reddish-pink tip. She gripped my hair and let the silky fabric pool at her feet to reveal a toned torso, round hips, and those long legs.

Her skin glowed under the stars. *She's here for me.* I repeated the words over and over in my head as I slid a hand down to her waist, over her lacy underwear, until my fingers rested between her thighs. Oh, she was ready for me.

Back at the fund-raiser, I'd almost come undone when my hand found her hairless sex and outer lips. I wanted to see it, taste it. I hooked my thumbs over her panties and let them fall to the floor. Her eyes flew open as if the spell had been broken. I was losing her. Why was she always running away from me?

"You're safe with me," I whispered in her ear, applying pressure over her sensitive spot.

"I know." She pressed against my hand.

At least she trusted me when it came to this. She was back, but not completely subdued like before. An active participant now, she pulled down on my tuxedo shirt. She fumbled with the top stud for a second. When it didn't come off, she moved down to my pants and unzipped them. It was my turn to be hypnotized. A naked woman undressing me with this much urgency, the same urgency I felt, was beyond erotic.

A groan escape my lips. I captured her mouth and kissed her hard before I helped her with the tuxedo cufflinks and studs, letting them fall on top of her underwear. With a triumphant smile, she pulled at my dress shirt, and it slipped off my shoulders. Her eyes never left mine. She pulled the undershirt over my head. A breeze brushed between us, though it did nothing to lessen the heat burning through me.

"I can't believe I'm here with you." She stepped into my embrace again, her soft skin finally touching mine.

"You have no idea how long I've fantasized about this moment. Having you living so close has been more than torment for me." I put my fingers in her hair. I'd thought about undoing her up-do all night. What a shame to put all that hair away. I placed my thigh between her legs and pushed gently against her.

"Cole," she moaned, eyes closed. I didn't think she realized she was doing it.

My hands hesitated over her backside, kneading each butt cheek. I wanted to touch and kiss every inch of her. One night wasn't enough, but one step at a time. I stood and got to work on the pins in her hair. With my arms over her head, she had full access to me. She sighed, and then her hands and soft lips were on me, leaving a trail of hot kisses.

Good God, woman.

I gripped my cock. I stepped back to watch her hair spill over her shoulders. The sight of her was more than I could bear. I picked her up by the waist and carried her into my bedroom.

"Why did you make me wait so long?" I muttered when she fell on the mattress, her legs slightly apart, waiting for me.

The view from up here was incredible—her hair sprawled about her, breasts rising and falling, the plunge of her waist and those muscular thighs. I almost climax just watching, but I wanted to savor this moment. She was here. After all this time, Valentina was in my bed.

I reached in the bedside drawer and pulled out a silver pack. Her gaze roamed from my face down to my chest. That smoldering look of hers made all kinds of promises as she watched me unroll the condom over my erection. My cock jerked in excitement, an aching need I couldn't control anymore. I grasped it tighter before I smoothed out the latex and kneeled between her legs. Running my hand up her thigh, I planted an open mouth kiss at the apex of her sex. She arched her back when my tongue pushed through the folds and found her button. I sucked on it, tasting all of her, slow and steady.

The inside of her thigh rubbed against the side of my face, and that was all I could handle. I worked my way up to her navel, took a handful of her breast, and thumbed her nipple while I sucked hard on the other one. I met her gaze and braced my arms on either side of her.

"Are you having second thoughts?" she asked, gasping for air, just as I was.

"I need you so much…it scares me." My erection pressed against her entrance.

She pulled me down for a kiss. Our lips touched, and I entered her with the full force of the desire I felt.

Her moan reverberated inside me. I responded in the only way I could at this point and thrust deeper into her. She tightened around me as her hips came up to meet me, sure of what she needed. *Jesus.* She had me at the very edge, but I slowed down for her. She was close, but not quite where I was. Holding her waist, I moved one knee under her and pumped hard. Again. And again.

"Derek," she called for me.

"I'm right here, sweetheart," I whispered against her neck as liquid heat surged through me. She tightened around me, and we found our release together with an intensity I'd never felt.

Chapter Sixteen
In the Light of Day

Valentina

"Champagne?" he asked.

"Hmm." I couldn't find my voice.

My legs didn't respond either. I flipped on my belly, and my hand landed next to me on the floor. I was on some sort of high. The earthy scent around us, the soft chenille fabric of the sofa that caressed my skin, and even the pale color of the cool travertine tiles were amplified…more vivid, more alive.

My gaze darted around the room as I tried to orient myself. The edge of the California-king bed sat on the far end of the room. How did we end up here? All I remembered was Cole inside me, his hands and lips all over me. My pulse raced again. I brought my legs together and giggled against the cushions.

Cool and fizzy liquid trickled down my back. A moment later, Cole's mouth was on me, drinking the wine that pooled there.

"If that's meant to get me up, it's having the opposite effect." I stretched slowly, and he continued his kissing.

"You taste amazing."

"I can't feel my legs." I sat and faced the fireplace. To my left, the Catalina Mountains were a distant shadow under the bright stars. This night couldn't be more perfect.

My hair fell over my shoulder, curly and messy. I raked my hands through it to smooth it out. After a few tries, I gave up. Fixing the curl once it settled in was impossible.

"You look beautiful." Cole knelt by my feet, setting a glass of champagne on the coffee table. He placed a macaron on my bare leg. His eyes were a bright blue as they lingered there. His hand moved up my thigh, and I held my breath. "That was one hell of a night."

God, I didn't think he could look any hotter, but he did. A serene energy emanated from him. He was comfortable in his own skin, even though he was as naked as I was. My fingers grazed the side of his face and curved around his lips, red and swollen from kissing. I wanted to ask him if it was always like this for him. Because I could honestly say I'd never had sex like that. Not ever.

He kissed the palm of my hand when I reached his lips. "Do you have any idea of what you do to me? Being with you is like nothing I've ever felt before."

He exhaled. His warmth breath caressed my skin, and my breasts came to life, nipples hard under his gaze. I took the macaron off my thigh and popped it in my mouth. Mainly because I was hungry, but also to ease the nervous energy building at the pit of my stomach. I'd never had a man stare at my nude body like this—or any other way, for that matter.

"This was a pleasant surprise." His hot fingers slid across my sex.

Just like that, I was turned on again, all thoughts of being naked forgotten. I leaned toward him, forcing deep breaths, as warm flurries dropped from my chest down to that hard spot between my thighs.

"But you didn't know I was going to be at the party."

"Oh." I looked down, realizing he was talking about my Brazilian. "I do it for me. I like how it feels." My cheeks turned hot.

"I like it too." His thumb made a wide circle across my outer lips. I shivered and pressed my forehead against his. I wanted him inside me again, filling me.

"Are you cold?" He traced the goose bumps on my shoulder. "It's like seventy-five degrees out."

The doors to the terrace were wide open, letting the cool night air in. Outside, the sky had turned a dark shade of pink, mixed in with puffy gray clouds. I guessed we had less than an hour before sunrise.

"Desert girl here," I said. "This is freezing for me."

"Okay. I would offer to light a fire. But we're in the middle of the summer. I refuse." He stood, the amusement written all over his face. He ushered me to the bed, pulled back the covers, and gestured for me to get in. I had at least sixty minutes. Our night wasn't officially over yet, so I got in.

My eyes followed him around the room as he fetched the plate of treats from the coffee table in the sitting area. His bedroom was bigger than the cottage, complete with vaulted ceilings and a fireplace, built to welcome in the desert and the abundant sunlight. He set everything on his bedside table and climbed in with me, using three fluffy pillows to prop himself up. I had four others on my side of the bed.

Leaning over him, I set my glass down. When I tried to move away, he held me in place. Being in his arms was better than I ever imagined. His body heat increased to somewhere between hot and scorching, and I melted into him. A hint of his cologne from last night still lingered on his skin, mixed in with sweat and sex.

"Where are you from?" I propped myself up on my elbow, while his hand gently drew a wide circle on my lower back. It was distracting, but I did my best to focus. I wanted to know everything about him.

"Atlanta." He flashed me a sexy smile.

I hadn't noticed before how a little wrinkle appeared on his right eye whenever he turned on the charm. "Deep South, huh?"

"Yes, ma'am," he drawled.

"Brothers, sisters?"

"Four brothers."

"Four? Wow, that's a lot of kids. Are you the oldest?"

"Yeah. How did you know?"

I shrugged. "You walk around like you carry the weight of the world. Firstborns always have this thing. Like they need to fix everything. Everything is their fault."

He laughed, his deep, smooth-as-honey laugh. "For someone who grew up an only child, you certainly know a lot about siblings."

"I have a lot of cousins. Fifty to be exact."

"Yikes. That's a lot of kids."

I nodded. "My mom is the oldest of eight."

"That happens these days?" he asked.

"That's not that far from five."

"Good point."

"What about school? Where did you go?" Time was slipping away from us, and I had a long list of questions.

"You know, this is stuff that's usually covered on a first date. If you hadn't been so stubborn, I would've taken you somewhere nice for dinner and answered all your questions."

"I wasn't being stubborn, just realistic. You're not really the *dating* type."

"I'm not." He shrugged. My chest hurt to hear him say it. I lowered my gaze. With a soft smile, he placed a finger under my chin and tipped my head up. "NC State. I did my masters at Georgia Tech."

I didn't know anything about the schools on the East Coast. "NC State, huh?"

He nodded. "Go, Pack." He made a hand gesture that looked like a dorky gangster sign. Derek Cole being cute sent a flutter across my chest.

"I would've guessed one of the Ivy League schools. Princeton or something." My fingers trailed his six-pack, or was that a twelve-pack? Jeez. I bit my lip, kneading his muscles, letting my hand go under the covers. His thighs were hard, like tree trunks, and super long. My arm was completely stretched, and I still hadn't reached his knee.

"My dad wanted me to go to Princeton. That's where he went. But NC State offered me a spot on their baseball team. And I really wanted to play ball. So I went with them." His chest expanded as he forced even breaths.

He closed his eyes, wetting his lips. I grinned when I realized my hand was inches from his erection. "Were you good at baseball?" I slid my hand up from his leg to his navel and rubbed the hair there.

"I was all right." He placed his free hand behind

his head to let me play my silly little game, while his other hand moved farther down my back. A slow electric wave spun from the pad of his thumb until it reached my core.

I traced the planes on his shoulder. Last night, I hadn't had time to really look at him. But now I could see clusters of freckles on the curve of his arm. His skin looked stark white under my fingers.

He cocked his head. "We look good together."

"So somewhere between baseball practice and homework, you decided to start your own company?"

He parted his lips, dark eyes on me, an invitation to do with him as I pleased. I wrapped my fingers around his shaft and slid them down to feel the length of him.

"Yes," he whispered in a raspy voice. He closed his eyes, and I did it again, hand up and down, holding him tight. "*Jesus*, Valentina."

He felt hard, really hard. It turned me on, and I realized I didn't have his self-restraint to play this game. I threw my leg over his and rubbed against him.

"You were doing so well." His throaty laugh was infuriating. I hit him on the chest and tried to get away, but he held me in place next to him, his heart pounding against my cheek.

"What happened to you?" The question came out of nowhere.

"What do you mean?" He reached for his glass, took a long sip of champagne, and put it back. Getting *real* personal information out of him wasn't going to be easy.

"Why did you stop going to work?" *And why are you getting a divorce and how soon is that going to be final*? No, wait. I didn't need to know that. The agreement was for just one night.

"The board kicked me out after they saw pictures of the cottage. I didn't fight it. I thought it'd be best for the company if I took time off. Let Bridget run things until the divorce was final."

"But she's been dragging it out? I heard you stopped going to the office almost seven months ago."

He nodded, pursing his lips. This was a sore subject for him. I shouldn't've gone there. I glanced down at my hands, cheeks flushed.

"Hey." He cupped my face. "I promise you I'm over her. The only reason we're not divorced yet is because she wants CCI. I couldn't let her have that. But that was before. Now I decided it's time to let go. I signed the papers… You did your job well."

I winced and turned away from him. "I never—"

"I'm kidding. Sorry. That wasn't funny. I signed weeks ago, and it had nothing to do with you." He looked up, lips pressed together. "Almost nothing to do with you. But now I'm waiting on my lawyer to give me the green light."

"Green light?" I ignored his comment. Did he sign because he wanted to be with me?

"He's doing due diligence to make sure this is my only way out."

"What happened between you two?" I couldn't help it. I wanted to know.

He shifted his weight on the bed and inched farther up. His hand had dropped to my side. I felt cold without his touch, but I pressed on.

"I wanna know," I whispered, sitting on my ankles next to him. Like a magnet, my hand found his belly. All soft skin and hard muscle.

Diana A. Hicks

"She cheated on me."

"What?" Who in their right mind would cheat on Cole?

"The cottage was her art studio. She slept there from time to time. You know, whenever inspiration hit her hard." He rolled his eyes at that. "One morning, I walked in and saw her having sex with our accountant. So cliché. I wanted to kill them both."

"That's when you punched a hole in the wall?" I cradled his cheek. My heart ached for him.

He nodded, let out a long breath, and placed three long fingers on my collarbone. "Broke my damn fingers. Didn't even notice until Em found me."

"I'm so sorry." I covered his hand with mine, holding it tightly against me.

"I deserved it."

"*No one* deserves to be treated like that." I inched closer to him. His side felt warm on my thigh when he leaned toward me too. I wanted him more than ever. I wanted to show him he deserved everything.

"We didn't love each other. I married her because it was convenient to have it all in one perfect package. You know. My company, my life, and wife. All in one pretty box. I was too lazy to go out and find a true companion. Bridget was as good as any, and she kept CCI running like a well-oiled machine."

"She didn't have to cheat. She's got some nerve asking for your company after what she did." My body tensed next to him.

He'd looked so broken the first time he'd stomped into Café Triste…and with reason. His entire life had just fallen apart, or rather, Bridget had torn it apart. I wished I'd had the courage to talk to him that day. Offer

162

him a bit of comfort. But even as broken as he was then, he was intimidating as all hell.

"Now I know I never loved her. What hurt the most was the betrayal. I trusted her with my life, and she just threw it away like it was nothing. On top of that, she's trying to take away from me something I worked so hard for."

"Your lawyer's right. You can't just let her take what's yours. You can't stop fighting her on this. Use me."

"What?" He turned his body toward me. His fingers trailed up my arm, brushing the side of my breast.

"I work there, remember?" I wasn't sure how I could help, but it seemed like a good idea. "I don't know. I could go in her office and see if I can find something you can use against her."

He laughed. " 'Preciate that. But it's not necessary. Dom's got it under control."

"I wish I could help."

"You've done more than you'll ever know. These past months, you've been my only constant."

"Me?"

He ducked his gaze. Was he blushing? "You were the reason I kept going back to the coffee shop. There was a strength about you. The way you sat there every morning, at the same time, for exactly one hour. The first time I saw you sitting by the bay window." He forced a smile, sliding his warm fingers to my nipple and around the curve of my breast, a faraway look in his eyes. "I felt like I was drifting into a dark ocean. You were a lighthouse in the distance. Every day, I went back to sit next to you and try to find my way back."

"And did you?" I blinked against the stinging in my eyes. How could someone cause him so much pain?

He nodded, eyes sparkling with unshed tears as he met my gaze. I didn't know what to say to that. It never occurred to me I might be the reason he kept going back to Cafe Triste. I ran my hands through his hair and kissed his cheek. The sunlight bounced off the puddles of rainwater outside and touched the edge of the bed. A kick in the stomach would've hurt less. Morning had come. No matter how hard we'd tried to make it last. Our time was up.

He held my waist tighter. "Don't go just yet."

He palmed my breast and tugged at my hardened nipple. Desire pooled quickly between my legs, tight and hot. He was using my own body against me. But I had my night. Today what I wanted didn't matter.

"Spend the day with me," he whispered as he reached for a silver packet on his bedside table.

I swallowed, watching him put on a condom. He looked manly and in control. God, I wanted him.

In a swift movement, my head was on the pillow and he was inside me, filling me completely. Heat pulsed at the apex of my sex. Damn, the man knew what he was doing.

"You know I can't." I touched his face. His stubble added to his sexy morning look.

With his eyes fixed on mine, daring me, he rocked slowly against my mounting need. Omigod, he felt good. He didn't play fair. How could he have this much control over me? A moaned escaped my lips as he entered me again and then stopped. My hips came up to meet him, but he stilled them with his hand.

Last night, he'd taken pity on me, as if he

understood my need. He'd made me climax in record time at least five times. But now he took his time, dangling the fruit in front of me, letting the ecstasy build, only to let it die again. He repeated the exercise twice more. My bud ached, but he refused to give me relief.

"Move," I begged with abandon.

"Spend the day with me." It was an order. The man didn't know how to take no for an answer. He suckled both my breasts hard, but when I try to move, he kept me in place. "Say it."

I inhaled. "Are you asking me out on a date?"

"Yes, ma'am." His gaze trained on me expectantly.

Only Cole could make *ma'am* sound sexual. He rocked again, hard and fast. I was being tortured. The blue in his eyes got thinner around his pupils as he hovered over me completely still, and completely maddening. His breathing was even, but every now and then his chest would hitch. He was affected by all this as much as I was.

I wiggled my arms from under him and focused my attention on his abs, brushing my fingers over his hip bone and the tight V-line around his navel. My free hand reached for the soft, brown hair on his chest. His skin was warm and smooth, but underneath he was solid as an oak tree. Damn, the man was hot.

Watching with hooded eyes, he smiled before he collected my wrists with one hand and put them over my head, pressing against me. He had me in a tight hold, and I was ready to combust.

How long could he keep this up, really? He had a lot of self-control. So he could probably do this to me all day. The idea didn't sound half-bad. Actually, it sounded amazing. Either way, he'd get what he wanted.

I nodded.

"Say it."

"I'll go out with you."

"Promise me. No running off at the last minute."

"I promise."

He gave me a wolfish grin. I wanted to slap him, but then he released my hips and drove into me with stunning accuracy and I found myself chasing another orgasm. My body tensed under him. All thoughts of hurting him gone.

"Relax," he whispered in my ear. "It'll come to you. You just have to be patient." His warm breath traveled down my neck, leaving a trail of goose bumps in its wake. He squeezed my ass and went deeper inside me. Then again and again, until as he promised, a long and satisfying orgasm found me.

"Cole," I whispered. Or maybe it was louder than a whisper. I couldn't tell and I didn't care. My heart pounded in my ears as heat rushed through me in waves and made me tremble.

He collapsed on top of me, sweaty and spent. "I'm never letting you go." He buried his head in my neck.

Our bodies were still connected when I felt him relax. I closed my eyes. After a few seconds, I couldn't find the strength to open them again.

"You promised. Don't forget that." His words were muffled by my skin.

I nodded before I drifted off to sleep.

The usual nightmare sipped into my dreams. He was there again. His dark eyes, furious and lethal. I'd made a mistake. I opened my mouth to apologize, but the pain kept me from speaking. All I saw were sparks in my head, followed by darkness.

You were nothing when I found. And you're still nothing.

I woke with a jolt.

What the hell?

Turning on my side, I saw Cole sleeping. A strand of blond hair on his forehead. I put it back in place and kissed his cheek.

At least now that he'd gotten this sex thing out of his system, he'd leave me alone. My heart raced. Yeah, a few hours ago we were still basking in the afterglow of the amazing sex we had. But how would he feel about it in the light of day?

You're still nothing. Max's dad had said those words to me over six years ago. They still hurt. Dammit. I had to go.

Slowly, I slid out of bed. Standing nude in the middle of the room, I looked around for something to wear. I padded outside and found the tuxedo Cole wore last night and his dress. I shook my head, remembering last night's auction. We'd left in such a hurry I forgot the bag of clothes I had brought with me.

I picked up the dress and hung it on the closet door hook. Or at least I assumed that was the closet. I didn't have time to explore. In a hurry, I laid out his tux on the bed and donned his white undershirt. It still had Cole's signature scent. I hugged myself, breathing him in, feeling warm all over. Dammit. I wanted to crawl back in bed with him.

With a sigh, I let my arms fall to the sides and trudged back to the coffee table to look for pen and paper. I scribbled a note and pinned it to the dress. A text would've been quicker, but he deserved something more intimate. I rubbed the sleeve of his undershirt and tiptoed out onto the terrace, taking one last glance at Cole.

Men like Cole didn't exist. Whatever fantasy I'd lived last night was over.

Chapter Seventeen
His Walk in the Clouds

Cole

Valentina was gone.

"Goddammit." I punched the pillow next to me.

Hanging on the closet door hook was the dress she'd worn last night with a note pinned to the tag.

I had to borrow your undershirt. Hope that's okay. Thank you for an unforgettable night.

She had neat handwriting. The smeared ink on the paper told me she'd written the note in a hurry. Why did I think she'd be next to me when I woke up? I rubbed the stubble on my cheek. Valentina had a way to set my blood on fire. Last night had surpassed all my fantasies of her. I eyed the bed. When I asked her to spend the day with me, I meant for us to spend it in bed, naked. Why did she leave?

I crumpled the piece of paper, cursing under my breath. If Valentina thought she could break her promise to me, she had a big surprise coming her way. I headed for the bathroom to take a shower—a warm one, for a change, the first one since Valentina moved in. After donning a pair of jeans and a T-shirt, I made my way downstairs.

In the kitchen, Em had breakfast set up on the counter. Giving me a knowing smile, she stopped me before I reached the patio door. "Good morning. I noticed the guest room was empty, so I figured it was safe to eat in here."

"Good morning." I sauntered into the kitchen, trying to look like I wasn't in a hurry.

"So. You finally got your way."

"What do you mean?"

"I caught Valentina doing the walk of shame about half an hour ago." She poured coffee into the mug in front of me.

That must've been quite a sight. I would've loved to see it. Valentina rushing across the lawn in nothing but my white undershirt, hair flowing wild. God, she hit me hard. All I could think about right now was seeing her again, preferably naked. And that gave me an idea.

"I'm seeing her again today."

Em smiled big. "That's unexpected."

"I'm gonna need your help." I slid onto a counter stool. Em gave me one of her looks, as if saying she didn't have time to play cupid. "Get the driver or the guards to help you. I need to get a lunch set up out on the overlook again. I thought we could watch a movie too."

She placed a hand over her heart, nodding. "I'll get it done."

"If you need help, you don't even need to ask me. Just go out and hire someone." We've had this conversation multiple times before. I didn't know how she did it all.

"Well, dear boy, if this girl keeps playing hard to get, I might need to." She shook her head, suppressing a smile. For whatever reason, she found this whole situation quite entertaining. "I think you've finally met your match…someone to have a real connection with."

"I enjoy her company. That's it." I headed for the door. Heat flushed through my body. I wasn't in the mood to wait until lunchtime.

Goddammit, Valentina. What's with all this running?

I knocked on the cottage door and crossed my arms over my chest in preparation for her excuses. She'd promised to spend the day with me. I was here to collect.

"You left," I said as soon as she opened the door.

She looked behind her, a dimple forming next to her mouth. "Good morning." She leaned on the doorframe and smiled.

I reached for her waist. I had something else I wanted to say, but I kissed her instead. Her hands went around my neck, breasts pressed against my chest as a slight moan escaped her lips. Just like that, my cock was ready.

"I had to come back for Max. Annie's mom needed to go home," she whispered. "Plus, I really needed a shower. Don't be mad." She caressed the side of my face. My anger, or whatever the hell it was I felt before she opened the door, vanished.

"I wasn't mad. Or I was. But you have the power to make all the bad go away." Why did that feel like a confession?

She laughed, shaking her head, as if she didn't believe me. If Max wasn't in the other room, she'd be out of that flower dress already.

"Are you hungry?"

"Starving." I pulled her closer and kissed the soft spot behind her ear.

She placed her hands on my chest. "Ham and eggs with coffee is all I can offer you right now." She raised a determined eyebrow.

"Fine. I get it. Max is like kryptonite. You seem to develop superpowers when he's around." I adjusted my pants and gestured for her to lead the way.

"That's not how kryptonite works." She laughed again, looking at me over her shoulder. Sexy. I followed her into the kitchen.

"All I know is that my persuasive powers diminish when he's around."

She placed a mug of coffee and a plate in front of me. Somehow she looked more beautiful than she had the day before.

I took a spoonful of eggs. They were great. "What's in this?"

"Goat cheese." She sat next to me and took a long sip of her coffee. "Get used to your faltering powers. He's going to be with us all day, as promised."

I ate more eggs. The goat cheese was really good. "He takes naps, right?" I glanced down to her cleavage to clarify my meaning. And also because I couldn't help it. Now that I knew what she looked like underneath her clothes, it was hard not to be turned on by the sight of her.

"No, he doesn't."

I took a long sip of my coffee. It was french press and very close in taste to a quad americano. "Why did you stop going to Cafe Triste?"

She smiled, and I was reminded that last night or earlier this morning I had confessed that she was the reason I went to the coffee shop every morning.

"I moved in with Annie for a few weeks while I

found a house. I didn't have time for coffee anymore. Also, their espressos are expensive. This is decent, no?" She drank from her mug. "I add steamed milk, and it almost tastes like a latte."

I nodded. "Yeah, it's pretty good." Nonfat latte was her beverage of choice. I'd spent many days staring at the *NL* letters scribbled in black marker on her cup. But that minor detail was nothing compared to all the other little things I didn't know about her. "So last night, I spilled my guts to you. It's your turn."

"What do you wanna know?" She gave me a one-shoulder shrug.

"Where're you from?" We both laughed at that question. After an incredible night, it seemed absurd that I didn't know something so basic.

"From here. Third-generation Mexican."

"What does that mean?"

"It means my grandparents immigrated to the States. My parents were born here."

"Oh, I get it. They're second generation. That makes you—"

"Third generation."

I shook my head. "I didn't know people kept track of that."

"It's a thing." She leaned back in her chair. "Don't you know about where you came from?"

"Sure. But it's not just one place. I have Irish and Scottish on my mom's side, and Greek and Italian on my dad's side. I'm a bit of mutt, really. "

She placed her hand under her chin, big sexy grin on. "I think I've heard this joke before."

"Yeah, I'm basically an angry drunk."

"You are not." She slapped my bicep.

173

I kind of was, until you.

My cock reacted to her giggles. *Focus.* "But we're talking about you."

She looked away. A bit of red crept up her cheeks as she exhaled slowly. So maybe Max wasn't full-on kryptonite. She reached for my plate, but I beat her to it. I got up and rinsed it in the sink, feeling her hot stare on me.

"Okay. What else? Let's see. Mom's an artist. She teaches at the community center. Dad's a retired cop."

"So artist plus cop makes a computer geek?" I sat and braced my arms on my thighs. Her flowery perfume made me wish we were back in my bed.

"Apparently." She let out a sigh, her gaze on my mouth.

I reached for her hand. "Did you love him?" What the fuck? Where did that come from? I couldn't possibly be jealous of the asshole who left her six years ago, though I did want to understand what'd happened there. So not jealous, just curious.

"What? Who?"

Out with it, Cole. Might as well.

"You said it'd been a while since the last time you had sex. Am I wrong in a assuming that it's been about six years?"

She pulled away and gripped her mug, her eyes focused on the coffee. I was such an asshole. But what was so special about Max's dad that she'd take this vow of chastity just because he disappeared? I really wanted to know.

"You're not wrong."

"Were you waiting for him to come back?" I swallowed, my pulse racing. Why was I afraid of her answer?

"No." The conviction behind her no sent a flutter across my belly, though the anger and fear in her voice were hard to miss. As if Max's deadbeat dad returning was her worst nightmare.

"He didn't just leave, like you said."

She shook her head.

"That bad?"

She nodded and looked down at her hands. I slowly rose to my feet. She trusted me enough to share her past, but I was afraid if I moved too fast, she'd run away again. I tipped her chin upward with my index finger, expecting to see tears. But she wasn't crying. She was out of tears for the jerk. Good. Whatever that guy did, Valentina didn't deserve to carry this with her.

A slow burn swirled in my stomach, and my fist itched to punch the asshole's face. Maybe it was a good thing I didn't know who he was or where he lived. Did he skip town? Leave her alone for good? Or was he still around? Tucson wasn't that big of a place. If he wanted to keep tabs on Valentina, it wouldn't be that hard. Was that the real reason for her chastity vow?

"Did he—"

"I'm ready," Max announced from the living room. He adjusted a backpack on his shoulder, his hair wet and combed to the side. He looked so much like her. Cute kid.

Valentina pushed me away. She jumped to her feet so fast I didn't have time to react. I had every intention of getting to the bottom of this. But for now, having her trust was enough.

One step at a time, sweetheart.

"You like hiking?" I asked Max.

"I love it." He headed for the door.

"Nope. Breakfast first." She pointed to a chair.

"Fine." Max dropped his bag and sat. The second Valentina put a plate in front of him, he started eating, only half chewing each bite. In two minutes flat, he'd scarfed down his meal, chugged the glass of milk Valentina set down, and bounced off his chair.

"Slow down," Valentina said. But it was too late. Max was finished.

"I guess we're leaving now." I stood and offered my hand to Valentina. She took it, biting her lip. A Sunday morning hike with her and Max felt right, familiar. I kissed the top of her head, trying to contain this thing simmering in my chest.

The walk to the overlook took us a whole hour instead of the usual twenty minutes. Max kept going off-road to touch the plants, climb a rock, or follow a creature to its hiding place. The kid knew the craziest facts about the desert and all kinds of animals. When I challenged one of his factoids, he pulled a book out of his backpack and flipped to a page where, in fact, a golden eagle was scavenging a deer.

"Oh my God." Valentina looked away.

"It's just a picture, Mom. She doesn't like blood," he whispered to me, and closed his book on scavengers of the world.

"This has been a very instructional walk." I winked at Valentina as I went after Max, who'd moved on to climb on a huge rock surrounded by tall saguaros and jumping chollas.

"Hey, look at that," he called out when he reached the top. He quickly dug through his bag and pulled out a pair of binoculars. "Mom. Cover your eyes."

"What?" Valentina's laugh was contagious. "What is it?"

"Yep. It's a vulture. And that's flesh." He riffled through his bag again and took out a book on vultures this time.

"Let me see that." I climbed up next to him.

"Right there." He pointed straight ahead.

"I'll be damn. That's pretty disgusting." I turned to Valentina.

"Gross." She covered her mouth, looking around her as if she expected the carcass to land at her feet.

"I guess it's true what they say. The world *is* a completely different place when seen through the eyes of a child." I jumped off the rock.

"I prefer my view with less scavenging." She winced. "I don't know why Dad keeps buying him those nasty books."

I chuckled. "That was pretty cool, though. Never seen that before." I looked back at Max, who was still scouring the skies with his binoculars.

"What the what?" he squealed. "Mom, can we go there? Mom. It's a playhouse." He slid down and took off running, his backpack bouncing all over the place.

"A what?" Valentina asked.

"I have no idea." I checked my watch. I honestly had no idea. It was still too early for my surprise to be here. "But I'm sure Em had something to do with it."

When we reached the overlook, Max was bouncing in a pirate-ship inflatable. So this was why Em had looked amused after I told her I was seeing Valentina again. She knew a whole day with Valentina meant I'd also be spending time with Max.

Across the way, canopy shades covered the pergola

177

by the paloverde. Inside, Em had a table laden with fruit bowls and pastry trays. She'd skipped the champagne I asked for.

"This is great. Thank you." Valentina planted a quick kiss on my cheek. She went in the tent and came back with two glasses of water.

"Thanks." I drank from the glass she placed in my hand.

We watched Max jump around the pirate ship, comfortable with the silence between us. When I turned to her, she regarded me. Then her face changed. The laugh lines were gone.

"Why are you doing this?" She drew a line on the dirt with her shoe, avoiding my gaze. "I'm sure there are other girls way less complicated than me."

"First of all, I didn't do this. As much as I'd like to take credit for it, this was all Em." I leaned closer. "Honestly, my entire plan consisted of getting you out here to convince you that your new no-sex rule is bullshit."

She shook her head once and shuffled a few inches away from me. Okay, so she wasn't ready to talk about that. Always running away.

"And second of all, you're not complicated."

"You are so stubborn." She crossed her arms. Her eyes sparkled under the sunlight. The glow in her skin was beyond distraction.

"Do you think you'll ever have more kids?" I asked.

"I think so." She nodded. "I feel like I missed out by not having siblings. I don't want Max to be an only child."

"Siblings? More than one, huh?" I raised both

eyebrows.

"Yeah. How about you? Do you see yourself with kids?"

"Definitely." I rubbed the nape of my neck. The answer came out of me before I had time to consider it. "I don't know. Up until now, I hadn't given it much thought. But I think, yeah, I do want kids." I racked my brain for the reason that'd brought me to this conclusion, but I couldn't think of one.

She smiled at the ground, her cheeks flushed. I wanted to hold her, kiss her again.

"What are you doing tomorrow?"

"Working." She raised an eyebrow. She could tell I was up to no good.

"What time?"

She laughed. "Eight thirty. Why?"

"Would you slam the door in my face if I bring you a latte in the morning?"

"Cole." Her tone of voice reminded me her no-sex rule was still in effect.

"It's just coffee." I put my hands up to show her my intentions were honest. They weren't exactly.

She squinted at me as she surveyed my face. I gave her my best innocent look, but she wasn't buying it. Her dimple appeared for a split second. What was she not saying?

"Come on. What are you afraid of? You think a sip of latte will make you want to tear off your clothes?" I winked.

She laughed and turned away from me. "You wish."

"You have no idea, sweetheart." My pulse raced.

Max rushed toward us. "Mom. Look. At. That. It's

a big screen."

Em had impeccable timing. My big surprise was here. We still had a couple of hours before sundown, but the screen setup would require a bit of time.

"We're watching a movie out here. It's really pretty at night," I said.

"Let's go see what movies they have." Max took off again.

"This is too much. I can't believe you had time to get all this together." She watched as two of my security guards set up the projector across from us.

With a chuckle, I stuffed both hands in the pockets of my jeans. "I wish I was as smooth as you think I am. *Las Nubes*—that's the name of the house—came with the equipment."

"The clouds?"

"Yeah. The previous owner brought me out here when I was trying to make up my mind about the place. He called it his "walk in the clouds." As soon as the stars came out and the movie started playing, I was sold. Made an offer that same night. I never found the time to come out here after that night, though." I took in a breath and exhaled. I'd been too focused on work, too busy wallowing in my own misery. Until today.

Valentina squeezed my arm. Those brown eyes of hers were full of longing. "It's time to move on."

Chest tight, I nodded once, fighting the urge to hold her, kiss her. Was *she* ready to give herself a second chance? "How about you? Are you ready to move on?"

Max charged toward her and pulled on her arm. "Come on, Mom. Look at all the movies they have."

Valentina took a few steps after him. When she

turned to me, the wrinkles across her forehead disappeared just as her dimple showed up. "I can do coffee."

Chapter Eighteen
The Ex

Valentina

A smile pulled at my lips as I opened the door. My heart did a little happy dance. There he was, Cole, looking as hot as heck and holding two cups of coffee with Cafe Triste's logo on them.

"Morning." He leaned in for a quick kiss on the cheek.

"Good morning." I balled my hands into fists to keep myself in check, trying to sound as casual as he did. I stepped outside and closed the door behind me. "Max's still sleeping."

"How long do we have?"

"About thirty minutes," I said. "Then I have to get to work."

"I'll take it." He handed me the cup with big *NL* letters on it. I assumed that was the nonfat latte. "Let's go sit by the pool."

I nodded. "You know, you're cutting into my yoga time."

"Yoga, huh? That explains a lot." He gave me one of his take-off-your-clothes smiles.

"I can show you sometime, if you'd like."

He let out a breath. "I would love to see that."

Heat crept up my cheeks. How was everything

about sex with him? Or was that me? "I didn't mean. Oh, forget it."

"That's going to be hard. Mental picture has already been saved." He winked.

Ditto. This no-sex business was going to be brutal, especially since I couldn't stop thinking about Saturday night. I couldn't stop thinking of his lips on my skin, his…

"So what's his name?" He asked as soon as we sat down, defusing the sexy thoughts in my head.

The way he'd asked, he made it sound as if we had been talking about this person the whole time. Unfortunately, I knew exactly who he meant. Was Max's dad the reason for Cole's visit?

"Who?" I asked.

"The ex." He clenched his jaw for a moment.

"Alex Maio. Why do you wanna know?"

He shrugged, sipping on his quad americano. But I wasn't buying the nonchalant act. Something about Max's dad bothered him. Was he jealous? The thought brought a flutter of butterflies to my stomach. Did Derek Cole care that much? Was Saturday night more than sex for him?

"Why are you still on this?" I asked.

"I don't like mysteries." He reached for my hand, and my heartbeat kicked into gear. "What happened?"

I gulped a mouthful of the latte and plunked the cup on the side table. Cole's warm fingers wrapped around mine. His touch was gentle, but the muscle along his jaw clenched tighter when I didn't speak. He'd come here to get answers. To be fair, he wasn't asking for anything he hadn't already given me. He'd shared so much with me the night we spent together.

Suddenly, I wanted to tell him the whole story.

"He was angry when I told him about Max. Called me names. Nasty stuff." I rubbed my chest to ease the pressure. "He made it sound like I'd ruined his life. He…" I'd never told anyone about what had really happened with Alex. I was embarrassed I put myself in that situation, that I didn't see Alex for who he was from the beginning.

"Go on. It's okay." Cole listened patiently, holding my hand.

"He said I only got pregnant to trick him into a relationship he didn't want. I was nineteen. A baby was the last thing I wanted. I swear that wasn't my intention at all." I looked away, but I felt lighter already.

"It takes two to make a baby." He put his finger under my chin and cocked his head. His eyes were full of compassion, serene. "Stop blaming yourself. He's a coward." He bit the inside of his lower lip for a moment. When he spoke, his words were soft, as if he was whispering a secret. "Yesterday I got the impression you were afraid of him. Why?" He clenched his jaw.

Now he knew what an idiot I was and why I couldn't fathom being in another relationship after Alex. "He had a very short temper." Heat flushed to my face. The tips of my ears burned. I'd hoped Cole would never find out what a coward I was, how small.

"Did he hit you?"

I ducked my gaze and swallowed a lungful of air. I nodded, feeling as if an anvil had been lifted off my chest. Slumped shoulders, I sat back in the chair. How did I manage to carry that with me for so long? When I glanced up, Cole's eyes said he understood.

"This was *not* your fault."

"It was a blessing he didn't want anything to do with us. Max growing up with someone like that… I just can't imagine what would've happened." A cold shiver ran through me at the idea of Max with someone as violent as Alex. "Can we talk about something else?"

"How's that latte?" He gave me his all-American-boy smile.

"It's great, thank you. I miss their coffee." I hadn't realized how much I'd missed sitting with Cole at Cafe Triste every morning, keeping each other company in silence.

"Me too." He braced his arms on his legs and surveyed my face.

Somewhere behind us, a waterfall muffled the sounds of the morning traffic. The real world seemed so far away. Alex and everything that happened six years ago felt so far away. I peeked at Cole over my latte. His body and face were fully relaxed, his gazed zeroed in on the city view below us. I sighed, and he clenched the coffee cup, long fingers digging into it as if it were someone's neck—Alex's neck.

I'd been so weak, letting Alex treat me the way he did. I hated that Cole knew that about me.

"I'm not that person anymore, you know?"

He nodded. "You got out. That shows who you really are. A strong and determined woman who deserves everything." He took my hand and brought it to his lips.

Strong? I smiled. He thought I was strong. A bubble full of giddiness bounced around in my belly. I glanced at my watch. I could stay here all day. But I had to get to work.

"See you tomorrow?" he asked when I stood.

The sunlight hit his face. God, the man was magnificent. I wanted to kiss him so badly, but kissing would lead to more, and I had a full day ahead of me. Crap. Did I say no sex *and* kissing or just no sex? I ran a hand through my hair, glancing upward. I couldn't keep my own rules straight anymore. No harm in a kiss, right?

What am I doing?

"Okay." I did my best to ignore the desire I felt, the heat, the sweat running down my back.

He shook his head once. In one fluid motion, he left his chair, wrapped his arms around me, and kissed me. A long, searing kiss to make me forget why Cole and I were not a good idea. He wasn't Alex.

All reasoning slipped away. I buried my fingers in his hair. I wanted his hands on me, but he just kept them around my waist. The man was impossible. How could he turn me on like this and not try more? I slipped my tongue past his lips, an invitation. He gripped me tighter, but his focus stayed on my mouth. Why? *Right. Because of my stupid no-sex rule.*

He pressed his forehead against mine, his breathing ragged. "If you're feeling inclined to change the rules again, now would be a good time, sweetheart." He nibbled the soft spot behind my ear, and my knees buckled. "Say it."

An image of him undoing my dress, his hands on my lower back, flashed in my mind. Cole touching me, licking champagne off my... *Okay. That's not helping.* We both stood still, entangled in this web of desire, my hands in his hair, his arms around me, both struggling to catch our breath. A standoff.

He wanted me to say it. And no, I wasn't above begging him for sex. But again, what I wanted was irrelevant here. If I didn't leave in the next five seconds, my resolve would crumble. If Cole got tired of me—and it was just a matter of time until he would—my heart wouldn't be the only thing at stake. I had to consider Max, too, and the family life I promised him.

One, two, three…

"I have to go," I said.

"You have to go." He released me, stepped back, and placed his hands in his pockets. Through his pants, I could see how much he wanted me. He didn't need that big of a clue to know I wanted him just as bad.

Four, five.

Dammit. I turned and left. His sigh followed me all the way back to the cottage.

****

"I'm in love with him." I confessed into my headset.

Annie had spent the last thirty minutes grilling me about Saturday night. She wanted all the dirty details, which I couldn't quite give her. I was at work. Plus, reliving that night had me almost panting into the tiny speaker near my lips.

I kept my story short. I told her how we went back to his house, had some champagne, ate homemade chocolate, and then he proceeded to make up for more than six years of celibacy.

"How many times did you come?" she asked.

"Oh my God. Why would you ask me that? Five," I quickly whispered. Maybe it was six.

She coerced a few more details out of me, but I never told her about Cole opening up to me. That moment was ours. For a few hours, it'd felt as if we were a real couple, a couple who had morning sex and shared secrets. I told her about Sunday too, how we explored the desert in his amazing backyard, had lunch, and watched a kids' movie under the stars.

Max had been in heaven when he saw the truck drive up with all the projector equipment. Between the hiking, the food, and movie, Cole had showed me a different side of him, his loving and carefree side.

I'd fallen for Derek Cole. And that scared the hell out of me.

"Oh, sweetie." Annie's voice had gone from teasing and probing to gentle. "I know."

"On Saturday, I convinced myself I only needed one night with him. You know, blow off some steam. But he's more than I thought, and he's so great with Max."

Her breathing broke the static for a second before the silence settled in again, into what felt like a long humming of *I told you so*. She'd warned me Cole was way out of my league. Dammit. Why didn't I say we could only have one week together, or maybe a year, a lifetime? God, who was I kidding? Cole would never go for a relationship that lasted more than a week. Not after what happened with his ex. Would he?

Bridget had managed to kill whatever inklings Cole ever had of settling down with a family. Wiping the back of my hand across my face, I spun in my chair to make sure I was alone and then ducked behind my monitor.

"In a way I'm glad you got it out of your system," Annie said. "Six years is way too long to go without sex."

"It wasn't a big deal until I met Cole." I rubbed the hem of my skirt between my fingers. "I've never felt like this for someone. Not even…you know."

"I know. Do you want to meet for a late lunch?"

"I can't." I flipped through the contract in front of me. I'd been reading the same formula in section B for the last half hour. "I still have to read a couple of contracts before I leave this afternoon. Rain check?" I peeled a sticky note off the pad, stuck it on the margin, and wrote a note for my boss. "Shit, she's coming my way." I sank deeper into my chair.

"Who? His ex?"

"Yeah. I'll call you later." I hit the Off button on my headset.

"Good morning, Ms. Dorva," Bridget said.

"It's de Cordoba." I rolled my eyes when she looked behind her.

"What?" A fat curl bounced in front of her face, and she put it back in place the same way she'd done last week when I first met her. The gesture had seemed almost elegant then, but now that I knew what she'd done to Cole, everything about her seemed two faced. Down to her fake curls, her perfect makeup, and acrylic french manicure.

I gazed into her eyes, betting her blue eyes were just as fake too. They weren't. Dammit. Truth was, she did match Cole in looks and level of sophistication. They shared the same life, same social circle. But she matched the Cole everyone knew, not the down-to-earth and genuine one I'd come to know the last couple of weeks. Nothing he ever said was calculated.

"My last name." I bit my lip. I shouldn't have corrected her. Regardless of what she'd done, I still needed this job. My pulse picked up the pace, and my ears felt hot. Did she know I'd told Cole about her plans?

"I can't say that." She waved a hand in front of her in dismissal. For a moment, she looked at me with a certain disdain in her eyes. Last week, she'd barely glanced my way. Now she studied me, as if trying to read my thoughts. "Christopher is in an all-day meeting today, and I wanted to make sure you knew Wednesday is your work-from-home day. It's part of a green initiative Derek and I committed to this year."

That last bit sounded like too much info. The *Derek and I* part stung a bit. "Christopher already discussed the VO schedule with me. He thought I should take Tuesday."

"Wednesday," she repeated, lips pursed and cheeks red. The woman didn't like being contradicted. "Make sure you have what you need to finish your reports from home."

"Yes, I'm sorry. I will." My voice quivered. I waited for her to ask me about our little so-called arrangement.

Luckily, her phone rang. Without saying good-bye or asking whether Cole had agreed to the divorce terms, she strolled away, with her mobile shoved against her hair. "This is Bridget Cole."

I was still reeling from the conversation with Bridget when Annie called back on my personal phone. With shaky hands, I pulled off my headset and tapped the green button on the screen. "Annie?"

A knock on my desk made me look up at Bridget's fingers snapping inches from my face. *Walk with me*, she mouthed while still on the phone.

I muted my mobile, taking long strides to keep up with her. Wow, she was tall. When we reached the break-room area, she grabbed an interoffice envelope and handed it to me. "I'm running late. Take this to my office." She left again without another word.

I unmuted my mobile and brought it to my ear. "I'm back."

"She knows," Annie said on the other end of the line.

"Who knows what?"

"The ex," she whispered. "I have a customer in here having lunch, catching up on her weekend gossip while she eats. You and Cole are all over the social section."

"Who reads the newspaper anymore?" A lot of people. I knew that. I just wasn't ready to face this particular news.

"I know, right? Here. I'm gonna send you a picture of the spread. The caption is hard to read. But it says Cole paid three times the price for the dress you're wearing."

My knees buckled. Glancing down at the screen, I waited for the picture to come in. I hardly recognized myself in it. And of course, Cole looked hotter than I remembered. A slow smile pulled at my lip. When I'd followed him out of the party, I'd only been concerned with the life-changing orgasm I had back in his tent and that we were headed to his house to do it all over again. In the picture, the lust in his expression made my mouth dry. I hadn't realized he wanted me that much.

"Are you still there?" She let out a loud breath.

"Yeah. I see it. So they saw us leaving together. What's the big deal?"

"The big deal is that *Mrs. Cole* knows. How could she not?"

She had a point. But Annie didn't know about Bridget's affair. How could Bridget be mad about Cole moving on with his life? Was this picture the reason she'd bothered to come all the way to my desk to tell me I had to work from home on Wednesday? Did she just want to size me up? My stomach rolled. She was probably wondering what Cole saw in me.

"You may be right. She's acting odd this morning, like she didn't ask me to sleep with Cole and get him to agree to her divorce agreement. Do you think she's going to kick us out of the cottage or fire me? Why didn't I think this through?" I put my head in my hands. What was I thinking? Well, that was just it. I wasn't. My brain had ceased all rational processing the minute Cole sauntered toward us at the party. The man had a way with words *and* his hands. "What am I going to do?"

"Did you tell Cole about Bridget?"

"Yeah." I headed for Bridget's office to drop off the envelope she gave me. I didn't want to give her yet another reason to fire me.

"Was he mad?"

"At first. But then…" A shiver went down my spine. I could still feel Cole's fingers on my skin as he slid the dress off my shoulders.

"Well, what's done is done. Just keep your head down at work. And more importantly, Valentina, stay away from Cole."

Keeping my head down at work wouldn't be a problem at all. Staying away from Cole was another matter entirely.

Chapter Nineteen
Alex Maio

Cole

Speak of the devil, and the devil shows up at your doorstep. What the hell?

After a coffee with Valentina, my morning was, as expected, uneventful. My afternoon, however, promised to be a bit more interesting.

"Let him through." I spoke into the house phone. "Don't tell him about the private driveway. Just send him here. I'll talk to him."

I set the phone down and strolled onto the terrace. Valentina wasn't back yet. With a quick glance at my watch, I headed downstairs. I had about an hour before she came home with Max. Different scenarios played in my head as to why Alex Maio, after all this time, was here looking for Valentina. His timing was impeccable. Was it a coincidence that he would come back into her life the minute she started seeing someone else?

Was that what we were doing?

In the living room, Em had a bourbon waiting for me. I pulled a swig from it, trying to sort out my feelings. Having this asshole in my house annoyed the heck out of me. I thought of Valentina and the fright in her eyes when she told me about Max's dad. She felt responsible for what happened. How could she believe getting pregnant by a worthless prick was her fault?

He did that to her.

No wonder she swore off men after that relationship ended. He'd made sure she could never trust anyone again. I smiled as the now-familiar desire streamed across my chest. She trusted me. She trusted me enough to tell me about him, and that filled me with contentment, even if the urge to do whatever it took to make her happy scared the crap out of me. But I couldn't deny it anymore.

My feelings for Valentina had gone from lust to something else I couldn't quite understand. Whatever I felt for her explained the irrational jealousy that burned in my gut every time I thought of Alex Maio. The hold he had on her. Her feelings for him. Even if those feelings were mostly trepidation. I looked down at my balled fists, forcing even breaths.

Before I got all hot and bothered over this guy, I needed to find out why he was here. This wasn't the time to lose my temper. I needed to handle this situation wisely.

Valentina's worst fear knocked on my door. Crossing my arms, I stood by the patio door and waited as Em showed him in. The asshole was nothing extraordinary. He seemed about Valentina's age, ear-length hair, dark eyes set in an oval face.

And a dark soul, no doubt.

He strolled into the great room, surveying the place with a look of disbelief, a smugness about him, as if he knew something I didn't. Did he honestly think he had a claim on Valentina?

"Good day, sir," he said in raspy, smoker voice that made me wonder if maybe he was older than I thought.

With a charming grin, he reached out. "Alex Maio."

"Derek Cole." I gripped his hand. Would Valentina be mad if I broke his fingers?

Something crawled down my back and made me cringe. Everything about Alex screamed danger. How the fuck did Valentina fall for a jerk like this one?

"I'm here for Valentina. Is she around?" The tone implied they were old friends. For whatever reason, he assumed I wouldn't know about him. I took a deep calming breath.

Valentina hadn't said much when she talked about him. But her body language filled in the blanks for me. She had a rehearsed story for what happened to Max's dad because he threatened her somehow. His charm was calculated. Anyone who took so much time and effort to appear friendly would care about keeping appearances. Certainly, he did the math when Valentina told him about the baby she expected. Walking out on a girlfriend would mark him as an asshole of epic proportions. Which he was. But he didn't want people to know that about him. Alex Maio wasn't the big mystery I'd made him out to be.

"She's not home."

"When will she be back?" He kept his eyes on the various knickknacks around the room.

I didn't want to tell him she was at work. If he was here now, he didn't know her schedule. I wanted to keep it that way. I wanted him gone. His gaze fell on my drink on the coffee table. A greedy spark hit his eyes as he went to sit by it.

"Don't sit down. You're not staying."

Big dark eyes snapped in my direction. "Excuse me?"

"You heard me."

I was flying blind here. A couple of days ago when Valentina told me about him, I asked Dom to run a background check on Alex. Mostly, I needed to satisfy my curiosity. I never imagined the asshole would show up at my doorstep this soon. I knew next to nothing about him.

"I know who you are. What you did." I gritted my teeth. My voice was laced with so much anger I didn't recognize it. I sauntered toward him, standing a good half a foot taller. I wanted to punch that smugness off his face. "What I don't know is why you're here."

"I'm here to see my family." He spread his arms.

I grew tired of his charade. "Let's be clear. You don't have a family here. What do you want?"

That smug smile pulled on his lips again, and something twisted in my gut. "Okay. Straight to the point. I like it." He scanned the great room as he wandered toward the patio door, craning his neck to see out. "Nice house you have here. You must have a lot of money." He pointed a long finger toward the pool. I wanted to grab him by the collar and throw him out.

I placed both hands on my hips. *Relax. He can't see the cottage from here.*

"That's none of your business." I moved in closer in case he tried to go outside.

He rubbed his jaw, wetting his lips. His strong cologne assaulted my nostrils. "But that's why I'm here. To talk business."

"Spit it out."

"Do you know how hard it is to stay away from my family? It's for their own good, but it still pains me, deeply. You know what I'm talking about. That tight body of hers." His tongue brushed his teeth, making a loud click. "She's so sweet." He rubbed his hand across his chest.

"How much?" I wanted this asshole out of Valentina's life for good.

"See? I knew you were a smart one. Val, she always had a thing for smart men."

Men? I couldn't help but be annoyed with Valentina. For the life of me, I couldn't figure out what she saw in this guy. A complete douche with no regard for his own son or her. At least his intentions were simple. He wanted money.

"For you?" He surveyed the room again. "Fifty grand."

"Okay."

His eyes lit up as a nasty grin pulled on his mouth, all charm gone. This was the real him. He took a couple of long strides, craned his neck toward the hallway that led to the kitchen, and spun around. As if he expected a cart of cash to roll into the room.

"I will give you five thousand now. The rest when you sign an affidavit where you give up custody of Max."

"Who?" He furrowed his brows and wrinkled his nose. "Oh…right."

"You're going to grant her full custody. And you will stay the fuck away from her. Because if you don't, I will beat the shit out of you."

"I'm with you. One hundred and ten percent." He rubbed the stubble on his jaw. "Fifty grand for the kid. And another fifty for Valentina. Come on. It's gonna be real hard for me to give up that sweet p—"

He didn't get to finish. His face smacked the patio

door, leaving streaks of blood behind. My hand pulsed in pain, but the satisfaction was worth it. So much for handling the situation wisely.

The loud crack his head had made when it hit the window prompted Em to dash into the room.

"I got this," I said to her.

Scared, she hurried back into the kitchen.

Slowly, the douchebag got up, hands on his knees for support. His face turned red as he struggled to deal with the pain and catch his breath. He hadn't expected me to do that. What the fuck did he think? That he could come into my own home, insult Valentina, and prance away with fifty thousand dollars of my money.

With a leering smile, he put up a hand in surrender and started toward the door.

Midstride, he spun and charged at me. He went straight for my gut, knocking the wind out of me with his head. I stumbled several steps back before I caught my balance. He rammed into me again. The side table collapsed under our weight, and books and other items scattered across the floor.

When I recovered, I gripped the front of his shirt and struck him across the face. I didn't wait this time. My fist connected with his jaw again. And once more, his level of strength was no match for mine. No, this wasn't a fair fight. I didn't give a shit.

He took a swing at me, slow and heavy. Could he even see through that swollen eye? Another swing. I ducked out of the way easily. On his next punch, I stood still. The loud smack of his fist against my jaw echoed in my head along with Valentina's words when she told me what he'd done to her. Was this what she felt when he hit her? Or was it much worse? I struck him again.

This time, I swung my arm around to connect with his side and let him have the full force of my strength. My knuckles felt raw, and warm liquid covered the skin, but I kept at him until he fell to the floor, almost unconscious. Out of breath and feeling deeply unsatisfied, I waited for him to recover.

When he stirred, I helped him up. Like a snake, he recoiled away from me. "Let's try this again," I said. Shaking, he shot me a dark and furious glance, lip curled. He knew this was a fight he couldn't win. I stepped toward him, towering over him, legs planted wide. "You will get your fifty thousand in exchange for Max's full custody. And if you ever come back…sniffing around my house…asking for more money… If you so much as speak Valentina's name, I will put you in the hospital first. And then in jail. Are we clear?" Sweat dotted the nape of my neck as anger buzzed through my body.

He nodded.

"Say it." I spit out the words.

"We're clear," he mumbled.

"My lawyer will contact you when the papers are ready for your signature. He will also file a restraining order against you. As far as you're concerned, Valentina never existed."

He rolled his eyes.

"You don't wanna fuck with me." I moved closer, fists at my sides. He stumbled and fell, his arm up to protect his face.

He sat on his ankles and wiped the blood off his lip. "All this for that chick. She must've done you something good. He shook his index finger at me. "I remember—"

At least, the asshole didn't disappoint. My pulse spiked as I grabbed him by the collar and half dragged him across the room toward the front entrance. I opened the door with my free hand and tossed him out. Exactly as I'd wanted to do the moment he waltzed in. I was glad I'd waited. We had a productive chat. And now he wouldn't be a problem for Valentina and Max anymore.

Out on the driveway, three security guards stood at attention. Em must've called them. Good. Now he knew the house was heavily guarded.

"Make sure he never sets foot in this place again," I said to the guards.

"Yes, sir," they all said in unison.

The little prick was scared shitless. That was smart of him. The gate was a half mile from the house. I stood by the threshold as the guards escorted him out of the property, and waited until all I could see was the dust his car tires left in their wake.

Frazzled, I trudged back upstairs. Em fussed around me, trying to put some kind of ointment on my hands. In the end, she settled for giving me a bag of ice to put on my knuckles.

"Are you going to tell me what that was about?" Eyes wide, she set a fresh drink on one of the tables out on the terrace.

"Just wrapping up some old business." I took a deep breath to ease the burn in my lungs and washed down the bad taste in my mouth with a swig of the bourbon.

"Why do I get the feeling this has something to do with Valentina? He looked familiar. Max's dad?"

I met her gaze and nodded. She let out a loud sigh. But other than that, she took pity on me and didn't dwell on it. Maybe I had no business meddling in Valentina's life like that. But I couldn't stand idle and watch as that asshole terrorized her again. The only reason she'd moved on with her life, why she lived in peace, was that she was certain Max's dad didn't want anything to do with them. I didn't want that peace taken away from her.

If he had found a way to reach Valentina, I had no doubt he would've played that card. Shake her up again to get her to pay up. I pegged him as someone who wouldn't be above using Max for his own gain. No doubt he'd come back because Valentina was with me. An easy payday, he probably figured. I didn't regret getting involved.

The now-familiar sound of gravel crunching under tires got my attention. Em mumbled something on her way out.

"Em." I called to her. "You have nothing to worry about. He's not coming back."

"Not after that beating." She chuckled. "The question is, how did he find out about you and Valentina?"

"I don't know. As far as I can tell, Annie is the only one who knows where Valentina lives. Not even her parents know."

"How indeed." She shook a finger at me before she left. "You have to be careful."

Over by the cottage, Valentina and Max headed inside, carrying grocery bags. If she had come straight home, she would've ran into Alex. They didn't deserve this. Now I understood her comment from the other day. *It really was a blessing he didn't want anything to do with us. Max growing up with someone like that…*

Just as he did with me, he probably showed his true colors after Valentina got pregnant. In his mind, he no longer had use for her. So he had no problem showing her the real him. The son of a bitch hit her. I should've beaten him into a pulp.

Max's giggles brought me back. I couldn't hear what they were saying, but something he'd said prompted Valentina to chase him. When she caught up to him, she tickled him until he wiggled out of her reach. His little backpack bounced all over the place as he darted toward the house. She stopped at her porch and glanced my way. I waved hello, and she returned the gesture with a bright smile that made my heart go into overdrive, and damn if my cock didn't react.

As Em had said, lately everything I did had something to do with Valentina. My anger and jealousy toward Alex, the insatiable need to be with her, to protect her and make her happy. It all stemmed from the same place. I was in love with her.

Chapter Twenty
Say You Believe Me

Valentina

On Wednesday, Cole stopped by to deliver another latte. We sat on the cottage porch, drinking our coffees, while a patchy drizzle made dimples on the puddles across from us. Just as we used to do before we met back at the coffee shop. Except now he looked at me and I stared back. And I couldn't stopped thinking about Saturday night.

"Punching walls again?" I pointed at the cuts on his knuckles.

"Ran into a wall." He shrugged.

"You're not gonna tell me?"

"Not today." He kissed my hand, sending a flutter of goose bumps up my arm. "When are you going to let me take you out on a real date?"

"What?" I almost spit out my drink. A real date? Like a couple? The image of the night we spent together was so vivid in my mind still. The idea of having a repeat of any of that made my legs feel weak. This felt different, though, as if he wanted more than sex.

He let out a long breath. "Would you like to go out with me? Tonight."

Do I want? Yes. I crossed my arms. "I can't. I

promised Max we'd cook dinner together."

Shoulders slumped, Cole lowered his head, rubbing the nape of his neck. The sad look he gave me wrapped itself around my chest and squeezed tight. The last thing I wanted was to hurt him, but I couldn't change my plans with Max.

"No outsiders allowed?" He raised an eyebrow, flashing me one of his charming smiles, and I melted a little in my seat and gripped his hand. "Lunch then," he said.

"Today?" My eyes flicked to my watch. "Like in five hours?"

He nodded.

"Tell me what happened to your hand." I had a pretty good guess what'd happened.

Yesterday when Max and I had come home, I saw Alex leaving the property. I couldn't tell if he'd seen me. He certainly didn't show it, but that didn't matter. The shock of adrenaline hit so fast and hard all I could see were dark spots. Everything that'd happened the day I told him I was pregnant came rushing back: the punches across the face because I'd ruined his life, the yelling, and his description of what would happen to my family and me if I ever told anyone Max was his.

In the end, Max's little voice brought me out of my panic attack. Then I saw Cole up in his terrace, having a drink as if nothing was the matter, and I convinced myself I'd imagined the whole thing. In an instant, all thoughts of Alex vanished. By the time Max and I had gone inside the cottage, I felt safe. But Cole's raw knuckles were proof I hadn't hallucinated Alex. Somehow, he'd found us.

"Oh, we're negotiating now." He sat a little

straighter, wolfish grin on. "How are you going to make me talk?"

"If you tell me, I'll meet you for lunch. I'm working from home today. I only have an hour, so we'll need to stay in."

"Are you sure? If we stay, we may end up doing something else." The lust in his expression promised this lunch would turn into another marathon of mind-blowing sex.

"What could you possibly do to me that you haven't done already?"

Leaning forward, he cupped my face and kissed my lips. I melted into him and cursed my own stupid no-sex rule. His breath on my neck sent shivers down my back.

"Sweetheart, there's so much more we haven't done. I'd like to get better acquainted with that tight little ass of yours…and these." His forefinger brushed the curve of my breast. "One night is not enough. Do you believe me now?"

"Oh." I nodded and shifted away from him. Noon could not come fast enough.

He pulled back and stood. "I'll see you at eleven."

I swallowed against the hum in my chest. "Noon. I have a lot of reports to do." I reached for his good hand and held it tight. "Now tell me what happened. It was Alex, wasn't it? "Deep down, I wanted him to say no.

The blue in his irises was almost gone. He clenched his jaw and met my gaze. "I was hoping you wouldn't find out."

"I saw him leaving. What did he want?"

"Nothing." A deep scowl flashed across his forehead. He shook his head once and treated me to one

205

of his smiles. "He's the biggest douchebag I've ever met, though. I hope you understand not all guys are like that."

"I know that now." I placed a hand on his chest, and he covered it with his. His heart beat hard against my palm.

"Are you sure? I wonder if this is why you're so quick to run away. To assume the worst in men. In me."

"Not you." Tears stung my eyes. I wasn't crying for Alex. I was crying for me and all the time I'd lost because of him. "You're different."

"I won't let him hurt you." He pushed the hair away from my shoulder, letting his fingers linger. "I promise."

I wrapped my arms around his waist and buried my face in the crook of his neck. He held me tight until I stopped crying.

"Come over when you're ready." He kissed the top of my head and tilted my chin up. "He's gone for good."

I nodded, and he turned to leave. My gaze followed Cole as he sauntered back to his house, his hands in his jean pockets, biceps bulging. Blowing out a breath, I wiped my cheek on my T-shirt and went inside. In the kitchen, Max sat eating a bowl of cereal he served himself. The bowl was full to the rim. Every time he took a spoonful, granola bits rolled off the dish and onto the counter.

"I see you're ready to go. Let's get in the car."

"Okay. I'm just finishing up my homework," he said.

My heart melted a little. Pre-K students didn't get homework, especially in the summer. But I didn't question it. Instead, I watched him trace letters with a crayon. He wrapped an arm around my waist and kept tracing. We deserved this happiness.

"Let's go, Mom. We're going to be late."

"Yeah. Grab your shoes."

We shuffled to the car side by side. Max waved at Cole when he saw him up on his terrace. "I like him."

"Yeah, me too." I sighed.

I drove Max to summer camp and made it back in twenty minutes flat. With flutters wreaking havoc in my stomach, I rushed through the list of tasks I had for the day. Every now and then, I would glance at the computer clock and the flutter would spread from my chest to below my navel.

Wait. What? Did I agree to a booty call with Cole? Oh crap. I buried my face in my hands. Cole was right—one night wasn't enough. If I were being honest, I was running out of reasons to push him away. Max liked him, and Cole was great with kids. More importantly, Cole wanted to be with me. We deserved a second chance. The question was, would Bridget let us have it? What would she do if Cole didn't turn in his signed divorce papers by Friday? I swallowed the lump in my throat and pushed the thought aside. He'd said he would handle things with Bridget, and I trusted him. In a few days, he would be free again.

Two hours and forty-two minutes later, I sent my reports to Christopher. I stared at the clock until the numbers got blurry. Lunchtime wasn't for another two hours, but I couldn't wait any longer. I rushed to the bathroom and got ready in record time, donning a simple belted shirtdress. Oh shit, I was going on a real date with Cole.

My heart threatened to push through my chest plate in anticipation. I shook my hands in front of me while I paced the living room. *Relax. It's just a date.* Why was this such a big deal? The clock beeped, and I almost jumped out of my skin. Jeez. It was eleven on the dot. Screw it. Rain pelted down on me when I dashed out the door and across the lawn, toward Cole's house. No amount of cool rain could diffuse this want I felt for him. I needed this.

A shudder went through me when I reached the steps that led to the grand terrace and his bedroom. The wicked smile that pulled at the side of my mouth turned into a full-on grin as I started up the steps.

Gosh, do I have to be so obvious?

I turned around and sprinted back downstairs. Taking a deep breath, I adjusted my dress and headed for the patio door that led to the great room instead. It was open, but I knocked anyway, suddenly feeling like an intruder.

I stepped into the living room and called out to Cole. "Hello?"

"Hello." A female voice came from the loft.

My stomached dropped. My whole world dropped. The voice sounded familiar. Was that Nikki?

"Valentina," Cole said from the top of the stairs. His hair was wet, and he looked hot as all heck in his oh-so-thin white T-shirt and jeans. A big smile formed on his face as he rushed down the steps.

Nikki came down from the loft and met Cole in the living room, where I stood frozen. A half-naked and sweaty woman would do that to anyone.

"What the fuck, Nikki?" Cole stepped back from her, brows furrowed, eyes darting from her to me. He reached for me. "Valentina."

My heart slowed to a painful beat until it squeezed into a tight ball. I couldn't breathe. Did he really not know she was in his house?

"Darling, who is this?" Nikki asked.

She knew who I was. I was Saturday. And I was here on the wrong day. I looked down at my hands, knowing I couldn't be mad at Cole. He never said we were exclusive. Instead, I was furious with myself. For letting myself think Cole would want a serious relationship with me. He obviously didn't. He just happened to have an open spot in his weekly rotation. And here was proof.

Nikki rushed to his side and whispered fast in his face. I couldn't hear what she was saying, and I didn't care. My chest hurt as I trudged toward the door. This was our good-bye, but without the closure.

"When I get back, you need to be gone." Cole's voice rumbled inside the house.

By the time I reached the lawn, my legs felt stronger. I broke into a run. At the fork in the pathway, I had the cottage to my right and the driveway to my left. I went left. I needed to put distance between Cole and me. A loud thunderclap followed by lightning in the distance made me run even faster to my car. Before I reached it, I ran into an oak tree. Or at least it felt like it. Cole stood between my Civic and me.

"Let me explain." His voice quavered. The sad and pleading look in his eyes cut right through me. "Please—"

"I think things were pretty self-explanatory back in there. Let me go." I sidestepped him, but he put out his arm.

"Not until we talk."

I moved toward to the cottage, but he blocked me again. On the second try, he bent down and reached for my legs. He slung me over his shoulder, knocking the air out of me.

"You're not seriously doing this?" I said through gritted teeth.

"No more running, Valentina."

As the rain continued in a relentless downpour, he sprinted up the grand staircase to his bedroom. With every step, my stomach bounced against his hard shoulder. I put my hands out to lessen the blow, but his back was wet and slippery.

He slowed his pace when we reached the landing. After a moment of hesitation, he strolled past the tables and chairs and dropped me onto his bed. He was on top of me, my hands over my head. I bit my lower lip, trying to catch my breath. Not much I could do to stop the tears from rolling down my temples.

"Let me go."

"I will. But please. Listen to me first. I didn't know she was here. And I sure as hell didn't invite her over." His whole body shook. He was inches from me. Water dripped from his hair onto my face. "You have to believe me. I haven't been with anyone. Not since I first saw you at the coffee shop."

I wanted to believe him. He had looked surprised when he saw Nikki in his living room. The knot in my stomach loosened slowly, and I let out a breath. He bowed his head and let out a small moan before he bent down to kiss me, a deep, hot kiss.

He pulled back, releasing my hands. Cold air seeped through my wet clothes. Standing by the bed, his gaze on me, he reached behind him and pulled his T-shirt off. Shoes and jeans came next. "Take off your clothes."

Desire pooled instantly between my legs. Heat unfurled slowly and left me weak. "No."

"They're wet. You'll catch a cold." He disappeared through one of the doors on the other side of the bed and came back with a white fluffy towel in his hand, still gloriously naked. Damn, that was a good look for him.

"I don't care." I crossed my arms. I had a hard time standing my ground while sitting on his bed, shivering.

He draped the warm towel around me, pulled me toward him. "Do it or I will."

I shut my eyes and reveled in the sweet rush of heat that sprung from my center and lingered for a moment before scurrying down to my toes. Too many days had gone by since the last time we were together. I undid the first button, aware of every inch of his skin within my reach. I slowed down my movements, and our gazes locked. If I took my dress off, my no-sex rule would go out the window. Or had it gone out the window this morning?

He pulled at the fabric tied in a bow around my waist, and his breath hitched when my shirtdress parted to expose my bare breasts. Yeah, the no-sex rule had gone out the window this morning.

"You're killing me," he mumbled. "Tell me you've reconsidered."

I nodded. "You were right. One night is not enough."

He cradled my neck, mouth hungry on mine while his hands peeled the dress off me. He walked me backward to the bed, and I plopped myself on the mattress, my gaze on him as he slowly knelt in front of me. His smile told me he planned to make me pay for making him wait this long. I closed my legs before he could position himself where he wanted. I didn't feel like giving in so easily, or maybe he just brought out the rebel in me.

His eyes settled on my sex, and I melted some more. "Why do you make me work this hard for you?"

I licked my lips and cleared my throat. I wanted to taste all of him. "I'm in your bedroom…naked. That's hardly me making you work hard for me."

He shook his head. That wolfish grin of his was back. Yeah, he was going to make me pay, and I couldn't wait. Wrapping his fingers around my wrists, he pulled me toward him. When I was within reach, he kissed me. His tongue gently pressed and teased until my lips parted for him.

Like magnets, my hands went to his shoulders and moved up to the nape of his neck. I loved his soft skin and the strength of his straining muscles underneath. I tunneled my fingers in his hair and breathed in his musk, that smell that was only his. He palmed my breasts, captured both nipples between the pads of his fingers, and applied a small amount of pressure. Holy shit. My clit reacted immediately, aching with need. What was that?

I let out a breath that sounded like something between a moan and sigh. He waited a moment longer. When he released me, the tightening around my hard bud lessened.

"You feel so good, so soft." He cupped my breasts again, and my pulse raced in anticipation. I bit my lip and waited. As soon as I relaxed my shoulders, he brought the peaks close together and moved down to kiss them. Again, he pinched my nipples and let the pressure build.

"Show me where you feel it," he whispered.

Omigod, show what? My hand reached for the inside of my lace underwear.

He blocked me with his elbow. "Show me," he muttered.

I arched my back. The aching desire at my core mounted. I wasn't sure how much more of that sweet agony I could take. I spread my thighs, falling back on the bed, undeniably under his spell. That infuriating grin of his appeared again when he hooked his fingers in my panties and pulled them off.

"Let me kiss it better." His hands on my waist felt cool against my hot skin as he bent down and captured my button in his mouth.

I nodded, unable to form the words. Or breathe, for that matter. He cupped my ass, kneading it and bringing me closer to him. His lips pressed against me expertly, soft and full. Within moments, I was merely a puddle of sensation. He palmed the apex of my sex. Each stroke in perfect synchronization with his electrifying tongue. I arched my back, ready to combust.

"Let it go, sweetheart," he whispered against my bud. His hot breath on my sex sent me into a whirlwind of ecstasy. Slow and hot, liquid fire sprung from my core and swirled down to my toes.

"Cole."

"Yes, sweetheart." He sat back on his heels, running a hand up my thigh, across my belly and breasts. "I've never felt skin like yours."

I couldn't move.

Taking ragged breaths, he reached for a wrapper on his nightstand. He took his time to smooth on the condom with precise strokes—to torture me some more, no doubt. I didn't want to wait. I sat up, and my hands landed on his chest, kneading anything I could reach, his rock-hard abs, his back, his ass.

His gaze met mine. *Omigod.* Cole wanted me as much as I wanted him. Slowly, he ran a hand up my leg, eased me back, and positioned himself on top of me. He entered me, hard, filling me completely, plunging into me. The need built up again. How was I going to get there again?

"You are so beautiful," he whispered. "And you feel so good."

Pulling out, he gripped my hips and guided me onto my belly. He kneaded my butt cheek and rubbed against me, letting me feel how hard he was for me. The bubble building up in my chest finally burst. I giggled, feeling giddy and complete. Nothing else mattered. We were meant to be together. Whatever problems we had outside this bedroom, we could work them out. I loved him, and something told me he loved me back. I'd seen the desperation in his eyes when he thought I was leaving, when he thought I didn't believe him.

I turned to look at him over my shoulder. "What happened to the lunch you promised?" I teased.

He chuckled. "Waiting downstairs. We can stop if you want." His voice sounded strained and ragged.

"Don't stop."

"Thank God." He pressed his lips on my shoulder before he entered me from behind. I buried my face in the covers, letting out a sigh, waiting for the climax I knew would come.

"Relax," he whispered in my ear, reaching deeper with every thrust, making my desire pulse hard. He increased the speed, and I squeezed tighter and tighter around him until I felt that burn inside me ignite, an intense and hot release. "Sweetheart. You're the only one I want. Say you believe me."

The peace and happiness his words brought me were better than any orgasm.

Well, pretty close.

"I believe you." The duvet muffled my words. "I love you."

Chapter Twenty-One
A Different Truth

Cole

I was well aware I looked like an idiot, smiling as if I were two seconds away from bursting into song. But I couldn't help it. Lunchtime was now my favorite time of the day. Well, spending it with Valentina was. I just couldn't get enough of her. And for once, she seemed content with our arrangement. The urge to run away had left her eyes. This pleased me more than I would've guessed. Checking my watch, I made my way downstairs. It was almost noon.

Halfway down the stairs, I halted. The clinking of glasses in the living room set my pulse into overdrive. Last time an uninvited guest came to the house, I almost lost Valentina. Although I had to admit, the make-up sex had been phenomenal. My pants got tight at the thought of her that da*y*, the little sounds she made every time she came.

No matter how good sex was that day, I couldn't risk another one of Nikki's silly games. The door guard had specific instructions not to let her in. I still couldn't figure out how she'd snuck in. I glanced down at the time again. Whoever was in the living room needed to be gone fast. I leaned over the banister before I reached the last step and spotted Dom.

"Well, I'll be damned, man. You're alive!"

"I've been busy." I patted his back harder than necessary. "Still drinking my booze, I see."

He shrugged, taking a long swig of whiskey. "You always keep the best shit. It's been two weeks, man. Where the hell have you been?"

"I'm expecting company, so state your business quickly."

He laughed. "I thought you had Fridays wide open."

"Fuck off. What do you want?" I had purposely not told Dom about Valentina. He wouldn't understand what she meant to me. Plus, he would most likely advise me not to get serious. Too late for that. At this point, I couldn't go for more than a day without seeing her. I needed her in the worst way possible. "I'm seeing someone," I blurted out. He had to know. I still needed him to draw up the custody papers for Max and arrange the payment for Alex Maio.

"Nikki?"

I laughed. "No. Not her. You'll get to meet her in a few minutes."

"Oh, man. Look at you. Are you really in…" He rubbed his eyes, shaking his head. "I can't even say it."

"I'm in love with her."

"Well. I never thought I'd see the day. *Our* boy's in love." He patted me on the back. "I guess it's true what they say. It can't rain every day."

"What do you mean?" My smile faded.

He finished his whiskey in one swig. "You want the good news or the bad news first?"

"Always the good news first."

Dom strolled back to the bar, poured two whiskeys,

and placed one in my hand. Lips pressed into a line, he gestured for me to sit down. "This is going to take a while."

I sat and sipped, blood pulsing through me. The alcohol helped eased my nerves some. It didn't take a genius to know this had to do with Bridget and the divorce. But, man, Dom had a way to dramatize things.

"Just say it." I set my glass on the coffee table.

"Bear with me. This is a long-ass story. So I told you I was going to sniff around Bridget's financials, right? Well, I couldn't find anything wrong. No credit card debt or big splurges of money, although the woman sure does spend a lot of money on Louis Vuitton."

"Yeah, I know."

"Anyhow, that's exactly what caught my attention."

"The LVs?"

"No, the fact that after burning through a couple of hundred thousand dollars in Vegas last month, none of it showed up on her account. So where did she get the money, right?"

I nodded, remembering for the first time the look in Bridget's eyes when we were honeymooning. The high of winning was everything to her. She'd lost a lot of my money those two weeks we were in Monte Carlo. But it never occurred to me that any of it was more than something to past the time or blow off steam.

"Turns out she has an account in the Bahamas. This account is under an LLC I didn't know about, but I was still able to get statements for it."

"I'm not even gonna ask how."

He shook his head. "I have my methods. Anyway,

this account receives payments every month, for the same amount." His eyes were alive with excitement.

I exhaled, watching him intently. Dom had put the puzzle together. Was Bridget having money problems? I sat a little closer to the edge of my seat.

"Now before I tell you where the money comes from, can you guess when the payments started coming in?" he asked.

A slow burn flared from the pit of my stomach up into my chest. Yes, I was over Bridget's betrayal. But this was something new. "It can't be when I hired her."

"No. Right after you got married. And I mean right after. Like that same night after, man."

This whole marriage thing had been Bridget's idea. Back then, I'd been so distracted by CCI I couldn't see beyond my office door. She'd been with me every step of the way as we worked to increase our revenue and get to the target goal for the year. For the life of me, I couldn't remember how we'd gotten involved romantically. One night we had sex in my office, and the next thing I knew she was planning our wedding. She'd been in a big rush too.

"Where's the money coming from?" I asked.

"Mostly CCI, but also your personal accounts."

I pinched the bridge of my nose. "She's been stealing from me? All this time, she's been screwing our accountant and stealing from me? Explain to me how this is the good news."

"I'm getting there. Despite the hefty monthly payments, her offshore account is almost empty. Get this—all the money has been flowing into another account in that same bank. No clue who the account belongs to or what kind of activity it's seen. Because the day I sent an inquiry to my contact, he promptly informed me that no such account existed." He paced for a moment, eyebrows drawn together. Was he afraid? This was something I rarely saw in Dom. "Then I found my car near the Nogales border, completely dismantled."

"What happened? Why didn't you call me?"

His cheeks turned red, as if he was remembering something. "It wasn't necessary. I handled it. And I had help. Sort of."

"Better the car than you, though, right? I'm sorry about your car."

"Yeah. They were trying to make a point. And don't worry. You already replaced it."

I sat back on the couch and raked a hand through my hair. We were going around in circles. We were out of time. "So now what? Back to square one?"

"Not exactly. We don't need to know what's in the account. It's perfectly obvious that Bridget went and got herself mixed up with a loan shark, a big one."

"Are you sure?"

"Trust me. I know a *crew* when I see one. I mean, who else would be able to act so quickly when I started looking into their business?"

"This is mob stuff, Dom."

He nodded. "No shit. My guess is her boyfriend introduced her. I did some digging on Frank. He's gotten himself into messes like this before." He shrugged and took another sip of his drink. "I guess their sudden love sprung from their mutual interest in gambling."

"They've been enabling each other's addiction." I finished his thought. So that was Bridget's big secret.

The reason she needed to keep CCI. A fucking addict. "How did we not know this prick was an addict? I'm sure we did a background check on him before he was hired on."

"I checked. You didn't do one."

I closed my eyes, clenching my jaw. "Bridget fast-tracked him."

"Not that it would've made a difference," he said. "We check for priors, not for whether or not they're friends with the mob."

Were they together when he came to work for me? Was this her plan all along? To con me out of my own company?

"So she figured if she keeps my company, no one would ever question why she's funneling funds out of the corporation." Heat flushed through me. I fisted my cold hands and tapped my forehead, wishing Frank were here so I could beat the truth out of him. "Was this her plan all along, you think?"

"Who the hell knows? She already canceled all bonuses for the year." Dom blew out air and refilled my glass, which reminded me this was the good news.

"Fuck. Shit. Fuck," I said.

"I hear ya, man." He knocked back his drink. "That's one fucked-up broad. I'm guessing she's going to suck the company dry, then sell it by the pound."

"Or worse, go public. But as screwed up as this is, I think we can use this to our advantage." A wave of hope washed over me, and I jumped to my feet. "I'll pay off her debt with the mob. And in return, she'll have to forfeit everything else. My company, alimony, and any other ties she might think she has with my family or me. I want that woman out of my life for good."

"Cole."

"No, Dom, this will work. Because if she refuses, I'll call for an audit and she'll end up in jail."

"I don't know. Based on the monthly payments bleeding out of her account, we're talking about a couple mil."

"I'll pay." I placed both arms on my hips. I was done with all this divorce bullshit.

"Cole, sit down." He took a long calming breath. "You still haven't heard the bad news."

"Just tell me." I leaned on the armrest. How much worse could things really get?

"Your divorce decree came in this morning. Apparently, Bridget's lawyer submitted a signed divorce agreement, in which you give her ownership of CCI."

Spots of bright light exploded in front of me, and blood surged through me, hot and fast. Resting my elbows on my knees, I pressed the heels of my hands to my eyes. My stomach churned with disgust for Bridget and her goddamn betrayal.

"Did she forge my signature?" I asked through gritted teeth, meeting his eyes.

Dom shook his head once. "That was my initial thought. I stopped by the court before coming here. They confirmed the signature is yours."

I sprung to my feet and raced to the library. I took the steps up to the loft two at a time. Random sheets flew off the desk as I trashed my office, riffling through the papers on my desk, looking for the damn documents. The agreement I'd signed four weeks ago was gone. Someone had come into my home and stolen it. I tried not to think of the implication. Someone close to me had betrayed me.

"How did she get the signed agreement? I had it here," I said. My legs felt heavy as I descended the stairs.

"She claims that an employee brought them to her. Outside of the courtroom, she approached me and let it slip that she had to pay a considerable amount for them."

I rubbed my chest and bit the inside of my lip. "Did she give you a name?"

"Yeah, wait. I have it in my inbox. I had to write it down. Not an easy name to remember." He fished through his back pocket for his phone. "You have to be careful with this, Cole. Since when does Bridget volunteer information that can incriminate her in a court of law? She's a lot of things, but dumb bitch isn't one of them. I don't know how this would benefit her. But I'm sure it does. Somehow. This entire situation just reeks."

My hands trembled as he scrolled through the email on his mobile. Only one other person knew about the divorce. Only one person had access to my life…and to Bridget.

"Here it is. Yeah, there was no way I was going to remember this. Valentina de Cordoba. Do you know her?" He must've read something in my face when he looked up at me. "Honestly, man, I have no way of confirming any of this. We could look at the camera feeds, but that'll take a long time to do. This came out of left field. I don't have a plan yet, but I'll come up with something. I promise. That bitch will *not* get away with this."

Valentina's name still echoed painfully in my ears. I shut my eyes, and all I could see was red. "Check your email again."

"What am I checking for?"

"Check your goddamn email again." My voice thundered around the room.

"It's here. Look." He showed me his phone. When he met my gaze, his mouth fell opened. "Oh man, Cole. I'm so sorry."

I was the biggest idiot. I deserved this for believing her sweet-girl act was real, for thinking her feelings for me were honest. That she didn't care about my money. What else did she lie about? Did she lie about needing a place to live? About Alex Maio? *Jesus Christ.* Did she send him to ask for money? I'd been flying blind that day because I only knew what she'd told me about him. But he certainly knew how to push my buttons. He knew exactly what to say to send me over the edge, to get me to rush in and save her.

She turned me into a pathetic imbecile.

I hoped she'd miss our lunch date. I wanted her to disappear because I didn't know what I'd do to her if she showed up now. Burying my face in my hands, I squeezed my eyes shut and let the tears flow. When I opened them, Valentina stood on the other side of the window, looking like an angel. The woman who I'd thought had walked into my life to save me hadn't been here for me at all.

Her hair flew in the wind, dimples adorning her smile, like some kind of dark angel. *She didn't do this.* She moved slowly. Why didn't I see it before? The way she hesitated with every step, calculating my reaction. She did it now. Her walk was a prowl, like a predator after its prey. *Me*. I rubbed my eyes. It was so hard to believe.

All those times she pretended to run away. Like an idiot, I gave chase every fucking time. She threw away my company. And for what? Money? I would've given her anything she asked for. Didn't I prove that the day she sent Alex? All she had to do was ask, and I would've laid the world at her feet. She didn't have to go and sell me out like this.

I was a fool for believing she felt my pain when I told her about Bridget and how I was about to lose my company. It was all a goddamn act. None of it ever mattered to her. I jerked to my feet. I needed to see it in her eyes.

In two strides, I closed the space between us. I cupped the nape of her neck and forced her to look at me. A moan escaped her lips, stirring the familiar desire in me, but I didn't back down. I ignored the pout of her lips and her small hands kneading my abs. Tears pooled in her eyes when I put my thumb below her jaw to keep her from looking away, desperate to find a different truth in her eyes.

Chapter Twenty-Two
Did You Think of Me?

Valentina

Cole shot me a dark glare when I crossed the threshold. My legs and hands trembled at the sight of him. I'd never seen him this furious. By the look on his friend's face, he hadn't either. I stepped back. Should I leave them to deal with whatever they had going on? I opened my mouth to speak, but the words wouldn't come out. What could I say? I should go, but that'd be like running away. In the last few weeks, Cole had shown me running was never the answer.

Whatever Cole was going through, we could face it together. I smiled. *Together* sounded nice. Even if we still hadn't addressed our feelings after I blurted out I was in love with him. I'd considered that maybe he didn't take my confession seriously because, well, I'd said it right after a mind-blowing orgasm. But that wasn't why I'd done it. I wanted him to know I was in love with him. Getting it off my chest had felt good. I'd given him time to digest the news, but now we needed to talk about it. Maybe not right this second, especially with Cole shooting daggers at me.

Stepping into the living room, I waved hello at the man standing next to Cole. He was almost as tall as Cole, with cobalt-blue eyes and dark, wavy hair. His skin was only a shade lighter than mine. The man was intimidating, but at this moment, he didn't look half as terrifying as Cole.

"Is everything okay?" I asked when both men just stared at me as if I had just committed a heinous crime.

Cole trod toward me, a vein throbbing in his temple, his eyes wet. My breath hitched. With a painful tug, he gripped my neck. His face was just an inch away as his eyes surveyed mine. Had he been crying? I wanted to tell him I loved him, but I couldn't get the words out. His hold on me was too tight. Pressing my palms on his chest and abs, I pushed him. His heart pounded so hard his chest strained, as if it were about to split open. He himself was about to spin out of control.

"Cole," his friend spoke. "Let's take a second to think this through."

"There's nothing to think through. It's all very clear to me now." When he released me, he fisted his hands so tight one of his scabs ripped and bled.

I'd been here before. I let my guard down, and somehow I ended up back where I'd started, at the receiving end of a man's anger. And just like the first time, I had no idea what I'd done wrong. *You said you were different. You said I could trust you.* The hatred in his eyes was too much for me to bear. I turned to leave, but Cole took a long stride and grabbed my wrist. I yanked my arm, but he caught my other wrist with his free hand and held me close to him. His breathing was ragged, and he smelled of liquor.

"You were never on my side, were you? That whole innocent act, you telling me the truth about Bridget—it was all lie. You've been working for her this entire time." His eyes searched my face again.

Tears rolled down my cheeks. "Cole, I told you the truth that night. I would never do anything to hurt you." I looked behind him to his friend.

Cole jerked my hands to get my attention back. "Answer me." He tightened his grip. "Or did you act on your own? You saw the opportunity to make some money and you took it. Was that it? You saw what a fool I was in your hands and decided you could get away with it?" His eyes were red and swollen with unshed tears. "Because of you, I lost everything. Goddammit, Valentina, you gave her my company. You threw my entire life away like it was yesterday's trash." Despite the anger in his expression, his voice quavered, lips so close to mine.

I pressed my forehead against his. "I promise. I would never do anything to hurt you. Cole, I love you."

"How convenient. Now you have feelings for me?" He shook his head. "Or was it Alex Maio? Did he make you do this?"

"Alex? What does he have to do with any of this? You never told me why you two fought."

His thumb rubbed the inside of my wrist. "Don't pretend. Tell the truth. Please."

"What did he tell you?" I asked him. Alex was capable of anything just to get what he wanted. I'd seen that firsthand.

"He asked me for fifty thousand dollars in exchange for you. To give you up, or whatever it is you two have." He pursed his lips and lowered his arms, forcing me to one knee.

"How could you think this about me? Please. You're hurting me." I yanked at my hands just as he released me. I lost my balance and fell to the floor. For a moment, I thought he'd reached out to catch me in his arms.

"And like an idiot, I agreed to pay." His pained expression broke my heart.

His friend wedged himself between us. "Enough. Cole." He offered me his hand, but I slapped it away.

I met Cole's gaze and stood, rubbing the scrapes on my palms. I hoped my eyes showed the same hate as his. "You paid for me? What? Why? Because I wouldn't sleep with you? Damn you, Cole. I'm not a thing." I wanted to punch him, hurt him. He couldn't possibly think that Alex had that kind of hold on me. Or that I would agree to something so repulsive.

He pressed a fisted hand to his forehead, biceps straining as if he was doing everything he could not to lose control.

"I thought you knew me. How can you believe any of this about me?"

"You were certainly very accommodating afterward," he said.

"You don't have to be so hurtful." I hit his chest hard, but it was like hitting a wall. It hurt me more than it did him. He wrapped his arms around me and pinned my arms to my sides, his face in my hair, his hot breath branding me.

With a growl, he pulled back and stared at me. "What about the pain you've caused me? Huh? Did you think about that? Did you think of *me*?" For a second, his gaze fell to my mouth, and I thought he was going to kiss me.

"When Nikki was here and it all looked like you had betrayed me, you asked me to believe in you, and I did. Now it's your turn. You have to believe me too. Or at least listen to me. Give me the chance to explain."

"I don't have to do shit for you." He released me, grabbed a glass off the table, and hurled it across the room. It hit the wall, and shards scattered everywhere. "Get out of my house. Now."

"Cole." His friend placed a hand on his arm.

Shoulders slumped, he trudged to the couch and leaned on the armrest. "You betrayed me. I let you in. And you repay me in the worst way possible." He stopped to take a deep breath. This was him using all the self-control he could muster, which I knew was a whole lot. "Get out." His words reverberated around the room, loud and menacing.

Thanks to the anger I felt, my legs managed to get me out of his house with some sort of dignity. I wanted to plead with him again. But I realized I had no idea what he thought I'd done to his company. Pressing the matter wouldn't help either one of us. The best thing for me to do was to do as he'd asked and leave. I crossed the lawn as fast as I could without breaking into a run. Behind me, Cole continued to hurl more things at the wall.

Chapter Twenty-Three
Talk to Him

Valentina

I went inside the cottage and slammed the door behind me, panting as I struggled to catch my breath and keep my breakfast down. My hands shook violently. I pushed back the hair plastered to my face and rushed to my bedroom to grab my big suitcase from under the bed. Lost in a blur of tears and accusations, I dumped the suitcase on the mattress and threw all my clothes in it. My head throbbed, but I couldn't slow down. No time for wallowing in self-pity. If I hurried, I could have the essentials packed before I had to pick up Max from camp.

Max. How was I going to tell him I'd lost us our home? I'd failed him. I couldn't give him the family he wanted for more than two weeks. Dammit. None of this would've happened if I hadn't let my guard down, if I hadn't let Cole in, if I hadn't fallen for him. If. If. And now here we were back to square one, and once again, it was all my fault. My own stupid fault. Like before, when Alex left me and I had to run back to my parents with my tail between my legs.

But I had no choice. My pride didn't matter. Max's safety, his happiness—that was all I cared about. I went to his room next and threw his clothes and coloring stuff in the same bag.

In under three hours, I was out of Cole's cottage and in line to pick up Max at school. My hands were still shaking, but at least the crying had stopped. I checked myself in the rearview mirror, using a wipe to clean up the smeared mascara. The red eyes could pass for allergies, I told myself, hoping Max wouldn't remember that he'd never seen me suffer from allergies.

"Hi, Mom." He climbed in the car. He sounded like such a big kid, but he wasn't. "You look sad, Mommy."

"Me? No. Just tired. I had a rough day at work." I waited for him to buckle up before I put the car in drive. It was now or never. "Hey, you know what I was thinking? I think we should go see *Abuela* this weekend. We haven't seen her in weeks." I toned down the happy voice when he didn't say anything. "Right?"

"That's a great idea. I miss *Abuela*. Let's go now." He sounded excited.

I glanced up, saying a little prayer. "You know what? Yeah, let's go now."

I pulled out of the parking lot and headed west toward Casa Grande. I had forty-five minutes to figure out what to tell my parents. Assuming I still had a job, I would need at least two weeks to find a new place to live. Would Bridget let me keep my job, even though I didn't help her get Cole's company? Now I understood why she didn't badger me about it on Monday. She'd already found a way to get CCI, but how did she do it? And why did Cole think I had anything to do with it?

But I couldn't worry about that now. First, I needed to make sure Max and I would have a place to stay. I needed a list.

1. Swallow my pride and ask my parents to let us stay

with them for a few weeks. At least two.
2. Find a new place.
3. Get my cousins to move my stuff, again.
4. Schedule pickup with Em.
5. Get over Derek Cole.

I mentally drew two lines under his name, rubbing my temple. *What happened, Cole? What did I do to make you hate me?* I peeked at Max in the rearview mirror. The hole in my chest grew bigger and pushed against my lungs. I swallowed the lump in my throat and focused on the road ahead.

By the time I pulled into Mom's driveway, I had a plan—sort of. I had no idea if it would help me get over Cole, but it would at least help in getting Max and me back on track. *Damn you, Cole.*

"Well, this is the best surprise," Mom said from the threshold, her arms opened wide as she waited for Max to run to her.

"We thought it'd be good to come and visit for the weekend." I was a jerk for lying to them. First about the unconventional living arrangements with Cole and now about the real reason for our visit.

Mom didn't question me at all, though, which felt like a punch to the gut. "See? I keep telling your dad my soup never fails. Every time I make my special beef soup, visitors show up. I can't believe it brought *you* this time. Come on in. It's almost ready."

I helped Mom set the table. I brought Dad his beer and even poured one for myself. He cheered me, a big smile on his face. The guy was just happy to have a drinking buddy. Or was that pity in his eyes? I took a long swig of my beer and sat down.

"How's that fancy job of yours?" he asked. "You

happy?"

I *was* happy. "It's great."

"You have to meet Derek Cole." Max saved me from having to elaborate on my "it's great," though his comment opened up a whole new can of worms.

"Oh yeah? Who is he?" Mom came out of nowhere, her eyes twinkling. She set a bowl of beef soup in front of me.

I swallowed hard and looked down, blinking fast. "He owns the house we're renting. He's nice."

"His real name is Derek Weston Cole…and…he has the coolest cat. His name is Pirate. And he's soft and comes over to our house, and we get to feed him." Max sat on his heels in his chair, and proceeded to tell Mom and Dad all about Cole, how we played baseball last weekend and had lunch by the pool. And…oh my God.

"He threw your mom in the pool?" Dad furrowed his brows. He opened his mouth, but Mom elbowed his arm.

My stomach dropped. Flashes of Derek's hands on me when we were under water swirled in my head. "Yeah, he just pushed me." I breathed out through my nose and shrugged.

Just like that, my whole charade was over. Mom and Dad exchanged meaningful looks. They knew why I was here. They knew that Cole was more than my landlord, that I was here because something had gone wrong. I'd fallen for the wrong guy. Again.

Yeah. No, I didn't learn my lesson before.

When dinner was over, Mom sent both Max and me to our rooms to get ready for bed. She wouldn't even let me help with the cleanup. Some things never changed, or at least when I was home, things quickly went back to the way they were. I was nineteen years old again, with a brand new baby, lost and confused.

I did what I was told, took a long shower, and brushed my teeth. Back in my bedroom, I found Dad had already brought my luggage in. If the oversize suitcase didn't confirm their suspicions, I didn't know what would. Why would I pack all our clothes for a weekend visit?

I dressed in my nightclothes and fell on the pillow face down, glad it muffled my sobbing. My heart was broken, and no list in the world could fix that.

A soft knock on the door brought me back. Mom didn't wait for me to answer. She pushed open the door and set down a plate on my bedside table—cookies and hot chocolate. That was her remedy for everything. I curled up, too embarrassed to tell her what happened. She sat on the bed and rubbed my arm. Through puffy eyes, I peeked at the clock. Midnight. I'd been sleeping for almost five hours. Tears tracked down my cheeks again. I had no control over them anymore.

"You can stay as long as you want. You know that." She fixed my pillows so I could sit up, then offered me a cookie.

"I screwed up again." I scooted up and took it from her.

"Don't say that, Val. Life happens. That's it." She got comfortable on the bed. The same way she had the night I told her I was pregnant and my boyfriend was as good as gone. Yeah. It was going to be another long night. "Do you want to talk about it?"

"I met someone." My voice was barely a whisper.

"What's he like?" She gave me a gentle smile. "Is

this the friend Max has been talking about all night?"

I nodded. "Everything was perfect. But he just turned on me. I'm not sure what happened." I wiped my face. My cheeks felt puffy and sticky.

"Do you love him?" She waved her hand. "Of course, you do."

"I'm such an idiot. I never should've let him get close."

"I'm glad you did. It means you've finally forgiven yourself. I've been worried about you all this time. You got your heart broken more than six years ago, and just like that, you decided you were no longer worthy of love."

"I didn't do that."

She laughed, smoothing the hair away from my face. "You were so set on doing your penance. There was no getting through to you. I tried to explain that life happens, that we all make mistakes. I tried to talk to you so many times, but you wouldn't have it." Her words were full of patience and understanding. "You deserve a second chance at love as much as anyone else."

Penance? Was that what I'd been doing? Punishing myself for falling for someone who didn't care about me?

No. I'd stayed away from men all these years because I wanted to focus on Max. He needed me. Mom made it sound as if I was using Max as an excuse. Was she right in saying I hadn't forgiven myself for what happened?

In a way, Cole had helped me find myself again. He'd showed me I was still capable of falling in love. That I deserved more. "Well, you'd be happy to know I tried. I tried really hard. But he's gone now." I rubbed my nose on my pajama top.

"Talk to him." She shrugged, patting my hand.

Talk to him? It sounded so simple. How could I do that when he couldn't stand the sight of me? Every time I closed my eyes all I could see was the hatred in his gaze. Tears crept up again, building up the pressure in my chest. Even if he couldn't love me because of what'd happened, I didn't want him to hate me like that. It hurt too much.

"He doesn't want to see me."

"For now. Give it time. If he's as good as Max says and if he really deserves your heart, he'll come around. And you'll get your chance to speak your piece."

I shook my head. "You didn't see him like I did. He was so angry, out of control."

"Sounds to me he was hurting as much as you." She put up her hand when I opened my mouth to speak. "Let's not get into it right now. I think you've been through enough for one night. Sleep. Things will be so much better in the morning. I promise." She kissed my cheek. "We'll figure this out, okay?"

She folded the sheet over my chest and tucked in the edge under the mattress. The way she used to do when I was little to keep the monsters away. On her way out, she turned on the nightlight and left with a wink.

I closed my eyes. Cole's words swirled in my head. Everything that'd happened earlier was a jumble of images. He had said so much to me, blamed me for so much. I couldn't keep any of it straight. Getting Cole back was impossible, but I had to at least try to clear my name. Maybe get him to hate me a little less.

Screw the list. Well, for now. First, I had to figure out how to get Cole to believe in me again. A slow burn swirled in my stomach at the thought of the disgust I'd seen in his face when he asked if Alex had put me up to this. God, he got to that conclusion fast.

Alex's return couldn't be a coincidence. Why did he come looking for me after all this time? Why now? How did he even know where to find me? If he had come to my parent's house, Dad wouldn't be here. He'd be at either the county jail or the hospital, which was why I never told Dad about what Alex did to me. Dad would've killed him. Did he reach out to Annie? No. She would've told me. A big piece of the puzzle was missing here.

I stuffed my hands in my hair and focused on what I did know. Cole had lost his company, and I was to blame. Alex was conniving, but not smart enough to pull off something like this. I kicked the covers, hands clenched. In Cole's eyes, I was just like Alex, a liar.

My pulse throbbed in my throat. I sat up. No more running. No more punishing myself for believing in Alex's lies. I paced the room as I rubbed my temples. *Think*. Tricking Cole into giving up his company would've required a lot of skill. Bridget. This had Bridget written all over it. But how did she pull it off?

Cole deserved better than this. Even if he didn't want me anymore, I didn't want him to go on thinking I had betrayed him. This time I wasn't going to hide under my bed and let my parents fix everything for me. Cole and I deserved to be together.

Holy shit. Am I really going to try and get Cole back?

A rush of calm washed over me, and everything

became clear to me. I had to find out how Cole lost CCI, and I knew where to start.

Chapter Twenty-Four
Or a Better Lie

Cole

I slumped into the lounge chair and gripped the armrests. Anything to keep me from going over to Valentina's house and make her tell me the truth.

Or a better lie.

Make me believe in you again.

At this point, I'd take anything. The pain Bridget's betrayal inflicted on me was nothing compared to what I felt now. This pain was a thousand times worse. Valentina had betrayed my love for her. And still, I refused to believe she would sell me out so easily. This couldn't be the real her. Had she seemed confused by my accusations? I pinched my nose, squeezing my eyes shut. Everything that'd happened last night, everything I'd said to her was a big blur, echoes. In my rage, I'd lost sense of reality and I couldn't think straight. Did I give her a chance to explain?

"I'm glad to see you're back to normal." Em set the rest of my breakfast on the table. The frown lines around her mouth said she didn't think this was normal or that she was glad.

I took a bite of the eggs. They tasted like cardboard despite the barbecued pulled pork she'd added. "I don't know what you mean."

"*Wednesday* is downstairs, asking for you. And you're up here. Hiding." Em poured coffee in a mug.

"Tell her I'm in a meeting."

When she didn't say anything, I looked up at her. She was glancing in the direction of the cottage. I threw my fork on the table, unable to stomach any more of the eggs.

"Relax, Derek. She's gone."

"Gone? What do you mean she's gone?" I rubbed my throbbing temple. A hot rod churned painfully in my gut.

"I mean, you asked her to leave your house. And she left." She picked up the empty tray and left me to continue my pity party of one.

"I didn't mean for her to move out." I whipped around in my chair. Em simply shrugged without looking back.

I picked up my phone and dialed her number. I gripped the phone with sweaty palms. Each ring chimed longer and louder than the last.

"Hello?" a man answered on the fourth ring.

I pursed my lips. Red blotches clouded my vision and my last shred of logic. That didn't take her long. I pressed the End button, threw my napkin on the table, and headed for Valentina's cottage. Not that Em would lie to me. I just needed to see it for myself. Did she really leave? To be with Alex Maio?

This morning I'd woke up wishing last night had been a nightmare. But it'd all been real. I pushed the door open and leaned my shoulder on the threshold. The furniture was still here. An ominous air covered every inch of the living room and screamed what I already knew.

Valentina was gone.

My eyes fell on the wall we'd painted together. Back then, I'd been grateful she'd patched the hole for me. No doubt she did it to gain my trust, an act to make me think she could fix everything that was fucked up in my life. I stepped into the living room. Her scent still lingered in the air, and my stomach twisted in a knot.

Cocking my head, I traced the discoloration on the wall with my fingers. My heartbeat slowed to a painful pace, intensifying the throbbing in my head. Because of Valentina, my life's work now lay in the hands of a fucking addict. How long before Bridget sold the company by the pound? Before all my people were out of the job? If she already canceled the bonuses for the year, as Dom said, we were looking at months. A year, at most.

Goddammit. I'd let them down. I didn't know what pained me the most: the loss of CCI, that Valentina was to blame, or the possibility that she was still involved with that asshole Alex. I squeezed my eyes shut. Images of his smug face, his smirk when he'd talked about Valentina and the *men* in her life flickered in my head. A scream escaped my lips. I balled my hand into a fist and pummeled the wall again and again, until the Sheetrock crumbled. Arms braced on my knees, I stared at the gaping hole in the wall. There. Now the cottage looked like it should again.

Out of nowhere, Pirate strolled in and went straight to Max's bedroom, as if he owned the place. I leaned on the wall, gulping air, knuckles bleeding, clothes covered in sweat.

"Since when do you come in here? You were banished from this house, remember?" I asked when he came back to rub his head on my pants. I followed him into the kitchen. "Were they feeding you?"

Pirate meowed in response. I shook my hand to ease the dull ache, while I searched the cupboards under the sink. I found several cans of cat food there, and a wave of hope washed over me. How bad could she be? If this was all an act, why take the time to feed my cat? I dumped the food on a plate she kept with the cans and set it on the floor for Pirate.

"What do you think? Is she as bad as they say?" He limped toward me and curled around my leg. "I don't believe it either." I sat on the floor next to him and scratched his ears while he ate.

When my legs went numb from sitting on the tile, I got up, but I couldn't make myself leave. Instead, I trudged toward her bedroom and her rumpled bed. I pictured her making room on the mattress for her suitcase, dumping her things in a hurry. How long did it take her to walk out on me? I went through the closet and drawers. All empty. A heavy weight pulled me down. I pinched my nose to stop the tears, but it was no use.

Where did you go? Please don't go back to that asshole. He doesn't care about you.

Feeling tired, I lay on her bed and buried my face in her sheets. Her smell was still on the pillow, her warmth. I inhaled, and for the first time since last night, my lungs didn't ache with each breath. The minutes slid by, or maybe I lay there for hours. I stayed in her bed and played our conversation over and over in my head. Or at least what I could remember.

She'd seemed sincere when she said she didn't know what I was talking about, and even shocked by my accusations. I closed my eyes, recalling her face and all the things she'd said. Was that fear in her eyes? I grimaced and bit the inside of my lip. Was she telling the truth? God, I wanted to believe her so badly. *Valentina, did you run away because you're innocent or because you're guilty?*

A cold shiver went through me, and I pulled the covers over me. A white undershirt fell to the floor. It was mine, the one she'd borrowed the first night we were together. She certainly didn't act like someone who was doing her boyfriend a favor. No, that night was real. She wanted me. The way she trembled under my touch, consumed by it. No one could fake that. No one could kiss like that and not feel anything.

Jesus Christ. What was I thinking, accusing her of colluding with Bridget and Alex? I could argue I was blinded by rage. But that was no excuse. I was a real asshole for saying all those things to her. The jerk didn't even know Max's name.

She'd also said she loved me. Why would she say that? A smiled pulled on my lips.

I jumped to my feet, rushed out of the cottage, and headed back to the house. None of this made sense. Valentina loved me. She couldn't have sold me out. If she was telling the truth, I intended to find out. I was an idiot for taking Bridget's word for it. She was an addict. At this point, she'd throw her own mother under the bus just to get one more high at the poker table.

At my computer, I punched my access code, sat back, and waited for the video feeds for the last two weeks to download. I placed my elbows on the desk and buried my face in my hands. Why did I send her away?

When the download completed, I set the files to autoplay and scanned the screen for Valentina's face. I hit paused when she first appeared, wearing a gray pencil skirt and a dark blue top. That'd been her first day at my company, in my building. Because of her, I'd begun to heal that day. Knowing she was there, surrounded by everything I'd built, I'd felt at peace.

Shit. This would be easier if she were here. This emptiness in my chest didn't threaten to choke me when she was around. I reached in my back pocket and fished out my phone. I wanted to hear her voice.

Guilty or not, I wanted her back.

I tapped on the Recents icon and spotted her name immediately. Maybe she'd answer this time and explain what the fuck was going on. The computer screen kept going in fast forward. Sitting back, I pinched my nose as my gaze shifted from the video to her name. And then, there she was again. One of the feeds showed Valentina going into Bridget's office to drop an interoffice envelope. I paused and rewound the image. The resolution on it wasn't all that great, but I could see her expression well. She didn't seem suspicious or even preoccupied. She simply dumped the envelope and left. No note or anything. Were the divorce papers in that envelope? Was this how she sold me out? In five seconds flat, she'd thrown my company away.

I threw the phone on the desk. This couldn't be her. I raked a hand through my hair, staring at her face on the screen.

"If you ask me, it all sounds too perfect to be real." Em stood in front of me. How long had she been standing there?

"What do you mean?"

"You're in pain, and that's understandable. You've been looking for this kind of connection with someone for a long time. I know you have. That's why it hurts so much. You opened your heart to her, and you got hurt again." She gave me her signature over-the-glasses glance, extra dose of pity. "It's hard to see things clearly, but give it time."

I rubbed my eyes. Everything seemed to be under a dark fog: my thoughts, Valentina's face, and every piece of evidence pointing a finger at her.

"If this was her intention all along, I think she'd would've gone a different route. Stealing doesn't seem to be her style." Em shrugged.

"Who knows what her style is?"

Em pressed her lips together. "All I know is that this doesn't add up. Or rather, it adds up too perfectly. Think about it."

"That's what I've been doing all morning. But the details are all fuzzy. There's nothing there to show me if she was telling the truth." I rubbed my temple.

"You don't need to remember what happened last night. Just look in there." She pointed at my heart. "See what you find. Hmm?" She smiled and left.

Chapter Twenty-Five
For Us

Valentina

I eyed my mobile sitting on Mom's kitchen counter. My hands itched to grab it and call Cole. But what would I say? It was too soon. He probably wouldn't even answer. Gripping the whisk, I whipped the batter faster.

"Whoa, easy. We do want lumps. I think it's good now." Mom pushed me out of the way to take over. "Just sit down. You're making me nervous."

I plopped myself down on the counter stool. "Sorry."

"You look better this morning."

I rested my head on my hands and swallowed my tears. "I don't feel better."

"Give it time." She poured the batter in the waffle maker. "So why is he so mad?"

"He thinks I made him lose his company."

"How did you do that?"

"No idea." I shrugged. "But I need to figure out what happened. I can't defend myself if I don't know what I'm guilty of, right? I was thinking about calling Em, his housekeeper."

"Housekeeper? Fancy." She slanted a glance at me over her shoulder.

I let out a breath. "You don't know the half of it."

"Does it bother you?"

"What?" I asked.

"You know, that he's loaded *and* white? Come on. The guy has two first names."

I laughed and shook my head once. With a triumphant smile, Mom turned her attention to the waffles. The cinnamon pumpkin smell was all over the house.

"I'm proud of him. He's achieved so much. And he's not even thirty." I sighed. "We have so much in common. It's hard to believe we grew up on literally opposite ends of the country."

Mom gave me her raised-eyebrow look, the one she saved for special occasions. Like getting the truth out of me. "Last night aside, does he make you happy?"

"Yes." I nodded. A smile pulled on my lips. "He's smart, kind, and generous. And tall and so freakishly hot."

Crap. Did I just say that out loud?

"Oh. I didn't realize things were that serious. Did you two already…you know?" She placed a hand over her mouth to hide her grin.

"Mom." I blushed and touched my forehead to the counter, arms covering my head.

"Well, good for you, honey. About time."

I peeked at her, raising both eyebrows. Why did I think she'd be mad at me?

"Go call this Em lady. Figure out what happened." She wiped her hands on her apron before she placed my hair behind my ear, the way she used to do when I was little.

Now that I had Max, I realized I would always be

her little girl. Just as Max would always be my little boy.

"You deserve to be happy. Don't give up now." She pointed toward the hallway. "Now go to your room."

I jumped off the stool and reached for the phone. Mom busied herself with breakfast as I rushed back to my bedroom. I called Cole's house, knowing Em would pick up.

"Good morning, Valentina," she said.

Her cheerful greeting disconcerted me for a minute. How did she know it was me? Oh right. Caller ID.

"Um. Good morning, Em."

"Would you like me to get Cole?"

"No," I blurted out. My heart did a couple of flips when she said his name. "I wanted to ask you when would be a good time to come get my stuff."

And also, did you happen to catch any of Cole's conversation with his friend last night? Any idea why he thinks I betrayed him?

Crap. I should've scripted something before I called. I had no idea how to pose the question. The static hummed for what seemed like an eternity.

"It's your house. You don't need my permission, dear. Come over anytime."

"Oh. Thank you." I puffed out a breath, hands cold and sweaty. "How is he?"

"As can be expected. Bad." She took a long pause. "You should come see him. Talk."

I shook my head frantically, even though she couldn't see me. "I can't. I don't even know why he's mad at me."

Her small laugh could barely be heard through the

speaker. "Cole signed his divorce papers a month ago. Someone took them and sold them to Bridget."

That was it? I'd spent all night dissecting our conversation, racking my brain for anything I might've missed, any clue to tell me what had unhinged him. The answer was so simple. Why didn't Cole take the time to give me two sentences to clarify things? I wanted to slap him, punch his chest again.

"It wasn't me." I gritted my teeth, wiping my cheeks and nose. "I love him too much. I could never do that."

"I know that. And I think he very much wants to believe that too."

"What about Nikki?" I was really reaching here, but other than me, only Em and Nikki had access to Cole's house…and his bedroom. A painful burn twisted in my belly. I sat on the bed and took a deep breath. How long before Cole went back to her?

"You think it was her?"

"Who else has had access to Cole's house?"

The long silence on the line was like a python coiled tight around my chest. Right. Cole brought a new girl every night. Any one of them could've done it. But Nikki was the only one who dared to show up uninvited. No doubt she felt she had some sort of claim on him.

The memory of Nikki's proud breasts in Cole's living room still hurt, but I forced myself to think about the day she was in his house. The second time I'd run into her. She was in the loft while Cole was upstairs taking a shower. She had a suspicious look about her. Hadn't she? She was sweaty and half-naked for no good reason. After our fight and make-up sex, Cole and

I never discussed Nikki again. But if they hadn't had sex that day, why was she half-naked? Did she do that to throw us off?

Well, it'd worked brilliantly. I ran out of the house, taking Cole with me. If she wanted to go back to the loft and take whatever she needed, she would've had plenty of time to do it after we left. Cole and I'd spent hours in his bedroom that day. A warm flutter touched my chest, but I pushed the thought aside. I had to stay focused on Nikki.

"Would you be able to give me her number?" My heart pounded.

Em didn't hesitate. "Of course, dear. Just a sec. I'll have to check the security logs."

Did I really have the guts to call Nikki and confront her? I had to do it.

For Cole.

For us.

****

This was a colossal mistake.

Earlier at Mom's house, I'd been on a let's-get-Cole-back high. Truth was, I didn't even know if he loved me enough to want me back. I was insane to think Nikki could help. What could she possibly do to change things? Confess to stealing the divorce papers and possibly go to jail? Not freaking likely.

I couldn't go through with this. Standing, I grabbed my purse and turned to leave. Too late. She was already here.

And Cole was with her.

I stood frozen by the condiment bar. My hands, my whole body ached to hold him, to plead with him. *It wasn't me.* I wanted to scream at him. Our eyes met. He

251

stared at me for what felt like hours. I opened my mouth to speak, but before I could utter a single word, Cole turned his attention to Nikki and the barista. Nikki leaned on the counter and ordered their drinks, shooting glances at me. Did she not recognize me? Of course she did. Her wicked smile said it all. Why did she bring him here?

Run.

My legs wouldn't move. I squeezed my hands into fists and wished Cole would turn to me and tell me that he believed me, that he was sorry.

"Is the restroom this way?" Nikki pointed to the back of the coffee shop.

The barista, who couldn't stop ogling them, nodded. Yeah, they were an impressive couple. Maybe all this was for the best.

"Grab a seat, darling," she said to Cole. "I'll be just a minute."

"I'm not staying," he growled.

Like a statue, an idiot, I stayed put and gripped the bar behind me to keep myself from crumpling to the floor. The barista handed Cole their drinks. He thanked her and walked toward me. Hot blood rushed to my feet, and every breath cut me, as if I'd inhaled tiny knives into my lungs instead of air.

"Excuse me," he said.

"Sorry." I moved over, slanting a glance at him.

His chest rose and fell, and his cheeks were red. If he was angry with me, he didn't show it. In fact, he didn't even acknowledge he recognized me. Anyone who saw us standing here would never guess Cole and I had history. That we spent an entire night making love and early mornings drinking coffee. That he knew all my secrets, and I knew his.

He set down the drinks, opened Nikki's mocha, and poured half the container of sugar into it. The hot liquid slapped out of the cup when he stabbed the coffee with a stirring stick and mixed. Like before, we were strangers again. As if I hadn't broken down over my latte a month ago when he'd offered me his cottage.

My stomach clenched as I realized this was what we would be if he hadn't come back to the coffee shop that day. If he hadn't given me a bunch of paper napkins and asked me what'd happened. If I hadn't opened up to him. But all that did happen. We couldn't undo it, just as I couldn't undo my feelings for him.

I love you, Cole.

"Fuck." The stirring stick snapped in his hand, and he tossed it in the garbage. And with that he darted out, leaving both drinks behind.

Nikki came out of the bathroom and made a beeline for the condiment bar. Hands on her hips, she scanned the room before she turned to me. "Well, that went well."

"I'm Valentina." It sounded like a confession.

"I know who you are." The blonde bombshell grabbed her mocha and sauntered toward my table while everyone ogled her. "We met last week at the benefit. I never forget a face. Nikki Swift." She offered me a slender hand.

"Oh" was all I could say. I shook her hand and lowered myself slowly into the chair across from her. Yeah, I was way out of my league here.

She reached in her bag and took out an elastic hair band. People around us stared as she put her shiny hair up into a high ponytail. She gave me a kind smile. If she was trying to ease my nerves, it worked. How did she do that?

Biting her lip for a moment, she grabbed a napkin off the table and pressed her lips against it. "You're here to talk about Cole."

"Yes."

"Shit hit the fan last night, I know." Her frank words startled me.

"Cole thinks it's my fault. But I know it was you." I didn't know for sure it was her, but I wanted to see her reaction.

A dashing smile covered her face. "You can't prove that."

Translation: It was me.

"No." I ducked my gaze.

"You and Cole." She sipped her coffee. "Hmmm." She pursed her lips and spit the coffee back into the cup. "What did he do to my coffee?"

I shook my head. "Sugar."

"I hate sugar. He knows that." She laughed. "I'm always amazed how love can turn a normal and intelligent person into a pathetic sap."

"Excuse me." This was *not* how I thought the conversation would go. I had a list of things I wanted to say to her, questions I was going to make her answer.

"Yeah, you and Cole with your sad puppy eyes." She turned to the barista and mouthed, *Can I get another one?* The barista nodded and got to work on her coffee. "I need a mocha in the worst way. Cole kept me up all night."

I winced. Her words exploded in my head and repeated over and over again. She spent the night with Cole? Darting my eyes to the window, I sat perfectly still and pretended that whatever they did last night didn't affect me.

She cocked her head, the way Cole used to do. "Relax. He just needed a bit of company. We spent all night *not* talking about you. Though he wanted to. Mostly, he drank and cursed. And I listened." She winked. "I'm a good listener."

A bubble rose in my chest. They didn't have sex. "Why did you do it? You ruined his life."

"Money."

"Wait. Someone paid you to do this? It wasn't your idea?"

She shook her head once. "Bridget. It was a dick move. Yes. And I deeply regret it. Cole didn't deserve that, but I need the money, and he has lots of it."

Of course, it was Bridget. Now it all made sense to me. She must've realized I wasn't playing her stupid game, so she decided to send Nikki to steal the signed divorce papers instead. That had to be it. When she saw our picture in the social section of the paper, she must've assumed Cole and I were sort of together. At the very least, she knew I had access to his house. I'd bet it didn't take much for her to figure out a way to blame it all on me. And Cole bought it. Certainly, Alex's visit didn't help my case.

I buried my face in my hands. "*Sorry* is not going to get his company back. And now he hates me."

She adjusted her weight on the chair. "He still has more money than he knows what to do with. Let me give you some free advice."

"Why the free advice?"

"Cole's a good guy. He deserves to be happy." Turning her attention to the barista, she got up and fetched her new coffee. She sat down. "Go see him. And this time, try to make more of an effort to talk to him. I all but served him to you on a silver platter just now, and you blew your chance."

"You brought him here on purpose."

"Yeah, I brought him here on purpose. God, you're hopeless." She sat back on her chair, bracing an arm on the table.

"Why?"

"This time Bridget won. And believe me—she won. More than you know." Her cheeks turned red. "But you two can still make this work."

I raised an eyebrow and shook my head. She hadn't been there yesterday when he'd kicked me out of his house. When his eyes showed me how much he hated me. Or here five minutes ago. He could barely stand being close to me long enough to put sugar in her cup.

In one blow, Nikki ruined Cole's life and broke my heart.

"Are you always this clueless? He loves you."

"You don't know that."

"He didn't sleep with me. That should be your first clue."

I shut my eyes. *Stop picturing them together. It hurt too much.* Jealousy aside, I wanted to help Cole. There had to be something we could do. I regarded Nikki as she sipped her mocha. This was one of the girls Cole kept on rotation. The one who broke us up. But Cole needed her. I bit my lip, swallowing my pride.

"You seem like a decent person. Help him," I said.

"I'm not a decent person. And it's not that easy. You don't want to mess with Bridget." She considered something for a moment. "Let me think on it. Maybe

I'll come up with something before I leave." She stood and headed for the door.

"Where are you going?"

She paused at the door. "Home. It's long overdue." Her smile made her look younger. "Ciao."

"Wait. Are you going to help or not?"

"I'll call you if I find something."

When she reached the curb, a cop had just finished writing her a parking ticket. She slowed her pace, a bright smile on. I couldn't hear what she said to him. But he blushed, mouthing the word *sorry* a few times as he tore the ticket in half and opened the driver door for her. How did she do that? At least she was on our side now. She seemed genuine when she'd said she would help.

My thumb hovered over Cole's name on my mobile. He needed to know this. But I wasn't sure if he'd listen.

Get out.

His words still rung in my head. I didn't want to go through that again.

I threw my phone on the table. Nikki was right. Bridget had won.

Chapter Twenty-Six
A Woman's Touch

Cole

Letting Nikki talk me into going out for a coffee was a bad idea. Even worse was agreeing to go to Cafe Triste of all places. Yeah, that was *our* place. But I had no idea Valentina would be there, wearing a pair of shorts that showcased her shapely legs. My knees had gone weak when I first saw her standing there, eyes red and swollen as if she'd been crying. Like the day my resolved to stay away from her crumbled and I talked to her.

Why didn't she run as she had that day? As she always did. Instead, she stood there. Why? So she could see what a mindless asshole I've become because of her. I'd wanted to hold her so badly, taste her lips, bury my hands in her hair and... *Jesus*. I'd come so close to telling her I didn't care if she'd given away my company. I didn't care about Alex or the money. I just wanted her back.

My mobile rang. I answered without looking at the phone screen. My eyes were glued to Valentina's face on the video feed on my laptop. "What?"

"Dom, here." He didn't take offense to my tone.

"What is it?"

"More bad news, I'm afraid. I just got Valentina's

financials. She received an amount for one hundred fifty thousand dollars two weeks ago."

What the fuck do I say to that?

I had nothing. Instead, I breathed loudly into the speakerphone.

"The money's still there, man." He let out a long breath before he continued. "If she was in a hurry to pay off her debt, she sure is taking her time now. Don't you think?"

"What do you mean?"

"The amount, give or take a few pennies, is what she owes to the Tucson Regional Hospital."

I sat up in my chair. "You really need to figure out the difference between good news and bad news."

"You think this is good news?"

"Maybe. I don't know. Can you send me everything you have? And let me know if she does anything with the money."

"Sure thing, man. Anything else?"

"No. That's it. Thanks." I hit the End button.

So Valentina did all this to pay off hospital bills? I knew about the debt. It'd been the reason she lost the lease on her other house…and the reason we met. If she had not broken down that day, we never would've found a reason to speak to each other. Some things were meant to be, I supposed. I wanted to believe that this thing with Valentina wasn't over. More than anything, I didn't want it to end like this.

As neatly as all the evidence against her was stacked, something still didn't add up. I'd come to know Valentina very well in the past few weeks. Her biggest flaw was the fucking plans she had for everything. Plans she stuck to with unholy resoluteness, no matter what. Wasn't that why she'd come to live in the cottage? If she was doing this for Max, it just didn't make sense.

My computer chimed when Dom's email came through. I clicked on the hospital invoice. It was a sucker punch to the gut. I had no idea Max had gone through surgery last year. And here I was only preoccupied with the state of my cock.

God, I am an asshole.

I buried my face in my hands. I couldn't be wrong about her. Sitting up, I opened the payment history file Dom sent. She'd made a payment just this week for the same amount as the previous month. At this rate, she'd pay off the balance in about twenty years. I'd bet that was on her list somewhere.

Why hadn't she used the money to pay off the hospital bill? That was the one-hundred-fifty-thousand-dollar question. Dom was right. If she was in a hurry, her actions now didn't make sense. Unless she didn't know she had it. I, for one, never check the balances on my accounts. Okay, that was a fucking stretch, but it was something.

Goddammit, I just wanted her home. I took in a long breath and released it. I thought of her calling out my name that first night we were together. She'd given herself completely and without reserve. Her face and the look in her eyes were so vivid in my mind. No one could fake that kind of passion. Raking my hands through my hair, I pulled at it to make myself snap out of it. Either Valentina was the greatest con artist of all time, or I was missing a big piece of this fucked-up puzzle.

Maybe instead of trying to prove her innocence, I

should be looking for the real culprit. Last night I'd been so focused on what Valentina had done I hadn't stopped to think about the other people in my life. Bridget was at the center of all this. The only one who stood to gain the most in the end.

Dom's words rang in my head. *Since when does Bridget volunteer information that can incriminate her in a court of law?*

She'd been so quick to point a finger at Valentina. Was she behind all this? She had to be. As much as I hated to admit it, she was the only one who knew all my faults and weaknesses, especially when it came to women. Valentina didn't fit the profile of someone I would fall for. When Valentina told me Bridget had ordered her to get me to sign the divorce papers, I knew she'd done it out of spite. No doubt she'd been pissed when she found out Valentina was living in the cottage. She'd done it to drive a wedge between us, to take away that last bit of happiness in my life. No, if Bridget had really wanted to hire someone to get me to turn over my company, she would've hired someone with a lot more skill than Valentina. Someone who, according to Bridget, was my type.

Mother fucker.

I picked up my mobile and called Dom.

"Yeah," he answered.

"Did you check Nikki's financials?"

"No. I mean, I figured she wasn't smart enough to orchestrate any of this."

I gripped my phone. "Dom, never underestimate a woman on a mission."

"Fuck. I'll get on that."

"No," I said. "Bring her in. I'm done fucking

around with her *and* Bridget."

His laugh echoed on the other end of the line. "Welcome back, man. Give me an hour."

I'd envisioned Dom showing up with Nikki in handcuffs or some other kind of restraint. Instead, he strolled in with an idiot smile plastered on his face and Nikki, wearing a skintight black dress, a couple of steps in front of him.

I waited in the living room, ready for a fight. Man, was I right before about never underestimating a woman with a plan. Now that she'd decided to drop the act, Nikki looked different, younger. The question was, what did she want now?

She gave me a lopsided grin. "Don't look so surprised, darling. I really do like you. I'm here to help."

"She was on her way here when I met up with her." Dom leaned against the wall, looking at Nikki as if he'd just seen her for the first time.

"Why the sudden change of heart?" I turned to him.

Nikki didn't wait for him to respond. "Your wife is a complete bitch, who decided to con me out of my two hundred and fifty thousand dollars. But that aside, this morning someone showed me you have something real here. Valentina—" She put up her hands when I advanced on her. Valentina and Max were off limits. "See what I mean?"

"You gave Bridget the signed divorce papers?"

She gave me a half nod, meeting my gaze. "In exchange for you." She smiled. "And two hundred and fifty thousand dollars. But after she got what she wanted, she decided you were enough. And I would've agreed, except last night I realized how much you love Valentina."

I opened my mouth to deny my feelings for Valentina, but it was useless. I was in love with her. "What do you want?"

"I need the money Bridget promised me…and one of your apartments outside of the country. Paris would be nice. In return, you'll have my full cooperation."

"It'll be tough to convince Bridget to give up CCI unless we have something to bargain with," Dom said. "What can you give us?"

"Frank, her boyfriend. He keeps records of all the money they've stolen. I heard him threatening her with it one time while we were having lunch. The jerk was asking her for more money. I've no idea what she sees in him." She crossed her arms, rolling her eyes. "Love is for fools."

"I bet I can get to him." Dom typed in his mobile. "If we can get our hands on those documents, we'll have enough to send her to jail. It'll be easier than proving she stole the divorce papers."

"Why did you do this to Valentina?" I asked.

"First, you have to understand it wasn't me." She sat at the end of the sofa. "Bridget went off the rails when I told her you were in love with Valentina. The picture from the benefit didn't help either. The look on your face, that mix of love and lust. Bridget was pissed. It was like you were no longer under her control."

"What exactly did Bridget hire you to do?"

"She wanted you to sign the agreement. I had to deliver CCI one way or another." She raised an eyebrow. "Would you ever forgive me, darling?"

Even after the divorce, after all she'd done, Bridget

still thought she had some claim on me. God, was I an idiot for giving her so much power over my life. A lazy idiot. With my nose buried in CCI business, I became an easy target for her and Nikki. A lump dropped to my stomach, and I tasted bile in the back of my throat. Bridget had gone too far this time. But one thing at a time. Valentina was innocent. Right now, that was all that mattered. She hadn't betrayed me. She was a victim in all this.

"What about Alex Maio?" I asked.

"Who?" She gave me puzzled look.

"Valentina's ex."

"Oh, that one. That wasn't me. Bridget asked me to talk to him, but he's a real lowlife. I didn't want to be associated with him. No idea where Bridget found him. I did deliver a message to him, though. Bridget asked me to set up a meeting and to tell him that she had a lucrative business proposal for him." She glanced at her hands for a moment before she looked up. "I'm sorry, but I don't know what kind of nasty business she had in mind."

"I have a pretty good idea," I said.

The prick played his part well. He'd strung a couple of sentences together, and just like that, he had me believing Valentina slept with me for money. And not only that, I actually considered she'd done it for him. How would I ever get Valentina to forgive me? I fished my mobile from my back pocket. We needed to talk. *No.* I threw the phone on the couch and met Dom at the bar cart. This was something I needed to do in person.

"Okay." Dom poured himself a drink. "If Nikki's lead pans out, we should be able to get Bridget to give you back your company. Just give me time to come up with a plan." He turned to me, eyeing Nikki across the room. "Is it bad that I'm turned on by all this? There's just something about a woman owning her business, you know?"

"Seriously? She almost ruined my life."

"I'm not saying I'm interested, man. Just saying it's interesting. But back to you."

"What about my money?" Nikki stood.

"If I don't get CCI back, you don't get paid."

Pouting, she placed her arms across her chest. "What about her account in the Bahamas? I bet there's something there you can use."

Dom shook his head once. "We know about that. It's best if we stay away from it. What else you got?"

Without Nikki's confession, getting CCI back would be hell, if not impossible. My gaze fell on Nikki as she made herself comfortable on the sofa. I should be angry at her, but that wasn't me anymore. I had to stay focused and salvage what was left of my life.

She beamed at me. "I know what you're thinking, darling. But with the number of girls you had parading through your house in the last six months, you can't really prove I was the one who took your documents. I'm not going to jail over this." She took the drink Dom offered her. "I'm on your side now. I'm of more use to you here than behind bars."

"She's right," Dom said.

Nikki wiggled in her seat, eyes wide and bright. "This is my favorite part. Let's brainstorm." Sipping from her glass, she patted the cushion next to her and gestured for Dom to sit down. "Why are you not calling for an audit?"

"Unless we know what we're looking for, it could be a year before we figure out how she's embezzling money," I said.

My first instinct had been to do just that. But at the rate Bridget was implementing changes within the company, there'd be nothing left by the time we gathered enough evidence against her. Time wasn't on our side. What we needed was a confession. Something to make her reconsider.

"Can you pay off her gambling debt?" Nikki asked.

I shook my head. "She has the upper hand. Why settle for a couple of million dollars when she can keep it all?"

"You're right," Dom said, sitting next to Nikki.

"That's it, then." Nikki sat up, her cheeks flushed. "I told you both that you needed me. We need to make her think she no longer has the upper hand."

"How do we do that exactly?" I plopped myself down on the sofa across from her, exhausted and wishing Valentina were here. But that was on me. I sent her away.

"Cole? Still with us?" Dom exchanged a meaningful look with Nikki.

"I'm sorry. What?"

"I said we'll need to take another look at Bridget's offshore accounts," Nikki said.

"Not unless you want that pretty Mercedes of yours to end up on the Mexico side of Nogales." I gestured toward Dom.

He gulped his drink before he spoke. "He's right. That's mobsters' stuff. We can't touch that."

"You can. You just need a woman's touch." She wiggled her fingers and reached for Dom's leg.

"You've done this before?"

She jumped to her feet. "Just get your checkbook ready, Derek. I'll take care of the rest." She kissed Dom on the cheek and then turned to me. "Am I allowed to leave?"

I stared at her. "You don't want to cross me again, Nikki. There won't be a second chance for you."

"I'll call you when I have something." She waved before she headed out. "Ciao."

"She's a good friend to have." Dom stared at her as she closed the door behind her.

"I hope she knows what she's doing. You can handle all this with Bridget, right?" I asked. Dom nodded, and I felt as if a heavy weight had been lifted off my shoulders. "I have something I need to take care of."

"Yeah, what's that?"

"I need to figure out how to get Valentina back."

Chapter Twenty-Seven
Pathetic

Valentina

On Monday, the traffic into Tucson sucked. After I hurled the Civic into a spot, I bolted to the badge reader, ID in hand. Made it with a minute to spare. This one-hour commute from Casa Grande would take a while getting used to. To make matters worse, I didn't have time to get coffee at home or stop for one on the way in. Crap. This was going to be a long day.

I dropped my bag at my desk and fired up my laptop before heading to the break room. I hadn't slept a wink last night. Coffee wasn't optional today. The brew we had on our floor was nasty, but it was hot, caffeinated, and ready to drink. The espresso machine we had when I first started working had been removed last week. One by one, all the lavish perks Cole had for his employees had been scaled down to the bare bones. No more playroom and definitely no more free meals. Bridget had taken pity on us and stopped at the coffee. The brew was free, but we had to pay twenty-five cents for the cup. I hadn't thought to bring a tumbler from home, so I was stuck paying the "membership fee."

"Good morning," I greeted the girl in front of me.

I was still fairly new, so I didn't know everyone by name. But she'd smiled at me before. Not this morning.

She looked me up and down and left the break room without saying a word. Jeez, I needed a lot of coffee to wake up in the morning, but I wasn't *that* bad.

Three cups of coffee later, my brain woke up and so did my bladder. I glanced at the computer clock. It was almost ten. Feeling proud of myself for not bursting into tears in three consecutive hours, I strolled to the bathroom. I'd also gone for almost an hour without thinking of Cole—his smell, his eyes, or his hands on me.

Damn.

Picking up the pace, I rushed to the ladies' room. I went in the stall at the end of the row and leaned on the wall, on the verge of breaking my three-hour record of no crying. I forced myself to breathe in and out, slowly. Everything that happened this past weekend went by so fast I still hadn't recovered from the whiplash. At this point, all I knew for certain was that Bridget had won. Just as Nikki'd said. She'd also said Cole loved me. I wished that were true. But she had no way of knowing that.

I thought of Cole's cold eyes when I first walked into his living room on Friday. A cold shiver ran through me and brought back the tears. I never wanted to see that Cole again. What we had, or almost had, was broken, and it couldn't be fixed. How could I ever get him to trust me again? All I could do now was to put it all behind me, start new, and forgive myself for making a mistake with Cole.

"Moms are not perfect," Mom had said when she found me bawling again in my room.

"Well, mine does a great job of not showing it," I'd said to her, feeling so grateful that she wasn't judging me for any of this. She was right, of course. Max didn't need the perfect mom. He needed a healthy and happy mom. I'd have to work hard on the happy part, but in time I'd get there.

But how much time? A day, a month, a year? How do I get over Cole?

I dug in my pant pocket and took out the Get Over Cole list I'd written on Saturday after my chat with Nikki.

1. Find a new apartment. Something close to the outskirts of town. And as far away as possible from Cole.

2. Start looking for a new job?

3. Let Annie set me up on a blind date?

4. Get over Cole?

It was a half-ass list. I'd never had to come up with a plan to fall out of love. I crumpled the paper in my fist and stuffed it back in my pants. For the first time since I could remember, I had no plan, and the idea terrified me.

The bathroom door creaked open, and two women barged in. Their hushed whispers echoed against the wall behind me.

"Oh, I know who you're talking about, the new girl. Latina, right?" one of the women asked. She had a girlish voice.

I rolled my eyes. How about the girl who had been programming the heck out of your stupid usage reports? I tiptoed back and climbed on the toilet so they wouldn't see my feet. A childish reaction, but I didn't need more awkwardness in my life. I thought I had done a good job of keeping my head down. Did I piss someone off? How?

"Yep. That's the one," the other woman said. She was already in one of the stalls.

"Her and gorgeous Derek Cole? How could she?" Girlish Voice said.

"I know. Poor Bridget. She had to file for divorce. But she's asking to keep control of CCI."

"Well, good for her. If that home-wrecker was looking for a quick promotion, she's going to hit a wall."

"A promotion? Honestly." The loud clank of the stall door opening was followed by water running. "I would've done it for free. Come on. Don't give me that look. You haven't seen the man in jeans. There's hot, and then there's Derek Cole hot."

They both giggled and strolled out of the bathroom.

I plopped down on the toilet seat, thinking of Cole coming down the stairs in worn jeans, wet hair, and shirtless.

Taking out my crumpled Get Over Cole list, I added another item.

5. Stop picturing Cole naked.

No. Scratch that.

5. Stop thinking of him. Period.

Things had turned for the worst, to say the least. By the time I found the courage to leave the bathroom stall, news of Cole's illicit affair had spread like malware through the office. Overnight, I'd become the reason for his divorce. Never mind that it was Bridget who cheated on him and stole CCI from him. What I knew to be true didn't matter. My coworkers had already digested whatever lie Bridget had fed them, and they'd passed judgment on it. The murmurs and the looks were enough to send me running. But I didn't flee as usual. I needed this job.

For the rest of the afternoon, I stayed in my cube as much as possible. They didn't know me. With a smile, I thought of Cole playing ball with Max. They didn't know Cole either. Explaining what had really happened was futile.

"Hello." Christopher leaned on the cubicle wall, lips pressed tight.

Had he heard the news? Crap. This would be easier if Cole wasn't so angry with me. His anger was the only thing that truly hurt in all this.

"How're you doing?" he asked.

"I'm good," I lied. "How about you?"

He paused for a moment, opened his mouth, only to close it again. "I just heard from Bridget. She's decided you're not a good fit for this company. I'm sorry. She wants you out of here by the end of the day. Um. I'll walk you out when you're ready, okay?" he said all in one breath.

"Christopher, I really need this job." I pleaded with him.

"I'm sorry, girl. But what were you thinking? You and Cole? I'm mean, yeah, he's as steamy as they come. But really? Did you think she wouldn't find out?" The disappointed look on his face made my stomach clench. He really needed my help with those reports. I'd let him down.

"It wasn't like that. I promise you. That was never my intention." I stood and reached for his shoulder, but retrieved my hand almost immediately. We'd only known each other for a few weeks. And even though we had connected from the start, we weren't that close. "I'm sorry. I—"

"You don't need to apologize to me." He made a dismissing gesture with both hands. "Get your things. You only have a couple of hours to clear out your desk." He pinched his nose. Was he crying? I touched his arm, and he embraced me in a bear hug. "I'm so sorry. I tried to get her to change her mind. There's just no talking sense into her."

My arms were pressed to my sides. I reached as best I could and patted him on the back. "Thank you for saying that."

"Of course." Taking deep, long breaths, he put up his hands in some sort of apology and left.

How am I going to tell Max and my parents I lost my job? No. That I got fired for sleeping with my boss's boss's boss's boss's husband.

There's pathetic. And then there's Valentina pathetic.

I glanced down, squeezing my eyes shut. Bridget didn't need an excuse to fire me. She'd spread the gossip about Cole and me out of spite. Breaking Cole and me up wasn't enough for her. Why? I hid behind my monitor and put my face between my hands. Hot tears dripped on the palm of my hands and scurried down my arm.

And here I thought the worst was over. I had let myself think Cole and I could be together. And now I was back to square one—dumped, jobless, and living with my parents. I was nineteen years old all over again.

Numb, I picked up the box Christopher had left on my desk and dropped my stuff into it. I didn't have much, a couple of picture frames, notes, books I'd brought on programming, and snacks. People went by my cube, staring, avoiding eye contact whenever I gazed at them. I was that car wreck they couldn't look away from. I wanted to crawl under my desk and never come out. This day couldn't end soon enough.

The collective humming of keyboards clicking and people chatting ceased completely, and the room went eerily quiet. Like those first couple of seconds after the lights go out and everyone is stunned speechless. Then, as if the figurative lights had come back on, the entire floor burst out into loud voices, talking fast. I couldn't catch what they were saying, but they sounded excited. I sat closer to the edge of my chair to peek over the cubicle panel. A gasp escaped my lips as my seat tipped over and dumped me on the worn carpet. What the hell? I jerked to my feet.

Cole strolled in through the door that led to the front lobby, his eyes surveying the room. A security guard caught up to him and handed him a badge. Cole said something and rested his hand gently on the man's shoulder, as if they were friends.

I ducked, hands pressing on my chest. *Shit.* When I checked again, the circle around him had grown wider than the aisle. Cole's lips alternated between a "Hi, how are you?" and his all-American-boyish smile as more people showed up. God, he looked good in a suit. I touched my fingers to my mouth.

He'd let his hair grow out since I moved into the cottage, which gave him that rebel-without-a-cause look. He'd combed it back, but a few strands refused to submit and streamed down to his forehead. I picked up the box and dropped it on the floor in frustration.

Why is he here?

Using my monitor as a shield, I snuck another

glance in time to see him saunter down the hallway. He looked calmed, not furious as he'd been on Friday. His step was relaxed, all loose hip and sexy. I didn't think it'd be possible, but he looked more beautiful than he did the first time he'd barged into Cafe Triste.

My eyes lingered on him. I could stay here all day, just watching him from a distance, as I did for so many months. But that wasn't me anymore. I wanted to run out and leap into his arms, kiss him until he said he believed in me.

I wasn't mad. Or I was. But you have the power to make all the bad go away. He'd said that to me once, after our first night together. If I went and talked to him, would he listen? Could I make all the bad go away? God, I missed him. It scared me to see how much.

I stepped out of my cube. I had to talk to him. He walked out of the circle of people and headed for Bridget's office, eyebrows drawn together, head held high. This wasn't a random visit. He had a plan. Scanning the faces in front of him, his eyes met mine across the room. He held my gaze, and I stopped in my tracks.

He didn't offer a hello. Or a smile. At the end of the row, he turned away from me as if he hadn't seen me. Tears stung my eyes, and I was glad all I'd had to eat today was the dry toast Mom shoved in my hands this morning on my way out the door. Talking to him wouldn't help. He hated me, and there wasn't anything I could do to fix it. Was he here to fire me himself?

You can't do this to me, Cole. He couldn't come in here and kick me out in front of everybody. It'd be too cruel. I had to get out of here. I couldn't let him humiliate me like this. Bridget had already taken care of

275

that. What more did he want?

"One, two," I counted under my breath while I threw the last of my stuff in the box. My hands shook uncontrollably. Eight...nine, ten... I raced to the door.

Chapter Twenty-Eight
Business First, Then Pleasure

Cole

"Business first, then pleasure, Cole," Dom said.

"I know." I glanced over my shoulder to see Valentina making a run for it. Of course, she was going to make me chase her. "Dammit, Valentina." I backtracked and went after her.

"Cole. What about Bridget?" Dom called after me.

"Handle it. You're the lawyer."

Valentina had a box in her arms, which slowed her down. *Small favors.*

I took longer strides to close the space between us. She was near the door when I grabbed her elbow and made her face me. She dropped the box, staring at me with wide eyes and that shapely mouth of hers slightly open. Picture frames and papers scattered across the floor, but she didn't flinch.

"No more running, Valentina." I cupped the nape of her neck. My heart beat fast from the run and the fear of watching her walk out on me. Again.

"Don't do this to me, please."

"Do what?" I met her gaze. The anger in her eyes wasn't there anymore. Not like I'd seen on Friday night when she'd dropped to the floor. I was an asshole for not helping her up. But the pain had blinded me to anything else. "I had a nice speech prepared. I was going to be very charming and all. But now that I have you in my arms again, all I want to do is kiss you. God, I missed you."

I looked over my shoulder to the operations gallery, where everyone stood around their cubes and gawked at us. Pulling her behind me, I walked us to the nap room next to the bathrooms. I shouldered the door open, and she let me bring her in.

"What—"

The door closed, and I leaned in to cover her mouth with mine, one hand on her waist, the other in her hair. Her lips were as sweet and soft as I remembered. Kissing her again was like a glass of water after a day in the desert with nothing to eat or drink. Heat built just below my navel when she wrapped her arms around my neck and her sweet tongue tentatively went past my lips.

Yes, sweetheart.

I nibbled her bottom lip, deepening the kiss. If I continued, things were going to get really embarrassing for me. My cock had a mind of its own whenever Valentina was around. Pressing my forehead to hers, I gripped her shoulders and pulled back.

"If you're here to fire me, you're too late." she said, out of breath.

"Does it look like I'm here to fire you?" I muttered against her lips. "No. I'm here to apologize. For being the biggest idiot. I should've listened to you. I should've believed you." Words weren't enough to say how sorry I was. I'd behaved like a complete jerk. She hadn't deserved any of it. "You didn't have to leave like that."

"You threw me out." The pain in her eyes made me want to punch a wall. But I was here to show her I'd grown. Not show her how big of an asshole I could be.

"I never meant for you to move out of the cottage. But I can see why you'd thought that. I'm sorry." I let out a long sigh, realizing how much I wanted to say this to her. "I love you. Come back to me. Please."

"What about your company?"

I laughed. "I'm confessing my love to you and this is all you have to say?"

"You know how I feel about you," she said with a two-dimple smile.

I ran the pads of my fingers over her cheek.

"Say it." I reached for her, my thumbs rubbing her ribs just below the line of her breasts. She grinned, understanding my meaning. It'd be so easy to spend the rest of my life playing this game with her.

"I love you too." She stepped into my arms and tunneled her fingers through my hair. "I love you, you stubborn man. Now tell me how we're going to get your company back."

God, she smelled good. "I like the sound of that." I wrapped my arms around her waist and picked her up. When we reached the door, she pushed on my shoulders.

"Where are we going?" She laughed. The sweet sound sent a rush of heat to my core.

"To get our company back."

"Put me down, then. Everyone here's had a field day talking about us today. Let's not give them anything else to talk about."

I released her and took her hand in mine. "Do you care what they think?"

A dimple touched her cheek. "No." She shook her head, as if the thought hadn't occurred to her until now. "They don't know us."

"It's just us. Nothing else matters."

Squeezing Valentina's hand, I opened the door to the small room and headed back to Bridget's office. No. My office. No one bothered to look away as we went by. I kept waiting for someone to break out the popcorn. Valentina squeezed my hand, her side flush against mine. When I faced her, her gaze flitted between our hands and the floor.

I could only imagine the kind of scrutiny Bridget put her through today. That was her style. Gossip. We would've gotten here sooner, but Nikki took longer than she'd said to get us the document we needed. Waiting around for her all morning had been hell. Dom, on the other hand, was all for coming up with a better plan and wanted to wait a few more days. No fucking way I'd let that happen.

I put my arm around Valentina and kissed her temple. She smiled up at me, shaking her head.

"We're gonna be okay," I whispered. Her soft hair brushed my lips. "It feels so good to have you in my arms again." All I wanted to do was take her home. But as Dom had said, business first, then pleasure. I was definitely planning on the pleasure part later. Four days was a long-ass time. The need to be with her was overwhelming.

Right. Let's get the business part out of the way.

To say that we marched into the middle of a shit storm was an understatement. Bridget's lawyer's voice boomed over the speakerphone, asking her to calm down. The crazed look in her eyes was something I'd never seen. In fact, I didn't think I had ever seen her lose control like this. It was safe to assume Dom had already told her about the affidavit.

When I shut the door, Dom came to stand next to me. "I don't think she fully understands the kind of shit she's in."

"That's her." She pointed a finger at Valentina. "She's the one who brought me the signed divorce papers. She said you had asked her to bring them to me."

"I thought you said she asked for money in exchange for the papers." I interrupted her ranting.

"Cole, I didn't," Valentina said with tears in her eyes.

Something twisted inside of me every time I saw Valentina cry. I squeezed her hand. "I know." I kissed her lips gently, went to my desk, and sat. Being back in my chair felt like coming home. "Sit down, Bridget."

"This is my company now. You can't come in—"

"Sit the fuck down," I projected my voice. She jerked in surprise, knowing very well I'd reached my limit. Her eyes went big as she eased herself into the seat across from me, her back perfectly straight. "Yes, CCI is now legally yours. But let's talk about all the illegal things you had to do to get it."

A click came through the speakerphone. Her lawyer had jumped ship. I turned to Dom, who simply shrugged.

"Some attorney you got there," he said to Bridget. "But something tells me he already knows all your dirty little secrets."

She squinted, giving me a sly smile. "I'm not giving you the company back."

"Yes, you are." I grinned. "By your earlier display, I'm assuming Dom already told you about the affidavit you're going to sign where you agree to forfeit your claim on CCI. Because you can't, in good conscious, take something your ex-husband worked so hard to build."

She snorted. "This business thrived because of me."

"It's also going in the shitter because of you." Dom dumped a stack of papers in front of her.

"CCI was well on its way to becoming what it is today when I hired you on. It wasn't yours to take." I shook my head. Whatever fucked-up reasoning got her thinking she could steal from me?

"You've been stealing from Cole for almost a year now. It didn't take long to find the trail of money you've been diverting to your account in the Bahamas." Dom threw a sheet that landed gently on the desk in front of her. Her eyes widened when she looked at the list of names on it. "Money laundry? That's so tacky. What else do I have here? Frank was so helpful this morning."

"That blessed idiot." She pinched her nose.

"He's your blessed idiot." He grinned. "With a thing for Nikki."

She pursed her lips, gripping the armrest. I glanced at Valentina in the back of my office. Her eyes were serene, sure I'd do the right thing. I wanted to be the man Valentina thought I was. A forgiving man. Forgiving Bridget was the only way out of this mess.

Our plan had been to get a confession out of her so we could legally and efficiently conduct an audit, which would land her in jail, leaving me in charge of CCI. A simple plan of quick revenge. Bridget would get exactly what she deserved. But that wasn't what she deserved. I'd blamed her for destroying our marriage for so long I'd convinced myself I was the victim here. She'd been a victim too. And if I deserved a second chance with Valentina, maybe I should do anything in my power to afford Bridget the same opportunity.

"I'm sorry I left you alone in all this," I said to Bridget.

Her eyes snapped up at me.

"A halfway-decent husband would've seen you were struggling with a disease. I failed you as a husband and as a friend. For that, I'm sorry."

"What are you talking about?" she asked.

"He's talking about your gambling problem." Dom always had a way of putting things simply. "The one that's going to land you in jail."

I shook my head at him. "Here's the deal you're going to take, Bridget. CCI will remain as is. Mine. And in return, I will not file charges for embezzlement. Also, you don't have to pay back whatever money you've already taken to pay off your debt."

She laughed, a shrill sound that made Valentina look away. Yeah, Bridget could be scary. "Just like that?" she asked. You're going to let me walk away?"

"Yes. Everyone deserves a second chance." I met Valentina's eyes across the room. She rewarded my good deed with a smile. "That's what I'm offering you."

Bridget followed my line of sight until she was face-to-face with Valentina. Valentina shifted her weight but didn't back down.

"I still owe them a lot of money." Bridget slumped

back in her chair.

"I know. I will settle that too. Provided you seek help and stay as far away as possible from us." I reached for the phone and dialed the extension for the security desk.

"Now, Cole. This isn't what we talked about," Dom said.

"I changed my mind." I shrugged. "Todd, how're you doing?" I said when the security guard answered. Todd had been with me since the beginning. He was loyal to me. "Could you come to my office? Ms. Bridget is leaving and will need help with her things."

In two minutes flat, Todd knocked at the door. Bridget looked around for something to take with her. But this was my office. Nothing here belonged to her. She had no other alternative than to accept my offer. Her eyes fell on the list of names in front of her. God only knew what that piece of paper meant to her. All Nikki could tell us was that this was our ticket out. With a sigh, she signed the affidavit Dom had put in front of her.

"Thank you." She clenched her jaw and left with Todd without saying anything else.

As the door closed behind her, a heavy weight lifted from my chest. In forgiving her, I'd found a reason to forgive myself too. I was finally free.

"You did the right thing." Valentina's words brought me back.

I nodded at her smiling face. "You forgave me so easily. I realized I needed to do the same and let it go."

"I'm Dom, by the way." Dom offered her his hand, ruining our moment. "We weren't introduced before."

Valentina shook it. "I know. Nice to meet you."

I rushed to her side. "Wipe that smile off your face. She's taken."

"I am?" she asked.

"Okay. I'm gonna leave you two lovebirds to figure things out." Dom went back to my desk, grabbed the stack of papers, and shoved them in his briefcase.

"How did you find evidence so fast?" Valentina asked.

"I didn't." He gave her a sly look. "Nikki stole this list from Frank. The document alone is worthless to us. But we figured if we could get Bridget to believe we had Frank's full cooperation, she'd realize she no longer had the upper hand. Owner or not, she'd still land in jail."

"I got the impression the list was more than what Nikki said." I tapped the piece of paper.

Dom nodded.

"What are those?" Valentina pointed at the big stack of papers.

Dom chuckled. "These are files from another case I'm working on. Telltale heart. Gets them every time."

I let out a long breath. "God, we took a big risk here. If she had called our bluff, that would've been the end of it."

"Honestly, man. I think your generous apology made her reconsider. That was very touching." He wiped a pretend tear.

"Fuck off," I said.

Valentina laughed. "He's right. I don't think she was expecting that. It confused her."

"Ah…*Dom's right* She utters my two favorite words." He placed a hand over his heart.

I gave him my *no, really, man, fuck off* look.

"Okay, I gotta run. I have to be in court in an hour. Nothing as exciting as your divorce, though." With a wink to Valentina, he rushed out.

"That guy is trouble." She frowned at him.

"Yes, it'd be best if you stay away from him." I wrapped my arms around her waist.

She giggled. "I thought he was your friend."

"Let's go." I couldn't wait to get her back to my bed. "As your new boss, I'm giving you the rest of the week off."

"You're not my boss. I got fired today." She gave me that look of hers. Those chocolate-brown eyes wide, soft, and wanting. Her red lips slightly parted. Yeah, that was the look. The one that said she wanted me. The one that made my blood boil.

"Is that why you had that box with you?" I asked. Bridget had fired her today, and she still thought letting Bridget go was the right thing to do. God, I was in love with her. "It's just as well. Contracts are boring. There's an opening in the development group. I know you'd be great there."

"Really? I'd love that."

"You'd have to work closely with the guy in charge there. And it'd be long hours, working 'til morning sometimes."

"Oh yeah. This guy sounds like a real hard-ass. Who is it?"

"Me." I winked. "We'll talk about it later. Let's go home," I said in between kisses. "I need to be inside you right now."

She blushed and let out a small whimper. When she mumbled an okay, I took her hand and strolled out of my office. Out on the floor, we were greeted by cheering and clapping.

"Welcome back, Cole," someone shouted.

"Can you believe this lazy crew?" I turned to Valentina. "They'll do anything to get out of doing their work. Get back to your desks," I called out to the room in general.

Valentina's laugh sent a surge of heat through me. I picked up the pace, in a hurry to get home.

Chapter Twenty-Nine
You Are Home

Valentina

I opened my eyes. The stark morning light came in through the open french doors. The view from Cole's bed was spectacular, especially from my side of the bed with Cole's beautiful profile set against the bright sunrays. I shifted to get a better look, and his grip tightened on my breast. The man wasn't kidding when he said he wasn't letting me go. Not even in his sleep.

He wanted me in his life. And *this* was certainly something I wanted to be a part of. But I wanted more from him. Even though he'd said he loved me, we hadn't talked about what we were exactly or where we were headed.

Last night I'd had every intention of bringing it up, but on our way home I made the fortunate mistake of pointing out how I'd never been in any other part of his house except his bedroom and the living area.

"Is that so?" he said with a half grin and a sparkle in his eye.

At the time, I had no idea what he had in mind. But the look on his face made my legs buckle a little. The minute we crossed the threshold, he kissed me, leading me to the library up in the loft.

"This is my office." He sat me on his desk and

pulled my pants off. I'd giggled and got to work on his tie, thrilled with the game.

I thought about the rest of the tour, and heat rushed to my face. Our clothes scattered all over the house. His hands and lips all over me as he took me from room to room. By the time we had found our way back into his bedroom, it was almost morning and I'd been too tired to even talk.

I moved again, peeling his fingers off my chest. This time his hand slid down my side and grabbed my butt cheek with a tight squeeze. When I looked up, Cole's smiling blue eyes greeted me.

"You're still here," he said.

"No more running." He'd made me promise last night. And for the first time in a long time, I didn't feel the urge to get away. "But I do have to go home today."

"Sweetheart, you *are* home."

His words melted my heart. "Max is waiting. I texted Mom last night to let her know I was staying here, but I have to get back today."

"Okay. I'll come with you."

"Really?" I raised an eyebrow. "If you do, you'll have to meet my parents."

He nodded. "I want to meet your family." His lips brushed against my shoulder, sending goose bumps down my arm. "I'd like you to meet my parents too."

"In Atlanta?" My stomach clenched. I wasn't ready for that.

"Yeah." He laughed. "Don't look so scared. I promise they're completely normal people. And they're going to love you."

"Won't they ask what happened with Bridget?" If they were Team Bridget, our first meeting would be very awkward.

"They never really agreed with that marriage. When they found out about the divorce, they were relieved."

The matter-of-fact tone in his voice made me happy. Bridget, the divorce—none of it hurt him anymore. He was truly over her and everything that had happened between them.

"And how would you introduce me?" I tried to keep my tone light, even though I was dying to know if he considered me his girlfriend now.

"How would you like to be introduced?"

I looked down at my hands. "Do they know about your other girlfriends?"

"No." He cupped my face. "You're the only woman I want in my life. If that's what you're asking."

"Yes. That's what I'm asking." I met his gaze.

I needed to get this off my chest and make it clear to him where we stood. It would hurt. But if he couldn't give me this, I was ready to walk away. He loved me. He'd proven that. But what he felt for me and what he could offer me in a relationship were two different things.

"Cole, if you still want to do your Monday-through-Friday-girlfriend thing, I can't be part of it. I won't."

"You're the only one for me. I promise. I want no one else." He caressed my cheek.

I kissed him. "I believe you." For now, girlfriend status was enough. "So how normal are we talking about?"

"My parents?"

"Yeah. What do they do?" I sat on my heels next to

him, and my thigh rubbed the length of his torso.

"Mom was a financial advisor but retired a few years back. Dad's a pediatrician. Like I said, normal."

"Your normal and my normal aren't exactly the same."

"Okay. Fair enough. But you have nothing to worry about. I know they'll love you." He pulled gently on my hair and pushed it away from my face.

"You're right. I should woman up."

"Yes. You should." He gave me one of his smiles.

I leaned forward and nibbled on his lower lip before I planted a wet kiss on him. "Let's go get Max."

"His stuff's already in his room down the hall." He laughed for a moment as if remembering a private joke. "Em said your mom was okay releasing all your belongings. But she put her foot down when it came to her grandson."

"That's *Abuela*. She'd been worried about me not being able to love again." I ducked my gaze, tracing my fingers on his freakishly hot abs. *Focus.* Cole needed to know how deep my insecurities went. I wanted him to know.

"I think her and Em had a good chat yesterday." He grabbed a strand of my hair and let it curl around his fingers. "She's thrilled for you. You deserve to be happy, Valentina. Never forget that."

"I know." I couldn't stop smiling. This beautiful man wanted me. It was going to be so easy to share my life with him. "Are you ready to go meet them?"

He nodded, placing a hand at the nape of his neck, biceps bulging.

He was doing it on purpose. Shaking my head, I threw a leg over the side of the bed and got up. If I didn't get away from Cole, he'd convince me to stay in bed all day. The idea sounded amazing, but we had things to take care of first. When I looked back at him, he watched me with smoldering eyes. I'd forgotten I was naked under the covers. He crawled on the bed toward me. How long would it be before this urgent desire we felt for each other went away? If the wolfish grin on his lips was any indication, I'd say probably never.

"You certainly know how to get my attention." His erection made my mouth water. The man was hot as all hell. "You are so incredibly gorgeous." He palmed my breast.

My nipples had already gone hard under his gaze. My resolve was crumbling, but I pushed him back. "I need a shower."

"Me too." He stepped off the bed to join me, standing almost a foot taller.

I ran my hands over every groove and soft hair on his flat stomach. He was real and he was mine.

"You have five seconds to get in the shower, or I'm taking you back to bed." His breathing was uneven, and his voice hoarse.

I liked having this much control over him, to know I wasn't the only one affected physically. He inched toward me, and I wiggled out of his reach. His laughter followed me into the bathroom, where I stood in awe, using the doorframe for support.

"What is it? Did you see a spider?" He nuzzled my neck.

"I've never seen your shower before. It's humongous."

"Well, let me give you the tour." His teeth grazed

my shoulder, and a warm tingling feeling rushed down to my toes.

The room was easily bigger than the cottage kitchen and living room put together. At the far right, floor-to-ceiling windows framed the mountains in the distance. To my left was a door I assumed was the water closet. Beyond that was the vanity and sink area.

"Shower or bath?" he asked. "Either way, I plan to make love to you in this room right now."

"Okay." I took a deep breath.

I eyed the massive tub, which sat against the wall straight ahead and took up only a small portion of the room. We'd have to give that a try soon. The shower had no doors, just a rain shower over our heads, four feet in length.

He turned on the water and the steamers. The warm water rushed through my hair and back. Even his shower was sexy. Pushing another button, he turned on the side jets. The spray tickled my backside and legs. On the tiki bench next to the standing towel rack, I found bottles of shampoo and body wash. I was right. The scent was lemon and verbena. I poured some of the soap on a puff and rubbed it against my belly to create a rich lather. When I turned, he was there, inches from me. His dark eyes said he'd waited long enough.

He bent down to kiss me, one hand at the nape of my neck, the other all over me, spreading the soap across my chest and down to my sex. Just like that, my body ached for him. I didn't have his self-control. I dropped the puff and buried my fingers in his hair. His hot mouth moved from my lips down to the peaks of my breasts while water dripped from his nose and onto my belly. Sharing the same water felt so intimate. I wanted this, every morning of every day.

He found my mouth again, our tongues touching gently while he kneaded my backside. Sliding his hands down, he caught me by the back of my thighs and wrapped my legs around his waist. His erection rubbed against me, and the sensation almost sent me over the edge. Gripping his muscular shoulders for support, I adjusted my weight, and he entered me with a strength that I'd come to expect from him. Familiar and all consuming. He thrust into me with purpose, deepening our connection. His mouth never left mine.

A billow of white heat rippled and spread from my core to my navel. In this position, he stimulated every inch of me. We stood under the rain shower, all hands and wet skin. I didn't want the feeling to end, but this was more than I could bare. He had me at the very edge.

"Now," I whispered.

His laugh rumbled between us as he carried me to the wall. Cold and slippery, the tile pressed against my skin, but I didn't mind because my entire focus was on his erection and the way he filled me. I rubbed his chest, taking in the heat emanating from his body. I held on to his neck and relaxed my body, letting him support my legs while he worked to get me the relief I craved. He kept at it until the ache inside me turned to liquid fire and I yielded to him. My moan echoed all around us, followed by his own groan against my shoulder.

"What have you done to me?" He released my legs. They felt like gelatin as they dropped to the floor, completely useless. But Cole had me pinned to the wall. I wasn't going anywhere. "Marry me," he whispered on my lips.

"What?"

The look in his eyes said it all. This wasn't the intimidating, sure-of-himself Cole. He'd opened his heart and showed me what he kept inside. I found fear in his eyes. As if I had the power to break his heart into a million pieces. He was mine.

"Marry me. Please."

Chapter Thirty
Are You Ready?

Cole

"Are you sure?" she asked, brows furrowed, still trying to catch her breath.

"You're impossible." I bent down to kiss her, pulse racing. "Please don't fight me on this."

"I'm not. It's just hard to think when you're all wet and naked in front of me."

I laughed. "Okay, fair point. Get dressed. We have a conversation pending." I kept my eyes on her face while I washed up quickly. She was right—thinking while we were both naked was impossible. "I'll wait for you in the bedroom." I kissed her forehead and left.

My initial intent had been to propose to her last night. But as soon as we walked through the door, I just couldn't keep my hands off her. And before I knew it, the night had turned into morning. I'd started to feel that if I didn't pop the question soon, I'd never get the chance. We'd just had sex without a condom. There was a high probability we were running against the clock here. The thought made me smile.

She strolled out of the bathroom thirty minutes later, wearing nothing but a towel. Her perfect breasts were barely contained. I swallowed. She just had no clue what she did to me.

"Any idea where we left my bra last night?"

I wet my lips. "Let's see. I remember taking your pants off in my office. Then we did that thing." She blushed. We would have to plan another tour of the house soon. "You only had your bra and underwear on when we went into the kitchen." I pretended I didn't recall the details of last night. I did. Vividly. But I was enjoying her blushing too much. I could do this all day.

She slapped my chest. "I'm serious. Wait. Was there an indoor soccer field?"

"Yeah. And I'm serious too. I'm thinking. Okay, maybe the living room? You definitely did *not* have your bra on then."

"I need my clothes." She laughed, and the towel inched down her front.

My cock reacted in anticipation. I raked both hands through my hair and blew out air. If we were going to get out of here, she really did need her clothes.

"I asked Em to bring your things here. Figured the cottage was paid off until the end of the month. If you were going to stay there, you might as well stay here with me."

"Interesting logic." She did her one-brow thing.

"Just trying to make things easy for you." I put on my innocent face.

"That's so sweet and high handed of you." She smiled and stepped into the closet.

It was high handed, but she'd left me no choice with her tendency to run away from me at every turn. Shaking her head, she picked up the clothes she'd worn yesterday off the sitting bench.

"I'm not even going to think about how these clothes got here." She covered her face with both hands.

"My guess?" I grinned. "Em brought them up while we were in the guest room. Don't be embarrassed."

She hit my chest, and a piece of paper fell out of one of the pockets of the pants she was holding. It caught my attention because I saw my name scribbled on it. I picked it up.

"Don't read that." She made a grab for it, but I held her hand until I was done reading.

1. Convince my parents to let us stay with them for a few weeks. At least two.

2. Find a new place.

3. Get my cousins to move my stuff, again.

4. Schedule pickup with Em.

5. Get over Derek Cole.

"You had a plan to get over me?" My heart squeezed tight. I'd come so close to losing her.

"That's one of three." She glanced at her hands, biting her lip. When she looked at me, she had creases on her forehead. "I had to move on. You were so mad at me Friday night. I thought I'd lost you."

I winced, thinking of how much I'd hurt her over the past few days. I crumpled the paper in my hand. "I'm so sorry." Sorry didn't begin to cover it.

"It's done." She eyed her clothes in the closet, which took up an entire section. She had a lot of clothes. "What if I had said no yesterday?"

I leaned on the doorframe. "My plan was to bring you here and make love to you until you said yes."

"That's exactly what you did." She suppressed a smile and ran her hands over the red dress I'd bought for her at the benefit.

"It's yours."

"Thank you. But you didn't have to buy it for me." She dropped her towel and let me watch her get her clothes on, while her breasts teased me with a back and forth sway. Now I had to spend the rest of the day knowing she was wearing lacy panties and nothing else under that form-fitting white dress.

"I wanted you to have it. And…I just didn't like the idea of you taking it off for someone else." I felt like an idiot saying it out loud. But all I could think of that night was that she was mine. I didn't want anyone else to have the dress she'd worn, the fabric that touched every part of her.

She shook her head, grinning. "I wasn't going to take it off in front of anyone. You know that, right? I was going to meet Annie in the dressing room and give it to her."

"Obviously, I wasn't thinking straight that night."

"Neither was I." She placed her hand on my chest, and my heartbeat picked up the pace.

"Have you decided?" I asked.

"Yes."

"Yes, you've decided, or yes, you'll marry me."

"I'll marry you." She stood on her tippy-toes and kissed me.

I cupped her face and got lost in her mouth, her skin, the smell of her. The scent of my body wash on her body made my cock stand at attention. Valentina was a part of my life.

I dug in the pocket of my jeans and pulled out a ring. A two-carat canary diamond that'd belonged to my grandmother. I never understood why I couldn't give it to Bridget when we decided to get married. This family heirloom was always meant for Valentina.

"I love you." I slipped the ring on her finger and kissed her hand.

"Cole, this is too much."

"You deserve that and so much more." I wrapped my arms around her and kissed her lips. "Now you have a new list to write. I want to be married to you as soon as possible."

Laughing, she shook her head. "Are you sure about this?"

"I've never been this sure about anything in my life. I promise you. This is what I want. A life with you."

Tears brimmed her eyes, and she nodded, letting out a sigh. "I want this too. I want you."

Her lips found mine. And just like that, I wanted to be inside her. I pinned her against the closet wall, hands over her head, as I kissed her neck and the mounds peeking over her dress.

Her hands kneaded the ridges on my stomach. "Let's go before we get sidetracked again."

When she pushed me away, I groaned and pressed my forehead against hers. "Okay."

Hand in hand, we walked downstairs. "Is that Dom on the couch?" she asked.

Now what? I raced down to the living room, picturing various scenarios in my head. He wasn't bleeding, so now I was pissed.

If he'd brought any women home, I swear…

"It's not what it looks like." He peeked over the pillow, his eyes on Valentina. "Wait. What do you think this looks like?"

I laughed at the worried expression that crossed his

face. Good. I wasn't the only one affected by that thing Valentina did with her eyebrows.

"What're you doing here? Dom, this is a no-women zone now."

Valentina joined me, trying to stifle a giggle. "Relax, Cole. You're the one who's not allowed to bring girls home. This is hilarious. What is he doing?"

"I've no fucking clue."

"You won't believe the night I had." He stopped to take the orange juice Em offered him and drank it as if his life depended on it. "I actually don't know how the hell I ended up here. She was at a bar. Emilia Prado's here, or she was. I went back to find her, but she vanished. Like a ghost." He buried his face in the pillows.

"Are you hungry?" I turned to Valentina. "Let's leave Dom to deal with his glorious hangover. I can't say I envy the guy."

"You're cute," she said.

"For freaking out over something I didn't do?"

"Hmm. I trust you, Cole. I know I have nothing to worry about. Do you trust me?"

"Absolutely, sweetheart."

****

"You're fidgeting." I took Valentina's hand in mine.

She looked out the car window at the unchanging desert landscape. "I'm not."

I slanted a glance at her.

"Okay, fine. I'm nervous. Just not sure we're ready for this. I mean, I'm ready for us to be together. But maybe we should've waited a few months to do the whole parent thing."

I didn't say it, but I felt the same way. All I knew at this point was that I didn't want to wait. I'd waited long enough for Valentina. Not to mention we were a mile away from her house and there was no going back—not that I wanted to.

Valentina's dad was what I had expected an ex-cop to look like. Built like an ox, with a look about him that said he'd seen a lot in his life. The kind of stuff most people never have to see.

"Nice to meet you, Mr. de Cordoba." I shook his strong and calloused hand.

"Please. Just Jav. Don't let the gray hairs fool you. I'm not that old."

"Mom." Max came out of nowhere and leapt into Valentina's arms. "I missed school today."

"I know." Valentina sounded relieved, probably because now she wouldn't have to tell him he'd have to switch schools. I wanted to hold her, apologize again. "I talked to your teacher, and she's okay with it. You'll see her tomorrow, okay?"

He nodded as he pulled on her shoulder to speak into her ear, his big brown eyes on me. "Is Derek Cole your boyfriend?"

She cleared her throat, standing a little straighter, gripping her skirt. "Um, yes."

"I knew it." He wrapped his arms around my leg. "Now Pirate can come to our house every day."

I hugged him back. "He's all yours, kid."

What an odd feeling. A good kind of odd. Months ago, I'd hit rock bottom in the worst way possible. If someone had told me that by the end of the summer, I'd find the woman of my dreams, I would've said they were out of their goddamn minds. Because of Valentina,

I went from having nothing to having a family. A wife, a son, and even a damn cat.

"I'm Mary, by the way." Valentina's mom gave me a tight hug. She was pretty with short dark hair and green eyes that sparkled when Max spoke. "Oh wow, you *are* tall."

"Mom." Valentina turned a deep shade of red. How much had she told them about me?

With a pat on my back, she gestured for us to come in. "You're just in time. Lunch is almost ready."

In the kitchen, Valentina sat at the kitchen counter, giving me a brilliant smile. She wanted me here, in her life. I couldn't wait to marry her and build something new with her.

"Want a beer?" Jav dug through an ice chest next to the kitchen door, which let out to the backyard.

"Yeah. I'll take one. Thanks," I said.

"Dad only drinks one brand." Valentina gave me an apologetic look.

"That's fine." I took the beer he offered. I'd drunk worse things in college.

"Okay. I'm gonna go check on the grill," he said.

"Need help with that?" I asked.

"Sure, thanks." He gestured for me to follow as he limped his way toward the door.

With a wink to Valentina, I went out to the backyard with him. The grill was smoking something fierce. Jav opened the lid and sprayed some of his beer on the flames.

With a shrug, he turned to me. "Improves the flavor."

"That's a good tip." I smiled and swallowed half my beer.

He rearranged the chicken on the grill, checking each piece. Probably to make sure it wasn't all burned. He rubbed his left leg and surveyed my face. "Some days are better than others," he said by way of explanation.

"What happened?"

He shrugged. "Cop stuff. Got shot three times, point blank." He sat on a lawn chair and swigged his beer. "One through the shoulder." He dug a finger on his right side and drew a line across his chest, down to his heart. "The heart and then the leg. I thought I was a goner. Doctors thought so too."

"Good grief," I said. Really, what else could I say?

"You know, the doctor couldn't get the bullet out of my chest."

I drew my eyebrows together. "It's still in there? How?"

"Yeah. Hell if I know. Big guy up there must need me here for something. Only way to explain what happened."

Valentina's dad was like a character out of a Jason Bourne movie. If Jav ever found out about Alex Maio, he'd pulverize the asshole. Was that why Valentina never said anything? She would never do anything to help that jerk. Whatever she did, keeping quiet about the whole affair was to keep her family safe.

"Is that why you retired?" I asked. He couldn't be older than fifty. Hardly retirement age.

He nodded. "Looks like you two patched things up."

The switch in topic took me by surprise. Guess we were done with the chitchat, if I could call it that. Was this his subtle way of intimidating me? Or a fucked-up way to open up and welcome me into the family?

Time to find out.

He'd gone straight to the point. I wanted to do the same. "Sir. I'd like to ask your permission to date your daughter."

He grinned. "I appreciate you asking. Shows your intentions are serious. I like that." He took a swig of his beer.

I did the same. "Well. I'm glad you like it because I'd like to also ask for your daughter's hand in marriage." I hadn't meant for it to come out so formal. Nerves, I guess.

He coughed, choking on his beer. He cleared his throat a couple of times and asked, "Isn't it a little soon for that? Dating is one thing, but marriage? That's…that's forever."

"I know. It's what I want. And if you think my decision requires more time, I'm willing to wait as long as necessary."

His laugh was deep. "When I first met Valentina's mom, I thought she was the prettiest girl I'd ever seen." He let out a breath, rubbing his leg. "Didn't take me long to figure out she was also the most stubborn."

"I think I know what you mean," I said. Valentina was the most beautiful woman I'd met. But she could be stubborn as hell. I thought of her no-kissing and no-sex rules and how much I'd enjoyed making her see reason. The passion and determination toward everything she did was why I loved her. One thing was for certain—life with Valentina would never be boring.

"You sure? Mary's stubbornness is nothing compared to Valentina's."

"I've been on the receiving end of it more than

once. I'm sure."

He barked out a laugh.

"Do we have your blessing? I know it would mean a lot to Valentina. To me."

"Looks like Valentina finally met her match," he said with a nod.

Valentina came out, carrying a salad bowl. She set it on the picnic table and turned to me. "Are you ready?"

"Yeah. I'm ready." I met her gaze.

Chapter Thirty-One
Right on Time

Valentina

I wrapped my hands around my cup of latte to keep them warm. It was hot outside, so naturally the AC was on full blast inside. I sat by the bay window at Cafe Triste and waited for Mr. Quad Americano, Cole. My Cole. The rain had gone from a downpour to a gentle drizzle. Soon the monsoon season would be over, and we could all go back to complaining about the dry heat.

In the past couple of months, Cole and I had managed to survive meeting in-laws, getting married, and honeymooning in Bora Bora. Cole's choice. He'd wanted a place where clothes were optional. After spending three weeks in an over-the-water bungalow, I'd have to say I was glad to be dressed again. A smile tugged at my lips. I looked around the coffee shop, hoping no one had noticed my hot cheeks.

And, yeah, we had our fairy-tale wedding. As Annie put it, why the hell not?

I'd never thought I would want a big wedding. But when Cole had asked what my dream wedding looked like, I came up with a pretty huge dream. Between Nikki and Annie, we had the perfect wedding reception out in Cole's backyard. Our backyard. We had over four hundred guests, half of which were my family. The other half were his friends and family. Cole had told the truth about his parents. They were totally normal, welcoming, and not at all fazed by the size of my clan.

Cole turned the corner. He stopped to wait for the light to turn green and ran his hands through his hair. I took a long sip of my decaf latte and blew out a breath. He still had that effect on me. Gosh, how did I manage to sit here for six months and not jump him?

His eyes met mine across the street. I exhaled, holding his gaze. The light changed, but he didn't make an effort to move. He gave me brilliant smile and headed toward me. Inside, the barista waited to take his order, her usual grin on.

"Quad americano, please," he ordered. "And a water."

Some things shouldn't have to change, I thought with a smile. Cole went past his table and sat next to me. Others could be improved.

"How was your day, sweetheart?" he asked.

"It was great. You?"

"Not bad." The man knew me better than anyone else. His look said it all. "You asked me to meet you here. You're dressed, so I'm assuming we're not here for a quickie." He flashed me a sexy grin that promised he'd make it worth my while if I was up for it.

"I got something for you." I dug through my shopping bags, embarrassed for what I had to tell him. No, I hadn't learned my lesson.

He sat back in his chair, intrigued. "Out with it, Valentina."

My eyes filled with tears. I had a cute plan to give him a silver rattle to deliver the good news. But now it seemed cheesy. Maybe the hormones were already kicking in. His face changed as he leaned forward. He cupped my face, thumbing my tears away.

"Sweet girl, don't cry." He ran his thumb over my cheekbones again.

"Cole, we're having a baby," I blurted out. "I had a nice speech prepared. It was cute and romantic."

"What?" He stood, knocking over the chair he was sitting on. He pulled me to my feet, a mix of panic and joy in his face. "Are you sure?"

"Relax. We're not having a baby right this instant." I giggled.

His deep laugh reverberated through the room. "Oh right. You're sure, though?"

I nodded. "The doctor confirmed it today. I'm eight weeks along. I can't believe I didn't realize it sooner. I just feel silly. After what happened with Max, I thought the next time I got pregnant, it wouldn't take me by surprise."

Cole and I had briefly talked about having kids. I knew he wanted them, although we had never agreed on a time frame. But now that we had a baby on the way, I really wanted this. I wanted a baby with Derek Cole.

It was so obvious to me now. It had never been about not making mistakes along the way. But rather about making mistakes with the right person. This time, I was sure Cole was the right man for me.

Wrapping his arms around my waist, he picked me up and did a half turn. "That's the thing about the best laid-out plans. A change in wind can come at any time."

"You're not mad?"

"Mad? Why would I be mad? This is incredible news, Valentina." He kissed me, a deep and soft kiss. "You make me so happy. I'm so in love with you."

"Me too."

"Let's take the rest of the day off," he whispered in my ear.

I would never have the strength or a good reason to say no this man. I melted into his arms as he kissed me again.

I could've spent my whole life planning, scribbling lists, and laying out perfect plans. But I supposed love had its own plan, even when we didn't want it to…when we couldn't find a way to forgive ourselves for our past mistakes.

Cole was the change in winds I never saw coming. And at the same time, the one thing I'd been waiting for. Looking back on it, we had the answer in front of us the whole time. For six months, to be exact. Literally staring us in the face. Love had been there waiting for us. In the end, it caught up to us.

Right on time.

Discussion Questions

1. Valentina promised her son he'd come to live with her after graduation. However, they never agreed on an exact time frame. Why do you think she set such a constrained timeline on herself? Why couldn't she wait until she'd had a year or two of income and could afford the rental she wanted?

2. Derek is an accomplished businessman who's not afraid to go after what he wants. Why did he wait six months to reach out to Valentina? Why not approach her as a friend?

3. After Valentina moves into Derek's cottage, Derek is relentless in his pursuit. What do you think was his plan for her, if he had no interest in a relationship?

4. Derek's relationship with his ex-wife was mostly business related. In the end, Bridget played the part of a jealous ex-wife. Do you think she had real feelings for him? Could they have worked things out if she hadn't been addicted to gambling? Why or why not?

5. After almost six years, Valentina finds a reason to forgive herself for getting pregnant her first year in college. Her parents and Annie were supportive of her. Why was she so hard on herself?

A word about the author…

Diana Hicks became an avid reader when she found her first romance novel tucked away in a corner of her high school library. The more books she read, the more she wanted to be a writer.

She has a master's degree in information systems and accountancy and for many years worked for a major Fortune 100 telecommunications company as an IT project manager (as one does when pursuing a career as a romance author).

These days, when she's not writing, Diana enjoys running half marathons, traveling, and indulging in the simple joys of life like wine and chocolate. She lives in Atlanta and loves spending time with her two children and husband.

Visit her at:
http://DianaHicksBooks.com
or at:
Facebook Closed Reader Group:
https://www.facebook.com/groups/DianaSexyReaders/
Facebook Page:
https://www.facebook.com/DianaHicksAuthor/

Thank you for purchasing
this publication of The Wild Rose Press, Inc.

If you enjoyed the story, we would appreciate your
letting others know by leaving a review.

For other wonderful stories,
please visit our on-line bookstore at
www.thewildrosepress.com.

For questions or more information
contact us at
info@thewildrosepress.com.

The Wild Rose Press, Inc.
www.thewildrosepress.com

Stay current with The Wild Rose Press, Inc.

Like us on Facebook

https://www.facebook.com/TheWildRosePress

And Follow us on Twitter
https://twitter.com/WildRosePress